FINDING
THE WORM

Also by Mark Goldblatt

Twerp

FINDING THE WORM

Mark Goldblatt

Random House 🏠 New York

Text copyright © 2015 by Mark Goldblatt
Jacket art copyright © 2015 by Joanna Szachowska

All rights reserved. Published in the United States by Random House Children's Books, a division of Random House LLC, a Penguin Random House Company, New York.

Random House and the colophon are registered trademarks of Random House LLC.

Visit us on the Web! randomhousekids.com

Educators and librarians, for a variety of teaching tools, visit us at RHTeachersLibrarians.com

Library of Congress Cataloging-in-Publication Data
Goldblatt, Mark, 1957–
Finding the worm / Mark Goldblatt.—First edition.
pages cm.
Sequel to: Twerp.
Summary: In 1970 Queens, New York, Julian Twerski, now in seventh grade, struggles to write an essay as punishment for an act he did not commit, worries about Beverly, the girl he likes, prepares for his bar mitzvah, and tries to cope with the serious illness of one of his closest friends, Quentin.
ISBN 978-0-385-39108-5 (trade)—ISBN 978-0-385-39109-2 (lib. bdg.)—
ISBN 978-0-385-39110-8 (ebook)
[1. Friendship—Fiction. 2. Sick—Fiction. 3. Bar mitzvah—Fiction. 4. Jews—United States—Fiction. 5. Schools—Fiction. 6. Conduct of life—Fiction. 7. Queens (New York, N.Y.)—History—20th century—Fiction.] I. Title.
PZ7.G56447Fin 2015 [Fic]—dc23 2014004052

Printed in the United States of America

10 9 8 7 6 5 4 3 2 1

First Edition

For Sal Salamone, who finished his book

Julian Twerski December 8, 1969

The Guidance Counselor

You know the noise the intercom makes when it comes on, the crackle you hear a second before the principal starts to talk? You can hear that noise a hundred times, and you know, just from the crackle, you don't have to pay attention. But then, the one time you *do* have to pay attention, the noise sounds different. The crackle sounds different. It sends a chill through you, and you know the principal is going to say your name. It's like that creepy old saying "Ask not for whom the bell tolls. It tolls for thee." Except instead of a bell, you've got that crackle.

It was the middle of second period when the intercom crackled, and the announcement came. I was in science class, converting Farenheit degrees to Celsius. Here's what Principal Salvatore said: "Will the following students please report to the guidance counselor's office: Lonnie Fine. Eric Haft. Beverly Segal. Julian Twerski. Howard Wurtzberg. Shlomo Zizner."

That's the entire Thirty-Fourth Avenue gang—minus Quentin, who'd gone into the hospital over the weekend, plus Beverly, who lives on the block and who hangs around with us sometimes. It didn't take a genius to know that something was going on with Quentin.

As soon as Beverly and I stood up, the class began to hoot, like the two of us had gotten in trouble. My heart thumped up into my throat, and my face went hot and then cold.

I thought Quentin was dead.

"Look, he's gonna bawl!" a guy two rows to the side of me said. At that point, I couldn't have cared less what he thought. What anyone thought. I left my books on my desk and rushed out the door.

Beverly was a couple of steps behind me. Once we were out in the hall, she ran to catch up and said, "He's going to be okay, isn't he?"

I was afraid if I answered her I *would* bawl, so I just kept walking.

"Julian!" she said.

The way she said my name made me mad. "You think I know more than you do?"

What I knew, what the entire block knew, was that Quentin was sick. Not just cold-and-flu-season sick. It was the third time in the last three months he'd gone to the hospital to get checked out. Beverly knew that as well as I did. She'd been there the first time, when he got dizzy tossing around a football. She'd been there the second time, when he threw up after a half hour of wolf tag, and then the third time, over the past weekend, when he sat down on the sidewalk for no reason and his eyes rolled back in his head.

She grabbed my shoulder, and for a split second, we stopped and looked at one another. Then the two of us started running toward the stairwell. Her long brown hair was flying out behind her as we hit the stairs. It looked like a comet tail as I trailed a step behind her. The entire time, I could hear my heartbeat. Not just feel it, I could *hear* it. It had gone from my chest to my throat, and now it was in my ears.

The guidance counselor's office was at the far end of the first floor, next to Principal Salvatore's office. It took us about a minute to run down the two flights of stairs and across the entire first floor, but that was a long minute.

The guidance counselor, Miss Medina, was standing in the hall outside her office, leaning against the door. The hall was deserted, so we saw her as soon as we turned the corner, but she would've been easy to spot even in a crowd. She's almost six feet tall and has curly blond hair that's piled up on her head to make her look even taller. I was trying to read the look on her face. What I focused on was her mouth. It was clenched in a tight smile—the kind of smile you get when you're forcing yourself to smile.

"Go inside and sit down with your friends," she said. "We're just waiting for two more."

Lonnie and Howie were sitting on wooden folding chairs pushed against the far wall of the office. They both glanced up as we came in, but then Howie turned his head and looked out the window. He always got squirmy around Beverly because he'd been sweet on her from the start of third grade until the end of sixth grade—when the rest of us clued him in that he had no chance with her. I sat next to Lonnie, and Beverly sat next to me, and for another minute we just stared down at the worn-out gray carpet.

That was when Shlomo staggered in. His face was pink from running, with a bead of sweat trickling down his forehead, and he was gasping for air. He held up his left hand as he caught his breath and straightened his glasses on his nose. Then, at last, he said, "You don't think he died, do you?"

"Just sit down," Lonnie said, and nodded toward an empty chair.

But Shlomo wouldn't let it go. "*Do* you think he died? I mean, he couldn't have just—"

"Sit down and shut up, all right?" Lonnie said. "You know as much as we know."

Shlomo slid into the chair Lonnie had nodded at, and bent his head down almost to his knees. It always took him longer to catch his breath, since he was out of shape. His breathing was the only sound in the room for another half minute, until Eric the Red walked in, followed by Miss Medina. Eric hustled to the last wooden folding chair as Miss Medina walked behind her desk. I thought she was going to sit down there, but instead she rolled out the chair and parked it in front of the desk, so that she was sitting right in our faces. She still had that same clenched smile on her face. It was scaring the daylights out of me.

Miss Medina said, "I'm sure you're all curious why you're here—"

"Did Quentin die?" Shlomo blurted out.

"No, no, no!" she answered, waving her hands back and forth. "Did you think that? I'm *so* sorry. Quentin is doing fine. He's a very sick young man, but he has the best doctors in the world looking after him. I spoke to one of them this morning, and he said Quentin has a tumor. It's in the back of his head, close to his brain. That's the reason he hasn't been himself lately. . . ."

"Tumor means cancer, right?" Shlomo said.

"It's a kind of cancer," she said. "I know that's a scary word, but Quentin has a good prognosis. Do you know what a *prognosis* is?"

Beverly answered, "Isn't it like a prediction?"

"Yes, it's like a prediction," Miss Medina said. "It's a medical prediction. It's the kind of prediction doctors make. Quentin's doctors predict he'll be back in school in no time. If all goes well, he'll be going to classes, doing homework, even shooting baskets in the school yard just like old times."

"Quentin didn't shoot baskets," Eric said.

"Maybe he will when he gets back," she said. "The point is, he'll be able to shoot baskets if he wants. Isn't that good news?"

"How long until he gets back?" I asked.

"You're Julian, right? The boy who keeps a journal?"

"That was last year."

"It's good to keep a journal," she said. "It's good to get your feelings down on paper. This might be an opportunity—"

"You still didn't answer Julian's question," Lonnie said. "How long until Quentin comes back to school?"

"And your name is?"

"Lonnie."

"No one can answer that, Lonnie. But sooner rather than later."

"So why did you pull us out of class?" Shlomo asked.

Miss Medina nodded. "That's a fair point. I didn't intend to frighten you, and I'm *so* sorry if I did. I just wanted to let you know that I'm here for you. It's natural that you'd be worried about Quentin. We worry about the people we love. We worry so much, in fact, that worrying can sometimes get in the way of the work we're supposed to be doing. It can become a distraction. Does that make sense to you?"

That was when Lonnie spoke up again. "I think about Quentin all the time."

"When you do, what do you think about?"

"You know—just stuff. Sad stuff, I guess. But it's a real distraction. I can hardly think about anything else."

"That's normal. It's very normal. And it's nothing to be ashamed of."

Lonnie began shaking his head, laying it on thick. "It's like, ever since he got sick, I'll be sitting at home, trying to do homework, but no matter how hard I concentrate, I keep thinking about Quentin. I can't stop myself, and like an hour goes by, and I've only done one math problem."

"How do you feel afterwards?" Miss Medina said.

"I just feel so . . . distracted."

"That's all?"

"I feel like I let myself down," he said. "Plus, then Mr. Montgomery chews me out the next day in math class."

Miss Medina nodded, then rolled her chair to her desk

and made a note on a pad of paper. "I'll have a talk with Mr. Montgomery."

"I don't want to get Mr. Montgomery in trouble."

"You're not getting him in trouble, Lonnie. I'm just going to talk to him."

"Thank you, Miss Medina," Lonnie said.

"What about the rest of you?" As she reached again for her pad and pencil, Shlomo leaned forward and was about to say something, but Lonnie shot him a look, and he clammed up. "So the rest of you are doing all right in your classes?"

"Yes, ma'am," we mumbled at the same time.

"But you'll let me know if that changes, right?"

"Yes, ma'am."

"That's a promise?"

"Yes, ma'am."

Second period was about to end as we left Miss Medina's office. That meant we had to rush back to our classes and pick up our books before the start of third period. There was no time to talk about what had happened—which was just as well. If I'd looked Lonnie in the eye, neither of us could've kept a straight face. I couldn't believe he'd come up with a get-out-of-jail-free card for math. It was his worst subject, and now he had the guidance counselor telling Mr. Montgomery to go easy on him. Lonnie might not be the greatest student, but he's the quickest thinker I know.

It was also a relief to know Quentin was going to be all right. Just the same, it was hard to see why Miss Medina had pulled us out of class like that—Shlomo was right about that much. The more I thought about it, the more pointless it seemed.

Beverly and I, meanwhile, were half walking and half running back to science class. We were near the stairwell at the end of the first floor when she tapped me on the arm and said, "That was *really* scary. Do you believe her?"

"Who? Miss Medina? Why would she lie to us?"

"You think she'd tell us if Quentin was dying?"

"No, but she wouldn't call us down to her office to lie to us. That would be stupid."

"So you believe her?"

"You were there, Beverly. You heard the same thing I heard."

"Why are you being so crabby?"

"I'm not being crabby," I said. "I just don't want to talk about it."

She stopped on a dime and grabbed my arm, which forced me to stop too. Then she took a step back and got a weird smile on her face. She pulled her long brown hair behind her and began to twist it into a knot. "I'll race you back to science class."

"What?" I said.

"C'mon, let's race back to science."

"What's the point?"

"The point is to see who's faster."

"We both know the answer to that, Beverly."

"I kept up with you, step for step, on the way down. I was *ahead* of you—"

"That's because we were running *together*," I said.

"So you *let me* keep up? Is that what you're saying?"

"Well, yeah."

"Then why not race me?"

"I'm *not* racing you," I said. "It's a stupid idea."

"Sixth grade was last year."

"What's that supposed to mean?"

"You were the fastest kid in sixth grade. You were faster than me last year, and I admit it. But things change, Julian. Different grade. Different school."

"Yeah, but it's still you and me."

"I've gotten *a lot* faster since last year. I'm five feet tall now. I'm as tall as you are."

"I'm not doing it, Beverly."

"Why not?"

"Because you're a girl!"

"So you're afraid of losing to a girl?"

"I'm not afraid of losing. It's just not a fair race." I

pushed open the door to the stairwell. "C'mon, the bell's gonna go off any second."

As soon as I opened the door, she shot through it and raced up the stairs.

"See you in science class!" she called back to me.

"C'mon, Beverly!"

She was making clucking chicken noises as she disappeared up the first flight.

Goofing on the Bus Driver

My sister, Amelia, who's starting college next fall, levels with me about most things. Not because we're *close* or anything. I mean, it's not like we sit around and have *Brady Bunch* talks. The reason she levels with me, I think, is that she doesn't like the idea of people kidding themselves. It's like she's allergic to it. "Get a grip" is one of her big sayings. What she means is *Get a grip on reality. Don't pretend the world isn't the way it is.*

When I told her that Quentin had a tumor, she did this thing where her eyes got real wide, and she brought her hands up to her mouth, but only for a couple of seconds. By the time she brought her hands down, she had that get-a-grip look on her face. "What are his chances?"

"His chances of what?"

"Julian, do you understand what's happening?"

"Miss Medina said he's going to be all right."

"Who's Miss Medina?"

"She's the guidance counselor. She spoke to Quentin's doctors."

"What if she's wrong? What if the doctors are wrong?"

"What you really mean is, what if Quentin dies? Right?"

"That's what I mean," she said, real calm. "Have you thought about it?"

"Yes," I said. Which was the truth. I mean, how could you not?

"And?"

"I need you to drive me and Lonnie to Jamaica Hospital tomorrow."

"What time?"

"One o'clock," I said.

"I have school, Julian!"

"C'mon, Amelia, you're a *senior*. I know you cut classes."

"Don't *you* have school?"

"Lonnie got us permission to leave early—as long as we get picked up in front of the school."

"Let me guess," she said. "He talked to Miss Medina."

"That's right."

She smiled. "Why don't you get Mom or Dad to do it?"

I just kind of stared her down.

"All right, I can cut out early and drive you there," she said. "But you'll have to take the bus home."

"Thank you," I said.

The thing of it is, I *didn't* have a grip on what was happening with Quentin. Not until I got to the hospital. Not until I walked into Quentin's room and got a look at him. His forehead and skull were wrapped in bandages and gauze, and there was a thick tube coming out of his mouth, and a narrow tube coming out of his right arm, and a medium tube coming out of his left side. I couldn't see how the side tube was attached, but it ran out from under his hospital blanket to a machine with pumps going up and down. The only good thing you could say about him was that he was awake. The lights were on in his eyes. They sparked up as soon as we walked into the room, and a couple of times he looked like he was trying to say something. But he couldn't because of the tube in his mouth.

Lonnie and I sat there with him for an hour, just yakking about stuff that was going on on the block, and every so often he'd blink back at us, which told us he was interested. That's the thing about Quentin. The guy *is* Thirty-Fourth Avenue. I don't know how to describe it, but he's the heart of the block. He's the kind of guy who squirrels don't run away from, the kind of guy other guys' moms love to pinch. I mean it. You sit Quentin down in the middle of a mah-jongg game, you might as well drop him into a tank of lobsters.

An hour after we got there, Quentin's parents came in and said he needed rest, so Lonnie and I left. We headed downstairs and waited for the bus and got seats in the back. For the first couple of minutes, neither of us said a word.

When I couldn't bear the silence anymore, I said, "He's going to be all right, right?"

Lonnie exhaled real loud. "You heard Miss Medina."

"You think she'd tell us the truth?"

"I don't know," he said. "If I knew, I'd tell you."

"Beverly doesn't think she'd tell us the truth."

Lonnie grinned. "Well, if that's what *Beverly* thinks . . ."

"You think there's such a thing as heaven?"

That made him laugh. "Where did that come from?"

"I'm just curious," I said.

"How the hell should I know if there's a heaven?"

"I didn't expect you to *know.* . . ."

"Use your brain, Julian! The only way I'd know would be if I was dead, which I'm not." He balled up his fist and punched me in the arm. Not hard, just enough to get my attention. "You see? If I was dead, you wouldn't have felt that. But you did. So I don't know the answer."

"I thought you might have an opinion," I said.

He leaned back. "Well, sure I have an *opinion*."

"What is it?"

"*If* there's a heaven, it must be full of old people."

"Really?"

"Who do you think does most of the dying? So I'm guessing, if there *is* a heaven, it's most likely like a humongous old-age home, except with wings and harps."

"What about kids who die?"

"I'm talking about the *majority*," he said.

I rolled the idea over in my mind. "Maybe there's a separate heaven for kids."

"So it would be like a giant sandbox, just floating around up in the clouds?"

"Maybe," I said.

"That's the dumbest thing I've ever heard," he said. "Sand is *much* heavier than clouds, so it would fall right through. We'd wake up one morning, and it would be raining sand outside."

"I'm not saying it *is* that. I'm just saying it could be."

"Yeah, and the moon could be made of Swiss cheese," he said. "Except it's not."

"The moon is *way* different than heaven," I said. "We *know* what the moon is like. Neil Armstrong flew a rocket to the moon. The last time I looked, no one's flying a rocket to heaven."

"You asked me my opinion. You got my opinion."

"Thanks a lot," I said, rolling my eyes.

He nudged me with his elbow. "You're welcome."

The bus rumbled and sputtered along Jamaica Avenue, then turned left onto Parsons Boulevard. It was a hard turn, and it sent us careening to the right.

"Do you want to goof on the bus driver?" Lonnie said.

"I don't know. I'm pretty tired. Plus, it's cold outside."

"C'mon, Jules!"

I took a deep breath, then stood up and walked to the front of the bus. "Excuse me, sir, can I have a transfer?"

The driver was a tall skinny guy with a bony face. "Why didn't you ask for it when you got on?"

"I guess I forgot," I said.

"Your pal need one too?"

"No, just me."

He tore off a transfer slip from the roll next to the coin machine and handed it to me. "Here you go."

"Thanks," I said. "I want to get off at the next stop."

"You sure cut it close, kid!"

He pulled the bus to the curb, and I hopped off. As soon as the doors slid shut, a gust of cold wind came up Parsons. It felt like a hard slap in the face. The truth I didn't mind goofing on the bus driver. But it was a lot more fun in July than in December.

I stood on the sidewalk and watched the bus pull away from the curb. Down at that end of Queens, Parsons

Boulevard is a real narrow street, with lots of twists and potholes, so I waited a long time—until the bus was out of sight. Then I tore out. The one good thing about the cold weather was that the sidewalks were deserted, so I didn't have to dodge moms pushing baby strollers or kids playing hopscotch or clusters of old people walking slow.

The first half block, the wind was hitting me so hard in the face that I kept blinking. I could feel tears leaking down my cheeks. But then, without warning, the wind changed direction. It came up behind me, and it pushed hard against the back of my coat, getting up underneath the hem, and for about ten steps I felt like, if I leaned forward another inch and lunged, I might take off. The only thing keeping me on the ground was knowing how hard the sidewalk was, and how much it would hurt if I fell. You know what it felt like? It felt like, if I could just get myself to believe it was possible, I could've flown.

Two blocks later, I caught up with the bus. I ran even with it for another block, hanging back so the driver wouldn't notice me. Then, when the next stop came into sight, I sprinted ahead. I got to the yellow line a good ten seconds before the bus, then put out my hand to signal for it to stop.

The driver recognized me the second he cracked open the doors. I was huffing for air as I handed him the transfer, and he shot me a dirty look, but he was also kind of smiling.

"Wise guy," he said, just loud enough for me to hear it.

Lonnie was grinning at me as I stumbled toward the back of the bus, still out of breath. He made room, and I slid back down onto the seat next to him. Then he gave me a quick shove, just playing around. "You look sort of familiar, but I can't place the face."

"Did you miss me?" I asked.

"Didn't think you'd make it."

"It wasn't even close," I said.

We sat quiet for a couple of minutes, listening to the rattle of the bus. I could feel my heartbeat coming down and the air coming back into my lungs.

Then, at last, Lonnie said, "If it's bugging you, you know who you should ask?"

"If what's bugging me?"

"Heaven."

"Who should I ask?"

"Magoo."

The bus hit a huge pothole right after he said that, which knocked us into the air and sprawled us out across the backseat. It sounds stupid, but that jolt convinced me to ask Magoo.

Magoo's Office

Rabbi Salzberg got a real scrunched-up look on his face when I asked him about heaven. He's pretty scrunched up to begin with—the kids at Gates of Prayer Temple and Hebrew School call him Rabbi Magoo. (It's not a respectful thing, to compare a rabbi with a cartoon character, except he really and truly does look like Mr. Magoo.) But when I asked him about heaven, he got an especially scrunched-up look, like he'd just bitten into the sourest pickle ever.

I was standing in front of the big wooden desk in his office, which always has, like, a blanket of dust on it, and he was sitting on the other side with his hands folded.

"How's that any of your business?" he said. "Why

don't you wait until after your bar mitzvah to worry about that?"

"But my bar mitzvah is next month," I said.

"Worry about your haftarah!"

So then I told him about Quentin, about how he might not be able to come to my bar mitzvah since he was in the hospital, and how no one knew how long he'd have to stay there. I even told him about the tubes going in and out of him and the bandages around his head. I blurted out the whole thing, and I got real emotional talking about it.

You'd think hearing about what Quentin was going through would change the look on Rabbi Salzberg's face. But he stayed scrunched up the entire time. Then, after I got to the end, he looked me straight in the eye and said, "So you're worried your friend is going to die and go to heaven?"

"Yes, Rabbi."

"Worry about your haftarah!"

"Rabbi, I have it *memorized*."

"Do you think that's the purpose of haftarah—to memorize words? What do the words *mean*?"

"I don't know what they mean, Rabbi. The words are in Hebrew."

"You're in Hebrew school, aren't you?"

"But that's not the kind of Hebrew we learn."

"Mr. Twerski, when you're standing up on that stage, reading the words of your haftarah, you'll be leading the congregation. Your family and friends will be listening to you. You'll be their guide."

"They don't know what the words mean either."

"Then *make* them understand. Be their guide."

"Lonnie got bar mitzvahed last year," I said. "Do you think he understood a word he was saying? But he made it through okay. You even told him what a good job he did. He said his haftarah, and I'll say my haftarah."

"No two haftarahs are the same."

"I know," I said. "Mine's half a page longer than his was. We compared them side by side. I don't think that's real fair, but I guess it's the luck of the draw. . . ."

"No two are the same because haftarah is more than just the words. That's the reason you have to study it. You have to let it become part of you, let it beat in your heart. You have to *learn* it, and then you have to *live* it. Study your haftarah, Mr. Twerski. Let God worry about Quentin."

"But you still haven't answered my question."

"What was your question?"

"Is there a heaven?" I said.

"Are you Jewish?"

That kind of caught me off guard, since we were talking about my bar mitzvah. I figured it had to be a trick. I thought it over for a couple of seconds, then said, "I think I am."

"You *think* so? That's it?"

"I'm getting bar mitzvahed."

"That's your only proof?"

I thought for another couple of seconds. "Well, I'm standing here talking to you, and you're a rabbi."

"What about your last name? Twerski sounds Jewish, doesn't it? So you must be Jewish. That's a logical conclusion, am I right?"

I nodded.

He slammed his fist down on the desk. "So you're Jewish because of logic?"

"Well, no, not *just* because of logic—"

He jumped to his feet, rushed around from behind his desk, and grabbed me by the shoulders. He smelled of cigarettes and fish, but I knew enough to take a deep breath and hold it as soon as he got out of his chair. He shook me a couple of times by the shoulders, then poked his right index finger into my chest. "What about what's in *here?* What about what's in your *heart?*"

"I'm Jewish in there too," I said, breathing out as I did.

He pulled back his finger. "That's good to hear."

I watched him walk back around his desk and sit down.

When he saw I hadn't moved, he shook his head. "Yes?"

"You still didn't tell me whether or not there's a heaven."

"Are you asking what I *believe,* or what the Torah *says?*"

"Is there a difference?"

"No."

"No, there's no difference? Or no, you don't believe in heaven?"

He almost, but not quite, smiled at that. "I'm sure God will look after your friend."

"But I want to know—"

"Judaism isn't about what you believe," he said. "It's about who you *are,* about how you *act.* If you ask a hundred rabbis about heaven, you'll get a hundred different answers."

"But there are only two answers, Rabbi. You either believe in heaven, or you don't."

"Maybe you should become a lawyer, Mr. Twerski."

I nodded again, even though it didn't sound like a compliment.

"The Torah doesn't tell us what happens after we die," he said. "It tells us to worry about the here and now. Your bar mitzvah. That's a good example of the here and now. That's what I suggest you focus on."

"Can you at least tell me your opinion?" I said.

He took a deep breath. "Here's my opinion, Mr. Twerski. I believe in heaven, and I believe in hell. I think heaven and hell are full of people just like us, except without elbows. The people in heaven and hell are sitting in front of long banquet tables—like at the reception after your bar mitzvah. But these tables go on and on forever, because heaven and hell are much bigger than one bar mitzvah reception."

"Why don't the people in heaven have elbows? That seems unfair."

"It doesn't matter—"

"I mean, I can understand why the people in hell don't have elbows—"

"Focus, Mr. Twerski!"

"All right," I said.

"So the people in heaven and the people in hell are sitting at long banquet tables, and the tables are loaded up with the most delectable food in the world—kosher, of course!—but no one has elbows, so they can't get the food to their mouths. But here's the difference. In heaven, the people feed one another, so everyone feasts. But in hell, the people are concerned only with themselves, so everyone starves. That's heaven and hell, in my opinion."

I rolled that over in my mind, tried to picture it. "Couldn't the people in hell just stick their faces in the food?"

"No!"

"Why not?" I said. "If they're sitting at the banquet table, and the banquet table is loaded up with food, why couldn't they just stick their faces straight into the food and eat that way? It would be real messy, for sure. But what do they care? They're in hell. How much worse could things get?"

Rabbi Salzberg stared at the ceiling and folded his hands together as if he was praying. After a couple of seconds, he looked back down at me. He had that sour-pickle expression again. "Mr. Twerski, you asked me my opinion, and I told you. Now go home, and study your haftarah."

"But—"

"Go!"

I turned around and walked toward the door.

Once I was out the door, he called after me, "I'm sorry about your friend, Mr. Twerski."

Ninth Graders

No one calls me Mr. Twerski except the rabbis at Gates of Prayer. Ninth graders sometimes call me Twerski when they pass me in the hall at McMasters, if they bother to talk to me, or Twerp, because it kind of sounds like Twerski—plus it's an insult, which is what ninth graders like. The rest of the world calls me Julian, which is my first name, or sometimes Jules, because it's shorter.

Lots of people know who I am on account of this long diary thing I wrote last year, which got passed around quite a bit. It was about running fast and skipping a report on Shakespeare and other stuff that happened back in sixth grade.

My English teacher, Mr. Selkirk, wrote an article about it for the PTA newsletter, and then the *Long Island Press* got wind of it and printed a story about how a kid from P.S. 23 wrote a book. Which I didn't. But it was long—you wouldn't believe how long if I told you. (Nine composition books long!) I've gotten a few months of junior high school under my belt since then, and I've grown up a lot, but I'd be lying if I said I didn't miss good old Selkirk every now and then. But what can you do? Life goes on.

Junior high is another world, of course. The difference between sixth grade and junior high is like the difference between a fishbowl and an aquarium, and ninth graders never let seventh graders forget who are the sharks and who are the guppies. They'll come up behind you and snag your books as soon as look at you. Nothing cracks up a ninth grader more than knocking loose a seventh grader's textbooks and binders and watching his stuff go tumbling and fluttering down a flight of stairs. Once you get past snagging books, chewing with their mouths open, and making farting noises with their armpits, there's not much more to say about ninth graders.

But of course there's got to be a worst of the worst, the absolute *ninth-est* of ninth graders, and at McMasters Junior High, that would be Devlin. If you want to picture him, think of a scraggly blond mop, except a mop has more meat on its bones and more brains in its mophead.

Devlin was the first guy to snag my books, on the first day of classes, and after he did it, he yelled, "Suh-nag!" Like the word had two syllables. "Suh-nag" is the ninth-grade version of "What are you going to do about it?" (What I did about it, in case you're curious, was pick up my books and then walk up the stairs to my next class.)

Devlin has a thing against me, by the way. Last June, I was out on a date for the very first time with a girl named Jillian—who, it turned out, he liked, and who, it turned out, also liked him. In the end Devlin kind of took over the date I had with Jillian, and he and Jillian wound up together. Which somehow, in his mophead of a brain, means I did him wrong. You'd have to be a ninth grader to makes sense of it. But here's the punch line: Jillian got zoned to a different junior high, nearer where she lived, so now she's not with Devlin, and she's not with me, and the only time I think about her is when Devlin glares at me in the hallways at McMasters.

So ninth graders are the worst, and Devlin is the worst of the worst. Eighth graders aren't quite as foul as ninth graders. They're kind of at an in-between stage—like milk that's about to go cheesy, but if you're thirsty enough, you think that maybe it's still drinkable.

I'm in the Fast Track Program, which means I'll skip eighth grade next year and go straight to cheese. (Except I won't, since I'll remember what it's like.) It also means

I'll wind up a year ahead of the rest of the guys from the block: Lonnie, Quentin, Eric the Red, Howie Wartnose, and Shlomo Shlomo. That's the entire Thirty-Fourth Avenue gang. We're not a *gang* gang—I mean like the Hells Angels. But we've been friends forever, and there's stuff that's happened with us that no one else knows about, so it's hard for an outsider to join in.

That's why—to get to the point—it would've felt wrong to go ahead with my bar mitzvah while Quentin was still sick. How could I have said the Hebrew words and not thought about Quentin lying in that hospital? It would've killed me every time I glanced down at the front row of the congregation, every time I noticed he wasn't there. If Rabbi Salzberg hadn't called my dad a couple of hours ago and suggested pushing back the bar mitzvah from January to the end of May, I'm sure my dad would've decided to do it on his own.

The four of us—Mom and Dad, me and Amelia—were sitting around the dinner table when the call from Rabbi Salzberg came. You could hear the relief in my dad's voice even before he hung up the phone.

Old Mrs. Griff

It was bitter cold this morning when I met Lonnie for the walk to school. The trip from the corner of Thirty-Fourth Avenue and Parsons to the front door of McMasters is about three-quarters of a mile—eight avenues north and five streets east. Lonnie and I sometimes walk it, sometimes ride the bus. The rest of the guys almost always ride the bus, especially during the winter. I was glad it was just me and Lonnie today, since I had to let him know the bar mitzvah was on hold until the end of May. He nodded when I told him—what else could he do but nod? It's not like I had to say why.

We went another few blocks without talking, just thinking thoughts. Then, to break the mood, he began razzing me about how much extra work I'd have to do on my haftarah. "With your brains, you'll know the thing backwards. You should do that, Jules! You should learn it backwards and then say it backwards in temple. Who's going to know?"

"C'mon, you know who'd know."

"I'm telling you, Magoo's going to make you say it standing on one foot. He's not going to let up until you cry uncle."

"Then I'll just cry uncle and get it over with."

"You might be a rabbi yourself by the time you're done with it."

We went back and forth like that for the rest of the walk, yakking it up about nothing, taking in the sights. Not that there were many sights to take in. It snowed a couple of weeks ago, and even though the snow was long gone from Thirty-Fourth Avenue, you could still see iced-over traces of it on the front lawns of houses as we made our way into Whitestone.

It's a nicer area than Flushing, at least the part of Whitestone we were walking through. There are no apartment buildings, nothing higher than two floors—just private homes until you get to Twenty-Sixth Avenue. That's where the two schools are, P.S. 23 and McMasters Junior High, right across the street from one another. But

I wouldn't want to live in Whitestone. It's too flat and too open. The neighborhood has no nooks and crannies, nowhere you can go with your friends where a half dozen neighborhood moms can't look out their kitchen windows and see what you're doing. There's nowhere like Ponzini— which is the abandoned lot off Parsons where we spend most of our time.

Still, if you take a step back, you'd have to say that Whitestone is nicer than Flushing. The streets are cleaner and quieter, and it's got old-fashioned mailboxes that sit on wooden poles, and during the spring it's got sparrows and robins instead of pigeons, and the people who live there own their houses and drive new cars and don't have to park them six blocks from their houses, since the houses come with garages.

The rest of the guys were hopping off the bus in front of McMasters as we turned the corner at Twenty-Sixth Avenue. Lonnie yelled to Eric, which got his attention, and he, Howie, and Shlomo waited for us to come up the block.

McMasters is a real school-looking school. The place is huge, which I guess it has to be, since it's got over a thousand kids. The building is four stories high and takes up half the block, and the yard takes up the other half. It's got reddish-brown bricks on the first floor, but after that it's just long glass windows, which glint in the sunlight, so it's kind of painful to look at on sunny days.

"My bar mitzvah got moved back to May," I told them as soon as we got within earshot of the rest of the guys.

Shlomo started to laugh. "You need more time to study?"

Howie swatted him in the back of the head, and the reason sank in.

"You think I should move mine?" Eric asked. "You don't think he'll still be in the hospital in March, do you?"

"Don't be an idiot," Lonnie said. "He won't still be in the hospital in March."

"How do you know?"

"Because by then—" Lonnie cut himself off. He didn't want to say the rest, and none of us wanted to hear it, even though we were all thinking it. "You're not going to have to move your bar mitzvah, okay? One way or the other, he'll be out of the hospital. Let's leave it at that."

It was just as well that the warning bell rang at that moment. We walked through the front doors of McMasters together, then went our separate ways. That meant fighting through crowds of kids rushing to their homerooms.

I like to take my time in the morning. There's only about a half-minute difference between taking your time and running like a maniac, dodging back and forth, ricocheting off other kids running in the opposite direction, so what's the point of knocking yourself out?

Plus, the hallways of McMasters are full of student art, paintings and drawings, and new stuff goes up each week. You'd be amazed at how good it is. Some of the art looks so much like the thing that it could've been done by a professional artist. It's a definite step up from the giant oaktag posters that lined the halls of P.S. 23. There's this one painting of the Bowne House—it's on the third floor, right after you come out of the staircase. The first time I noticed it, it stopped me in my tracks.

The Bowne House, in case you don't know, is a big historical site in Flushing. Quakers used to worship there. So I guess it's kind of inspirational. But what got to me wasn't the Quaker stuff. It was the way the artist had laid on the yellow paint so that you could almost feel the heat from the fireplace coming through the windows. You can't, of course. I've reached up a half dozen times and touched it, and the paint is cold. But then you step away, and the warm glow comes back. Truthfully, I can't believe a *student* painted that thing. I've tried to read the kid's name, which is in the lower right corner, but I can't make it out. If I could, and I met the guy, even if he was a ninth grader, I'd shake his hand.

My homeroom is on the third floor, room 301. It's

reserved for seventh graders in the Fast Track Program, so the rest of the kids call it the Spaz Track (which is the *nicest* thing they call it). Really, though, it's just an average classroom. You've got your blackboard up front, your American flag off to the side, your teacher's desk, and then five rows of student desks with five desks in each row. Nothing special. But I *do* like the posters of famous authors, with quotes underneath: "We are what we repeatedly do. Excellence, then, is not an act but a habit." That's by Aristotle, an ancient Greek author. I mean, how could you *not* stop and think about it?

Room 301 also comes with Mrs. Griff, the oldest teacher I've ever had. She's hunched over at the waist and has white hair the color and shape of a dandelion. But she also has a sense of humor about it—about being old, I mean. She told us the first day of school to think of her as a "sweet little old granny . . . who's not afraid to kick your butts if they need kicking." There are a few guys who take advantage of her, tossing paper airplanes and shooting rubber bands when she turns her back to write on the board. She'll hear them sometimes, then wheel around and say, "Now cut the shenanigans!" That cracks up the class even more. But what's the point of doing stuff if the teacher's too old to catch on? Where's the challenge?

We're only with Mrs. Griff long enough for her to take morning attendance and write a few announcements and reminders. Then we split up and head to our first-period classes. We don't see her again until the end of the day, when she takes afternoon attendance, writes a few more announcements and reminders, and lets us go home.

This afternoon, though, Mrs. Griff pulled me aside after she dismissed the class. She didn't make a big deal of it. She just kind of got in my way as I was heading out the door, and put her arm in front of me. Then she nodded toward my seat. So I went back and sat down. When we were the only two people left in the room, she walked over, leaned against the desk next to mine, and said, "Beverly mentioned that you and she have a sick friend."

"Yeah," I said.

"You're probably expecting me to give you words of encouragement."

I looked up at her. "Isn't that what you're going to do?"

"I'm going to tell you to persevere. Do you know what that means?"

I shook my head.

"It means to keep going," she said. "That's the last I'll say on the topic."

She nodded at the door, and I got up and left.

Say what you want about old Mrs. Griff. But she kept it short and sweet.

The Accusation

You'd think one visit to the guidance counselor's office would cover me for the month. But as second period was winding down and the teacher, Mr. Gerber, was talking about how inert gases can't fit any more electrons in their outer shell, the intercom began to crackle that certain way, and then Principal Salvatore came on and said my name just like I knew he would. I had to report to Miss Medina's office.

The class hooted again, of course, and Beverly glanced up at me with a confused look. But I was kind of relieved. Since no one else got called, I knew it had nothing to do with Quentin. So I grabbed my books and coat, because

I knew the period would be over before I got back, and headed out the door.

Miss Medina was waiting for me, again, right outside her office on the first floor. She was rubbing her forehead with her fingertips. It was a nervous-looking thing to be doing. It made her look like a student, except for how tall she was.

She led me into her office and sat down behind her desk. I didn't sit, since I didn't know how long I'd be there. Her expression was different from what it was like when she talked to us about Quentin. She was staring me down, waiting for me to say something. I had no idea what she wanted me to say.

After maybe ten seconds, she said, "Julian, do you have anything you want to talk about?"

"I don't think so."

"Are you certain?"

"Is there something you *want* me to talk about?"

"Don't fence with me, Julian."

"Miss Medina, I don't know—"

"I understand there's a work of art you're fond of."

"Do you mean *Judith Beheading Holofernes*?"

"What?"

"It's a painting by Caravaggio. I wrote about it last year for Mr. Selkirk. . . ."

She crossed her arms over her chest. "How would I know that, Julian?"

"Then I don't understand what you mean," I said.

"I gather there's a work of art here, *at McMasters,* that you admire."

"You mean the Bowne House painting?"

Miss Medina didn't answer. Instead, she reached down behind her desk and came up with the painting. She set it on the edge of her desk and held it upright so that I couldn't see her face behind it. All I could see of her were her hands on either side.

"Yeah," I said. "I like that one a lot."

She stood up but continued to hold the painting in front of me. "Now, Julian, is there anything you want to tell me?"

"About what?"

"This is *not* a joke," she said. "No one is laughing."

"I'm not laughing either. I don't know what you're talking about."

"Look in the lower right-hand corner."

I glanced down at the corner of the painting, where the signature was—the one I could never quite make out. The letters *JT* were scratched into the surface of the paint. It looked like whoever did it had used a house key or a pocketknife or something.

"Wow, who would do that?" I said.

"I don't know . . . Julian Twerski." She said it with an extra-hard stress on the *J* and *T*.

I guess I kind of laughed, which, looking back, wasn't a smart thing to do. "You don't think *I* did that, do you?"

"Do you think it's funny?"

"No, but why would I mess up a painting I like?"

"Would you mess up a painting you didn't like?"

"No, I wouldn't mess up a painting either way."

"Julian, this is *serious*," she said. "Principal Salvatore is talking about suspending you."

"But I didn't do anything."

"You've never touched the painting?"

I was about to say no, but then I caught myself. "No, I've touched it. I touched it a few times because I wanted to feel the paint. But I didn't mess it up. I guess I shouldn't have touched it. I *could've* messed it up if I accidentally knocked it off the wall—"

"Then you admit you *could have* messed it up?"

"But I *didn't*," I said. "It *didn't* fall off the wall."

"Julian, your initials are carved into the surface."

"Why would I do that if I were going to mess up the painting? It would be like waving a flag and yelling, 'Hey, look, Julian Twerski is the guy who messed up this painting!' It would be stupid."

"You're a very clever young man," she said. "Maybe you're clever enough to think you could use that argument."

"But—"

"Look," she said, stashing the painting back behind her desk. "I realize you've been under stress because your friend Quentin is sick."

"I started keeping a journal, like you said."

"That was only a suggestion, Julian. It's irrelevant to this conversation."

"But you said it, and I'm doing it, and I'm glad I'm doing it."

"I'll mention that to Principal Salvatore. But you've got to meet me halfway."

"Halfway to where?"

"You've at least got to apologize," she said.

"But I didn't—"

"Julian, I have an eyewitness who says you did it, who *saw* you doing it."

"Did my friend Lonnie tell you that? Because he's a real practical joker. . . ."

"No, it wasn't your friend Lonnie," she said, "and no, again, this is *not* a joke."

"Then I don't know what to say."

"Just say you're sorry. If you do, I can talk to Principal Salvatore about the stress you've been under."

I thought it over. "But I really and truly didn't scratch the painting."

She took a deep breath, then let it out. "Follow me."

I followed her out of her office and into the principal's office, which was right next door. Miss Medina nodded at the secretary in the front office, who nodded back, and then we headed past her and through a glass door. As we walked in, Principal Salvatore was sitting behind his desk, staring out a huge window that looked onto the street. He was a short guy with black hair, a real round head, and dark stubble on his face. He didn't have a beard, but he looked like he needed a shave. He always looked that way.

Miss Medina and I sat down on folding chairs in front of the desk.

He cleared his throat and said, "I gather we have a problem."

Miss Medina looked at me like I was supposed to talk. I kept quiet.

"I see," Principal Salvatore said. "You're Julian Twerski, right?"

"Yes."

"You were suspended from sixth grade last year—for a full week."

"Yes."

"You injured a handicapped boy. Is that right?"

I looked off to the side but nodded. I felt the shame of the thing all over again. "We egged him."

"Egged him?"

"We threw eggs at him." My voice got shaky when I

said that. Talking about what we did to Danley Dimmel always curls me up on the inside. "We apologized to him, but that doesn't make it go away."

"Do you carry a knife with you to school?"

"No!"

Miss Medina interrupted. "Julian isn't violent, Principal Salvatore."

"Ah." He drummed his fingers on the desk. "Did you think you deserved to get suspended for that incident?"

"Yes."

"So you accepted responsibility?"

"Yes."

"That's good, Julian. But it's water under the bridge. What matters is what you do in *my* school, not the mistakes you made in the past. Is that clear?"

"Yes."

"Now tell me about the painting," he said.

"Miss Medina thinks I messed up the painting of the Bowne House. It's not her fault for thinking that, because someone told her I did. Except I didn't do it. That's the honest truth."

He leaned forward. "Is that the story you're sticking to?"

"I don't know what else to tell you," I said. "I didn't do it."

"What would you do if you were in my position, Julian?"

"I guess if I thought I had the right guy, I'd suspend him."

"That's a very honest answer," he said.

"Am I suspended?"

He shook his head. "I gather your friend is ill."

"Quentin," I said. "His name is Quentin."

"Do you worry about Quentin?"

"Yes."

"What Quentin is going through, does it make you angry?"

"I don't think 'angry' is the right word," I said.

"Miss Medina thinks I should let you off with a warning."

I glanced at her, and she said, "Under the circumstances—"

"But I really and truly didn't do it, Principal Salvatore."

"Do you see, Julian?" he said. "That's the core of my dilemma. How can I let you off with a warning when we can't agree on what I'm warning you about? That would make no sense."

I shrugged. I didn't know what else to do.

"I gather you're a writer, Julian."

"I like to write, yeah."

"Are you a good citizen as well?"

"I don't know what you mean."

"I'm asking if you consider yourself a good citizen."

"I guess," I said. "I try to be."

"Do you know what it means to be a good citizen?"

"Yes, I think so."

"I want you to tell me what it means to be a good citizen."

"Being a good citizen, in my opinion—"

"No, Julian," he said. "I want you to write an essay on good citizenship. I expect it to be at least two hundred words. And I expect it on my desk Monday morning, before first period. Do I make myself clear?"

"But I didn't do anything!"

"This conversation is over."

Principal Salvatore spun his chair around and slid open a file drawer. As he started to riffle through papers, Miss Medina got up and tapped me on the shoulder. She nodded at the door, which meant I was supposed to leave.

So I walked out, shaking my head.

There was only one guy in the hallway as I left Principal Salvatore's office. It was Devlin. He was halfway down the hall, near the center stairwell. As soon as I noticed him, he began to smile in a sly, sarcastic way. Then he ducked into the stairwell, and a second later I heard his footsteps running up the stairs.

December 20, 1969

The Principle of the Thing

I actually meant to write the stupid essay on citizenship when I sat down at my desk last night, but I couldn't figure out how to start. So instead I wrote about how I got roped into writing the essay, and then, by the time I got finished writing *that,* I was so worked up that I couldn't do it. Well, I guess I could've done it, but I didn't do it. It's just wrong.

I *didn't* scratch up that painting. If I wrote the essay, it would be like saying I did it—even if I said straight out in the essay I didn't do it. Which I didn't. So I put down my pen and closed my composition book. Except then I couldn't fall asleep. The whole situation was gnawing at me.

Looking at it from their point of view, I can understand

how Miss Medina and Principal Salvatore think they're doing the right thing. I'm sure they think they're going easy on me, asking me to write a 200-word essay. That's not even one full page. I just counted up the words I've written in the last three paragraphs, and the total is 179. That means by the time I get to the end of this sentence, the total will be over 200. There, you see? I just counted it up again, and it's 219. It's not like it's hard to do, coming up with 200 words.

It's the principle of the thing.

That's one of my dad's big expressions: *It's the principle of the thing.* Until now, I've always thought of it as his way of saying, "I'm going to cut off my nose to spite my face." Like the time he asked old Mr. Dong, our landlord, if he could park his car in the driveway in front of our house. It's just a two-floor house, with the Dongs on the first floor and us upstairs, and the Dongs don't even own a car, so the driveway is always empty. My dad offered Mr. Dong an extra twenty-five dollars a month. But Mr. Dong wanted fifty. My dad told him to forget about it. He said he could've afforded the fifty dollars, but it was the principle of the thing. It made no sense to me.

Until now.

It *is* the principle of the thing between me and Principal Salvatore—which is kind of a funny sentence if you say it out loud. Two hundred words means even less to me than fifty bucks means to my dad. But it's just not right. I *didn't* scratch up that painting.

The thing was still gnawing at me when I woke up this morning. I woke up earlier than usual—or earlier than usual for a Saturday—and wolfed down a couple of unfrosted cherry Pop-Tarts. Then I headed across the street to Lonnie's house. He lives on Thirty-Fourth Avenue, like the rest of us, except on the other side of Parsons, at the far corner—which means, if you get technical about it, he's the only one of us who doesn't live on the actual block. It wasn't even nine o'clock when I got to his front door, and I stood there for about half a minute in the cold air deciding whether to knock or ring the doorbell like I always did.

Just as I put out my hand to knock, the door swung open. Lonnie's mom, Mrs. Fine, was smiling at me. She said, "Good morning, Julian. Do you want breakfast?" Those were the words she said, but with Mrs. Fine it never quite sounds like the words. She was in a concentration camp in World War II, and the Nazis did bad things to her tongue, and now whatever she says comes out thick and wet, and real sad to listen to. (It makes my mom cry sometimes, though never in front of Mrs. Fine.)

She led me back to the kitchen, where Lonnie was sitting, finishing off a plate of Mallomars. That's the other thing about Mrs. Fine: she's real good-natured. She lets Lonnie eat whatever he wants, whenever he wants. Cookies for breakfast? No problem.

"I didn't hear the doorbell," Lonnie said, looking up.

"Julian was too polite to ring it," Mrs. Fine said . . . except, again, the words didn't come out like that. She grabbed my hair and messed with it, which is what she likes to do, then left us alone.

Lonnie held out his last Mallomar to me, but I shook my head.

"What are you doing here so early?" he said.

I sat down across the table from him. "I woke up and couldn't go back to sleep."

"The guys won't be around for another hour."

"Yeah, I know."

"I got a couple of dead Spaldings," he said. "Do you want to roof 'em?"

"Maybe later."

"Something's bugging you."

"Yeah."

"I can always tell when something's bugging you. That's the reason you're a crappy card player."

"When was the last time we played cards?"

"Never," he said.

"Then how do you know I'm a crappy card player?"

"I'm just saying you *would* be a crappy card player *if* we played cards."

"Then I guess we're never going to play cards," I said.

"That's just as well, because I hate cards."

"Then why are we talking about cards?"

"You want to talk about what's bugging you?"

So I told him about the thing with the painting. He listened to the entire story and didn't interrupt, not even once. After I was done, he still didn't speak. He reached out and popped the last Mallomar into his mouth. He took a long time chewing it, and while he was doing that, I could see his brain working, rolling over what I'd told him.

Then, at last, he said, "So who's the worm who told Miss Medina you did it?"

"I don't know," I said. "If I had to guess, I'd go with that guy Devlin."

"The guy who looks like a mop?"

"He was standing outside Principal Salvatore's office when I got out, and he had a sly look on his face."

"What's he got against you?" Lonnie asked.

"The thing with Jillian, I guess. . . ."

"*He* stole her away from *you.*"

"Lonnie, the guy just doesn't like me," I said. "It's not logical."

"You think he'd scratch up a painting just to get you in trouble?"

"He's a *ninth grader*," I said.

"All right, I see your point."

"So what would *you* do?"

"You mean, if I had to write the essay?"

"Yeah."

Lonnie grinned. "I'd probably get you to write it for me."

"Be serious! Do you think I should write the essay?"

"Why wouldn't you write it?" he said.

"Because it's not fair."

"And?"

"There's no *and*," I said. "It's not fair. Why should I write the essay if it's not fair?"

"But it's a two-hundred-word essay. You could knock it out in, what? A half hour?"

"I could knock it out in fifteen minutes. But that's not the point."

"I don't see the problem," he said.

"It's the principle of the thing."

"Oh, it's the *principle* of the thing."

"Don't say it like that. It matters."

"It only matters because you're you," Lonnie said. "Suppose you woke up tomorrow and, for no reason, Presto the Magician had turned you into a raisin."

"But that would never happen. . . ."

"Say it did. Would that be fair?"

"No!"

"How would you feel about it?"

"I'd think it was unfair," I said.

"Wrong!"

"How do you know it's wrong?"

"You'd be a raisin, which means you *wouldn't* think it was unfair, because raisins don't think."

"That's just stupid."

"Look, you're a raisin. You don't understand what's stupid and what's not stupid. You don't understand what's fair and what's not fair. That's the key to the whole thing. You've got to think like a raisin. Which means *don't think*. Just do what you need to do."

I shook my head and took a deep breath. "So you want to roof the Spaldings?"

"What roof?"

"You pick."

"I was thinking the Dorado," he said.

Five minutes later, Lonnie and I were standing in front of the Dorado House, glancing up at the roof. The Dorado is in the exact middle of the block—I've stepped it off—halfway between Union Street and Parsons Boulevard.

"You want to go first or throw first?"

"I'll go," I said.

What that meant was I'd climb the fire escape on the side of the building to the roof, which was six stories up. Then Lonnie would throw the rubber balls up to the roof, and I'd throw them back down to him. After he roofed them ten times, we'd switch.

I walked around to the side of the building, jumped up, and caught the bottom rung of the fire escape ladder. As I was hanging there, about to chin myself up, I heard a voice. "Hey, Twerski, what are you doing?"

It was Beverly Segal. She lives in the Dorado House. She was pushing her bike out the side door.

"What does it look like I'm doing?"

"Does Coco want a banana?"

"Very funny," I said, still hanging.

"Hey, Coco, why don't you race me?"

"I'm *not* racing you, Beverly."

"I guess you're Coco the chicken," she said. "I thought you were Coco the monkey."

"Yes, I'm Coco the chicken. That's the reason I won't race you."

She flapped her arms at her sides and started to laugh, then hopped on her bike and pedaled away.

You know, if I were a raisin, I'd race her—just to get it over with.

Except I'd lose, because I'd be a raisin.

That was what I was thinking as I climbed the fire escape.

December 22, 1969

Good Citizenship

Here's the essay on good citizenship I
wrote for Principal Salvatore:

No. No. No. No. No. No. No. No. No. No. No. No.
No. No. No. No. No. No. No. No. No. No. No. No.
No. No. No. No. No. No. No. No. No. No. No. No.
No. No. No. No. No. No. No. No. No. No. No. No.
No. No. No. No. No. No. No. No. No. No. No. No.
No. No. No. No. No. No. No. No. No. No. No. No.
No. No. No. No. No. No. No. No. No. No. No. No.
No. No. No. No. No. No. No. No. Ness. No. No. No.
No. No. No. No. No. No. No. No. No. No. No. No.
No. No. No. No. No. No. No. No. No. No. No. No.

No. No. No. No. No. No. No. No. No. No. No. No.
No. No. No. No. No. No. No. No. No. No. No.
No. No. No. No. No. No. No. No. No. No. No.
No. No. No. No. No. No. No. No. No. No. No.
No. No. No. No. No. No. No. No. No. No. No.
No. No. No. No. No. No. There, I think that's
exactly two hundred words (counting the
words in the parentheses).

I slipped the paper under the door of Principal Salvatore's office first thing in the morning, then rushed off to homeroom and waited to hear my name over the intercom. I was curious whether he'd suspend me for a couple of days or for a full week. Either way, I'd catch up on the work I missed, and that would be the end of it, but no way was I going to write an essay on good citizenship. It would be like admitting I scratched up the painting.

But homeroom came and went, and the intercom never crackled. Sitting in first-period social studies, I began to think that maybe Principal Salvatore cracked up at what I wrote, and decided to let the whole thing drop. But Miss Medina was waiting for me outside the classroom door as social studies ended. She handed me the paper and shook her head, then walked off. On the back of the paper, Principal Salvatore had written:

Julian, I read your "essay" on good citizenship, and I gather you want me to suspend you. That's the reason I'm not going to do it. But I'll expect a real essay on my desk the Monday after Christmas break. And I'll expect an essay each Monday until you take the assignment seriously. You clearly don't know who you're dealing with.

—Dr. Salvatore

The Tzedakah Dollar

It's Christmas Eve, but it's hard to get in the mood because of what's going on with Quentin. Christmas is a big deal on Thirty-Fourth Avenue, even if it drives Rabbi Salzberg crazy. He says you're either cream or milk . . . you can't be half-and-half.

What he means is you're either Jewish or you're not Jewish, and if you're Jewish, you're supposed to celebrate Hanukkah, not Christmas. Like that's ever going to happen. *Yes, Rabbi, I'd much rather get eight crappy little presents, like dreidels and shoehorns and handkerchiefs, than one really good present, like a slot car race track.* (Which was what I got for Christmas last year.) But here's the thing: we get Christmas presents, but we also get the dreidels and shoehorns and handkerchiefs for Hanukkah. Plus, we light the candles, so it's never a Hanukkah versus Christmas thing. It's both.

Quentin's family is the same way. So is Eric the Red's and Howie Wartnose's—Howie's parents go the whole nine yards and put up a real tree! If you look in their window at the Hampshire House, you'll see a lit-up menorah sitting on the windowsill, with a lit-up Christmas tree standing right behind it. Mike the Bike, who's a Catholic, saw that a couple of years ago and called Howie a dirty Jew—except it sounded more like "doity chew," because that's how Mike talks—and then rode off real fast before Howie could get hold of him. But it was a stupid thing to say, because the next week, when school started up again, Howie jumped him during recess. Then, at the end of the day, he jumped him again and broke the kickstand off his bicycle.

The only Hanukkah-but-not-Christmas guys on Thirty-Fourth Avenue are Shlomo and Lonnie, which makes sense, because Shlomo's dad is by-the-book strict and Lonnie's mom was in the concentration camp. The Jewish stuff is a major thing for them. I mean, it's a *thing* for all of us. It's not like any of us are worming our way out of Hebrew school. But it's not a *major* thing.

The funniest thing that ever happened on Christmas happened just last year. It didn't happen on Christmas exactly, but it happened *because of* Christmas. It was a week later, so it was right after we egged Danley Dimmel. (Which wasn't funny at all.) But what happened with Quentin's Christmas present—that was the funny thing.

Quentin got twenty bucks for Christmas last year. His dad woke him up on Christmas morning and slipped him a twenty-dollar bill. Just like that! None of us had ever had a twenty-dollar bill before. Not even Lonnie, who would sometimes wave around a ten-dollar bill he got for working in his father's candy store. But a *twenty*—that was just unreal!

I can't tell you how many arguments we had over what Quentin should do with his money. Shlomo kept saying he should buy a set of walkie-talkies, but Howie kept saying he should buy a Saturn V model rocket kit. The only thing we ruled out was Eric's idea. He wanted Quentin to get a year's subscription to *Mad Magazine,* which Quentin would never read, since he didn't like to read, but Eric would read over and over, because he loved *Mad Magazine.*

It was the Thursday after New Year's, late in the afternoon, and the five of us—Quentin, Howie, Eric, Shlomo, and me—were walking up Parsons Boulevard to Hebrew school. Lonnie wasn't with us, because he'd gotten bar mitzvahed a couple of months before, so he didn't have to go anymore. (It always feels weird when Lonnie's not there. He's kind of the glue that holds the gang together.)

We were halfway to Gates of Prayer, just crossing Northern Boulevard, when Eric asked us if we'd remembered to get tzedakah dollars from our moms. Tzedakah, in case you don't know, is charity money the rabbis collect for poor people. Except in Hebrew school it's not a choice. You *have* to cough up that dollar every week, and then you have to walk up to the front of the classroom, with the rest of the kids watching, and you have to fold the dollar in half and slide it into the tzedakah box—or else you get a note home to your parents.

So Eric asked us if we'd remembered, and Quentin got this nervous look on his face, and right off we knew he'd forgotten his tzedakah dollar. None of us had an extra one, so it looked like Quentin was going to get that note home. Except then he pulled out the twenty-dollar bill.

"What good is that?" Shlomo said. "You think the rabbi's going to make change?"

"Then I'll just put in the whole thing," Quentin said.

I'm not sure who said what, because the sentences got jumbled together, but Howie and Shlomo and Eric shouted over one another, "You're out of your mind!" and "You've got to be kidding!" and "Over my dead body!"

Quentin laughed, but it was a panicky laugh.

"Look," I said, "why don't we just go into the deli and get change for the twenty?"

That's what we did. I took Quentin's twenty, and the five of us walked into the Parsons Deli and up to the counter. I did the talking, and the old guy behind the cash register was shaking his head before I even was done asking the question. "No change without a purchase," he said.

"C'mon!" Howie cried. "What's the big deal?"

"Either buy something, or get out of my store."

So I glanced around and saw a box of Bazooka bubble gum. One piece for one penny. I grabbed one piece and gave the guy the twenty-dollar bill.

"You got to buy something else," he said.

I looked up at him and said in a soft voice, "I think that's against the law."

Which I was pretty sure was true.

He stared me down. I looked him in the eyes, but I tried to do it in a hopeful way, not an angry way.

"Give me the damn twenty," he said.

He took the bill, opened the cash register, and handed me back a ten-dollar bill, a five-dollar bill, and five ones.

"Don't we owe you a penny for the bubble gum?"

"It's on the house," he said. "Now get out of here."

Problem solved, right?

So a couple of hours later, we're sitting in Rabbi Salzberg's classroom, and we're getting near the end of class, and he pulls out the tzedakah box from the bottom drawer of his desk and sets it down on top of the desk. As soon as he does that, we all reach for our dollars, and that starts the parade up to the front of the room, one by one, in alphabetical order.

When Quentin's turn comes up, he's got this big smile on his face, and I'm feeling pretty good about that smile, because it was my idea to get change at the deli . . . except then, as he passes by my desk, I notice he's got the ten-dollar bill in his hand instead of a one. I reach out to grab him, but it's too late. He's out of reach. I call his name under my breath, but he can't hear me. Quentin is still smiling as he folds the ten-dollar bill in half and slides it into the tzedakah box.

I thought Howie was going to strangle him on the walk home from Gates of Prayer. Eric and Shlomo were yelling at Quentin and cracking up at the same time. You should have seen Lonnie's reaction when we told him what had happened. He was rolling on the floor, gasping for breath. I don't think I've ever seen him crack up so hard. I mean, we razzed Quentin for months afterward. None of it bothered him. The guy is just good-natured.

He kept saying how he still had ten dollars, and that was more money than he'd ever had before. You know, to this day, I have no idea what he did with that ten dollars.

Except here's the thing: the more I think about it, the more I think Quentin did it on purpose. It's nothing I can say for sure. But he always got this look on his face when we were arguing over what to do with his twenty-dollar bill. It was like the entire thing made him feel weird. I think maybe he meant to get rid of all the arguing in the tzedakah box.

Good Citizenship

Here's the second essay on good citizenship I wrote for Principal Salvatore:

> Last week, I learned that good citizenship
> is more than just writing "no" over and
> over, which shows a negative attitude.
> So: Yes. Yes. Yes. Yes. Yes. Yes. Yes. Yes. Yes.
> Yes. Yes. Yes. Yes. Yes. Yes. Yes. Yes. Yes.
> Yes. Yes. Yes. Yes. Yes. Yes. Yes. Yes. Yes. Yes.
> Yes. Yes. Yes. Yes. Yes. Yes. Yes. Yes. Yes. Yes.
> Yes. Yes. Yes. Yes. Yes. Yes. Yes. Yes. Yes. Yes.
> Yes. Yes. Yes. Yes. Yes. Yes. Yes. Yes. Yes. Yes.
> Yes. Yes. Yes. Yes. Yes. Yes. Yes. Yes. Yes. Yes.

Yes. Yes. Yes. Yes. Yes. Yes. Yes. Yes. Yes. Yes.
Yes. Yes. Yes. Yes. Yes. Yes. Yes. Yes. Yes. Yes.
Yes. Yes. Yes. Yes. Yes. Yes. Yes. Yes. Yes. Yes.
Yes. Yes. Yes. Yes. Yes. Yes. Yes. Yes. Yes. Yes.
Yes. Yes. Yes. Yes. Yes. Yes. Yes. Yes. Yes. Yes.
Yes. Yes. Yes. Yes. Yes. Yes. Yes. Yes. Yes. Yes.
Yes. Yes. Yes. Yes. Yes. Yes. Yes. Yes. Yes. Yes.
Yes. Yes. Yes. Yes. Yes. Yes. Yes. Yes. Yes. Yes.
Yes. Yes. Yes. Yes. Yes. Yes. Yes. Yes. Yes. Yes.
Yes. Yes. Yes. Yes. Yes. Yes. Yes. Yes. Yes. In
conclusion, good citizenship is saying
"yes" all the time.

I slid the paper under the door of Principal Salvatore's office as soon as I got to school, and Miss Medina handed it back to me an hour later. Principal Salvatore had written on the back:

NO. Try again.

The Big One-Three

Dad woke me up this morning just after sunrise. He does that every year on my birthday. He sat down hard on the side of my bed, which bounced me about a foot off the mattress, and I went from fast asleep to wide awake in that second I was in the air.

The first thing I saw, after my eyes focused, was him grinning down at me. Then he said, "I tell you, Jules, you don't look a day over twelve!"

That's his routine, every birthday, as far back as I can remember. That same dumb joke, year after year, except the number keeps getting bigger. I don't mind, to be honest. It's the only day he does it, and it seems to mean a lot to him.

I yawned and said, "What did I get?"

"You're thirteen, and you're still expecting a present?"

"Yeah."

"All right, kid, I'll bring you home a pack of Camels."

"Good enough," I said.

He snatched the pillow out from under my head, which sent me rolling over. Then he clobbered me across the shoulders and back with it, just kidding around. After that, he got up and left for work.

Now here's what you need to know about my dad: he's maybe the most regular guy on the planet. Nothing ever changes with him. It's not a bad thing, but it also makes him real predictable. Like, for example, he always buys presents for me and Amelia about a week before our actual birthdays and always hides them in the same place . . . on the floor in the back of the closet in his and my mom's bedroom. He stashes them underneath a pile of dress shirts he doesn't wear anymore because he sweated through the collars. So every year, a few days before my birthday, I sneak into the closet and check underneath the pile of shirts to find out what he got me.

What he got me this year is a Bobby Murcer–autograph baseball glove.

I'll act real surprised when he hands it across the table tonight after dinner. That's part of the routine too. Plus, it *is* a great present. He knows how bad I need a new glove, and he knows Bobby Murcer is *my guy.* I've followed him since he was a rookie in 1965. Even after he got drafted into the army, I waited two years until he got out, and then I followed him again. I even kept a scrapbook the first couple of years—I pasted in the newspaper box score of every game he hit a home run. So, yeah, my dad couldn't have done much better with his present. And any other year, getting a Bobby Murcer baseball glove would have been the highlight of my day.

But Quentin totally stole my dad's thunder.

It was around three-thirty when the telephone rang. Amelia raced into the kitchen to answer it, which is what she does whenever the phone rings, and then she let out a shriek, but a second later I heard her apologizing in a soft voice. That got my curiosity up. I couldn't make out what she was saying, though, so after a minute, I forgot about it. The next thing I knew, she was standing outside the door to my room, which is as far as the phone cord stretches, smiling ear to ear, telling me I had a call.

"Who is it?" I said.

She handed the phone to me and stepped back to watch my reaction.

I stared at it for a second, then brought it to my ear and said, "Hello?"

Then came a whispery voice I didn't even recognize. "Jules?"

"Yeah . . ."

"It's Quentin."

It was one of those times when your brain short-circuits, when you want to say ten things at once, but nothing comes out of your mouth. I couldn't spit out a single word. I might as well have put the phone to my armpit and made farting noises—that's how shocked I was. I mean, the last time I saw the guy, he had that tube-thing in his mouth.

After about ten seconds of gagging and sputtering, I came up with "How do you feel?"

"Not too bad."

"So . . . er . . . is the food okay?"

Amelia slugged me in the chest when I said that. Not hard—she wasn't mad. But she was staring at me with a real frustrated look, as if to say, *That's it? That's the best you've got? That's all you have to say to the guy?* It *wasn't* all I had to say. That's for sure. But I wasn't going to get gushy over the phone, which I knew was what she wanted. That's something girls never seem to figure out, not even if they're seniors in high school, like Amelia. Guys don't get gushy with one another. That's how it works. I'm not saying it's good or bad, but that's just how it is. If I got gushy, I would've felt wrong afterward. Not only that: *Quentin* would have felt wrong afterward. He would've felt like I was getting gushy because he was sick, which would have reminded him of how sick he was. Why would I do that to him just to make Amelia happy?

"It's pretty good," he whispered. "I got orange Jell-O."

"I got a Bobby Murcer baseball glove. I mean, I didn't get it yet. But my dad's going to give it to me tonight. He hid it in the back of the closet, but I found it. Today's my birthday."

"Yeah, I know," he said.

"Oh, yeah, I guess that's why you called."

He gave a whispery laugh that almost made me bawl. "Dope!"

"We pushed back my bar mitzvah. . . ."

"Why?"

"Because of you. Because you're sick."

Amelia slugged me again, but I just ignored her.

"You didn't have to do that," he said.

"No, I wanted to. We all wanted to, even Amelia. It was like a family decision."

There was a long pause. "How'd your dad get Bobby Murcer to sign the glove?"

"Murcer didn't sign it *himself*," I said. "It's just a glove that's got his name on it."

"Oh."

"Dope!"

That made Quentin laugh again, even softer than before, and then he coughed.

"If Murcer had actually *signed* it," I said, "I'd never be able to use it, because I wouldn't want to mess it up. I mean, I'd keep it around the house. But then I'd still need a glove I could play with."

"That makes sense. . . ."

Quentin's mom got on the phone at that point and said the conversation was tiring him out, so he had to rest. I told her I understood—which I did—and said goodbye, and I heard her tell him goodbye for me, and the next thing I heard was the click and buzz of her hanging up.

Amelia took the phone from my hand, because I was still kind of in shock, and she said, "That's a pretty superb birthday present, isn't it?"

"Yeah."

"You really love that kid, don't you?"

"C'mon, Amelia!"

"I'm just teasing you, Jules. You don't have to say it to me."

"I'm *not* going to say it to you."

"But at least say it to yourself," she said.

"What's the point of saying it to myself?"

"Because if you can say it to yourself, you can say it to Quentin."

"You just want to hear me say it."

"He's real sick, Julian—"

"He's getting better! You just spoke to him yourself!"

"Don't take that chance," she said. "Say what needs to be said."

"This is stupid. . . ."

"If you don't, and something happens, you'll regret it the rest of your life. Trust me on this one."

By then, I'd heard enough. I stepped back into my room, snatched my coat from the hook on the wall, and headed outside to find Lonnie. I wanted to tell him I'd talked to Quentin while the thing was still fresh in my mind.

January 10, 1970

Saturday-Morning Services

Today would've been my bar mitzvah, the day I was supposed to become a man . . . if it hadn't gotten pushed back until the end of May. So my dad got it in his head that I should go to Saturday services at Gates of Prayer. Alone. Because, I guess, that's what men do. Except no way was he going to get up early, put on a suit, and spend the morning in temple.

I asked Lonnie if he wanted to come, and you can guess what his answer was.

So off I went at eight-fifteen, in a blazer and dress pants, just as the sun had started to warm up the air. I walked real slow, squinting into the sun. Once I got to temple, of course, that was the end of sunlight for the next hour and a half—an hour and a half of squirming on a hard wooden pew, staring into a back-to-front prayer book, and keeping my yawns to myself. Unfortunately, Lonnie's mom noticed me walk in. I'd been planning to sit in the back row, where at least I could get in a couple of good stretches, but she stood up and waved me forward. Then she gave me a long hug, like she hadn't seen me in a year, and made me sit next to her in the front row.

If there's one thing worse than sitting through Saturday-morning services, it's sitting through them with Mrs. Fine. I don't mean that in a bad way. She's my favorite of my friends' moms, and I'd say that even if she weren't so generous with Mallomars. Plus, I know the Jewish stuff gets to her on account of what happened during World War II. But that's why sitting with her is so awkward. It's like sitting next to a bag of cats, the way she yowls and moans the Hebrew words, the way she hunches up her shoulders and shakes, the way she rocks back and forth with her eyes closed, the way she sobs to herself, and meanwhile you're right there next to her, faking like you know what's going on, feeling people's eyes on you, wanting to pat her on the back and tell her it's going to be all right, that the service is going to be over in another hour . . . except you know, because of how worked up she gets, she wouldn't hear you regardless.

So, yeah, sitting next to Mrs. Fine in temple is real

awkward. On the other hand, it *does* make you think deep. It makes you think about what happened to her, and it makes you realize how good you've got it. It's the same thing, in a way, with Quentin's tumor. It makes you feel guilty, almost, on account of he's sick and you're not. It's like—I don't even know how to explain it. It just hits you. Like you're running down the block, running to get home for dinner, and the wind is whistling in your ears, and you're taking deep breaths, and the air just comes and goes like it's nothing, and then, out of nowhere, you remember Quentin is stuck in that hospital bed, with those tubes going in and out of him, and it just doesn't seem fair.

You think about stuff like that, sitting in temple next to Mrs. Fine, because you can't *not* think about it. It seems like the natural thing to do. So I figured as long as I was there, I might as well get into the spirit of the thing and pray a little. I said a quick prayer, which I felt bad about afterward, because, looking back, it's not the nicest prayer. But here's what I prayed: I prayed that when Quentin got out of the hospital, he wouldn't get all religious like Mrs. Fine.

It was maybe another ten minutes until Rabbi Salzberg said the last "amen" and the service ended. I jumped up and was about to cheese it. But then, a second later, I felt Mrs. Fine's hand take hold of mine, and she lifted my hand to her lips and kissed it. It felt wet, the kiss, because it had tears mixed in with it. She looked down at me afterward, and her eyes were tearing up, and she said, "You're a good boy, Julian."

I nodded. What else could I do? But I was thinking: *Tell that to Principal Salvatore.*

Then she let go of me. I grabbed my overcoat and walked away, not too fast but not too slow either. The side door of the temple was open, and sunlight was pouring into the place, and I was maybe ten feet from fresh air and freedom. But at the last second, Rabbi Salzberg shuffled to the edge of the stage and called out my name: "Mr. Twerski!" He was close enough, and enough people were standing between us, that I couldn't pretend not to hear him.

I turned and called back, "Yes, Rabbi?"

"Come here, Mr. Twerski."

I took a couple of steps toward the stage, but then I heard my name again. It came from outside. I glanced over my shoulder, toward the side door, and was blinded by the sun. But I knew the voice. It was Lonnie's. "Hey, Jules!"

"Mr. Twerski," Rabbi Salzberg said, "I'm right here. Are you confused?"

I spun back around. "Sorry, Rabbi, I've got to go."

Saying that, I rushed out the door.

As soon as I stepped outside, Lonnie grabbed the

sleeve of my coat and started to pull me through the crowd. We were weaving in and out, walking fast until we got to the sidewalk, and then we took off running. I had no idea where we were going, but I was glad to be in the open air, feeling the sun on my face, making a quick getaway from Gates of Prayer.

After a couple of blocks, my dress shoes were cutting into my feet. I slowed down to a walk again, which caused Lonnie to slow down too. We were both huffing and kind of laughing.

"All right," he said, "I think the coast is clear."

"You don't think the posse's coming after us?"

"Well, Magoo is definitely going to kill you."

"Yeah, but what can he do? *Today, I am a man.*"

That cracked up Lonnie, which cracked up me.

"Where are we going?" I said.

He was smiling. "I got something to show you."

There's a crinkle-eyed look Lonnie gets on his face when he knows he's outdone himself. Right then, he had that look. We were walking along Roosevelt Avenue toward Bowne Street. He turned right on Bowne, and I followed him for another block and a half. It wasn't hard to figure out that he was leading me to the Bowne House. There's nothing else on that street.

The closer we got, the queasier I began to feel. You don't mess with the Bowne House. You don't mess with a *painting* of the Bowne House, and you sure as heck don't mess with the real thing. What I mean is . . . it's the *Bowne House*! It's a historical site. Tourists from Manhattan take the train to Flushing just to see the thing. But in a weird way, that calmed me down. I mean, how bad could it be? Lonnie's a practical joker, for sure, but he's not out of his mind.

We came up on the west side of the house. It's not much to look at, to be honest, given that it's such a big deal. Really it's just a two-floor wooden house with peeling paint that used to be brown but now looks more tannish gray. It's got a tall brick chimney, which kind of stands out, and a big oak tree in the backyard. But otherwise, you wouldn't give it a second look if you didn't know how historical it was.

The place was deserted, which you'd expect, since it didn't open to the public until noon. So Lonnie and I took a quick look in both directions, then hopped the three-foot stone wall that separated the sidewalk from the backyard lawn.

He grinned at me. "Notice anything different?"

"You didn't break a window, did you?"

"C'mon, Julian, why would I do that?"

"Okay, so what *did* you do?"

"Just look around," he said.

I put my hands in my coat pockets and took a stroll.

The ground underneath the grass was hard, which I was grateful for, since it meant mud wasn't caking on my dress shoes. I was glancing up and down, side to side, trying to pick out anything that looked wrong. After I'd covered the yard, I walked along the edge of the house, running my fingertips along the wood slats.

"You're ice cold," Lonnie called.

I stepped away from the house and drifted back toward the yard.

"You're getting warmer. . . ."

"Did you carve the tree?"

"I wouldn't hurt the tree, Julian. What did the tree ever do to me?"

"Then I give up," I said.

"Do you want a hint?"

"Yeah."

"Don't go out on a limb," he said.

"What does that mean?"

"It means what it says."

"Then I don't get it."

"Don't go out on a *limb*, Julian."

Suddenly, it hit me. I looked up, almost straight into the sun. It took a second for my eyes to adjust, but there, about three-quarters of the way up the tree, was a worn-out pair of black high-top sneakers. They were dangling from a narrow branch by their laces, which were knotted together. The dark color of the sneakers blended in real well with the bark of the tree. You likely wouldn't have noticed them unless you were looking straight at them. Sooner or later, though, they were sure to get noticed.

"How could you do that, Lonnie?"

"How could I not?" he said.

"C'mon, it's the *Bowne House*. If it were just a tree from the block—"

"You're the one who gave me the idea when you were going on and on about that painting. So, in a way, it was *your* idea. . . ."

"Lonnie!"

"I'm just joking with you, Jules. Don't be such a Goody Two-Shoes."

"I'm *not* a Goody Two-Shoes," I said. "I just don't get the point of it. Why would you even want your sneakers here? Who's going to see them?"

"They're not *my* sneakers. They're *Quentin's*."

"You stole Quentin's sneakers?"

"He left them at my house last year," he said. "They didn't fit him anymore, so we were going to tree them, but then it started to rain, and we just forgot about them. My mom found them a couple of weeks ago in the basement. That's when I got the idea. I even wrote Quentin's name in them—"

"Lonnie!"

"What?"

"You're going to get him in trouble."

"I didn't write his *last* name," he said.

"How many guys named Quentin live in Flushing?"

"What difference does it make? The guy's got a *tumor*. What do you think is going to happen? You think the cops are going to show up at his hospital room and arrest him? Not to mention they'll know he *couldn't* have done it himself, because he's in the hospital."

"What about after he gets out?"

"If he's out of the hospital, that means he's in good shape. So it's win-win."

"That's not even what 'win-win' means."

"I know what 'win-win' means, Jules. Do you know what 'tribute' means?"

"Yeah, but—"

"Don't you think Quentin deserves a tribute?"

"Of course I do."

"Then case closed," he said.

Good Citizenship

Here's the third essay on good citizenship I wrote for Principal Salvatore:

My sister, Amelia, reads lots of books. Not
just the ones she has to read for school.
She takes books out of the library on
Union Street and reads them just because
that's what she likes to do. Last week, she
finished a book called <u>Love Story.</u> It made
her cry her eyes out at the end, and when
I asked her why she was crying, she said,
"Love means never having to say you're
sorry." I think good citizenship is the

exact opposite of love. It means saying
you're sorry for stuff you didn't do. So
I'm sorry. I'm sorry. I'm sorry. I'm sorry.
I'm sorry. I'm sorry. I'm sorry. I'm sorry.
I'm sorry. I'm sorry. I'm sorry. I'm sorry.
I'm sorry. I'm sorry. I'm sorry. I'm sorry.
I'm sorry. I'm sorry. I'm sorry. I'm sorry.
I'm sorry. I'm sorry. I'm sorry. I'm sorry.
I'm sorry. I'm sorry. I'm sorry. I'm sorry.
I'm sorry. I'm sorry. I'm sorry. I'm sorry.
I'm sorry. I'm sorry. I'm sorry. I'm sorry.
I'm sorry. I'm sorry. I'm sorry. I'm sorry.
I'm sorry. I'm sorry. I'm sorry. I'm sorry.
I'm sorry. I'm sorry. I'm sorry. I'm sorry.
I hope that makes me a good citizen.

As usual, I slid the paper under the door of Principal
Salvatore's office as soon as I got to school, and as usual,
Miss Medina handed it back to me an hour later. Principal
Salvatore had written on the back:

I'm sorry, try again.

January 14, 1970

For the Quakers' Sake

I couldn't stop thinking about Quentin's sneakers. It kept nagging at me, the picture of them dangling on that branch, swaying in the breeze, waiting to be noticed. On the one hand, it was a decent tribute to Quentin, but on the other hand, it was also disrespectful to the Quakers. It was both. But the more I thought about it, the more the disrespectful part outweighed the tribute part.

Last night, when I couldn't stand it anymore, I decided to climb the tree and take them down. I felt pretty skunky about it, knowing how much thought Lonnie had put into the thing, and how much trouble he'd gone through to get them up there. It was like a work of art, in a way. It was something he had accomplished, and I hated to ruin it. But I figured he'd made his point. He'd shown it off to the rest of the guys on the block, and he'd even taken a Polaroid and brought it to the hospital to show Quentin. There was no need to keep it going.

So I waited until after dinner and told my mom I was headed over to Shlomo's house to trade baseball cards, but instead I headed up to the Bowne House. Lying to my mom made me feel even skunkier than I already did, but I couldn't very well tell her the truth.

The Bowne House might not be much to look at during the day, but after dark it's downright creepy. What I mean is it's got a cemetery feeling even though no one's actually buried there. Don't get me wrong. It's not like I believe in any of that haunted house stuff. Besides, from what I've heard about Quakers, they'd be the most polite ghosts ever—they'd hover around, saying prayers, eating oatmeal, telling you to have a nice day.

I guess what creeps me out about the place is just the fact that it's so old, the fact that real people were walking in and out the doors, living their Quaker lives, worrying about their Quaker stuff, not having the slightest clue that a kid named Julian Twerski would someday climb that old tree in the backyard and take down a pair of worn-out sneakers. They likely didn't even know what sneakers were! But I was doing it for *their* sake, for the Quakers, as much as for Lonnie and Quentin. How could it be that they'd lived and died without knowing what I was doing for them?

As I turned onto Bowne Street, I shook my head to shake loose those thoughts. I wanted to get up the tree, get the sneakers, and get out as fast as I could. But the second I hopped the stone wall and landed on the scraggly grass of the backyard, I had a feeling I wasn't alone. I squatted down as low as I could get and looked side to side. No one was there. But the feeling of not-aloneness was strong. It sent a shiver across the back of my neck, which came at the exact same time as a cold gust of wind. It gave me second thoughts. I decided to come back another night.

"Help me, Julian!"

It was a girl's voice, a whisper, but still loud. It was coming from above me.

I looked straight up. "Who's there?"

"Please, please help me!"

"Where are you?"

"I'm here, Julian!"

That was when I realized the voice was coming from the tree, right around where the sneakers were dangling. I glanced up and saw a shadow clinging to the branch maybe five feet below them.

"It's *me*, Julian!"

"Beverly?"

"Help me. I'm stuck. I can't move," she said.

"What are you doing in the tree?"

"Please!"

"All right, I'm coming." The lowest branch was just out of reach, so I had to jump straight up to catch hold of it. After I pulled myself up, there were plenty of other branches to grab for balance. Beverly was another twenty-five feet up and ten feet out from the trunk, hanging down like a human hammock, with her arms and legs wrapped around the branch.

"Hurry!"

It wasn't a hard climb. The branches were close together, and you could pretty much step up from one branch to the next. It didn't get hairy until the branch below Beverly's, which was thinner than the lower ones. I could feel it starting to sag as soon as I put my weight on it, so I dropped down and shinnied out until I was right underneath her.

"All right, I'm here," I said, then tapped her foot.

"Don't touch me!"

"All right . . . but what do you want me to do?"

"Race me," she said.

"What?"

She started to crack up. "My hero!"

"Are you stuck or not?"

"What do *you* think?"

She spun around and sat on the branch, then squirreled out the last five feet, reached up with her left hand, and snatched down Quentin's sneakers. Then she dropped them. It took a long time for the sneakers to thud onto the ground. It kind of spooked me, how long it took. The sound of them hitting down seemed like it came from about a mile below us. I'd never climbed so high, not even in a neighborhood tree. I doubted Beverly had either. Not to mention she was so far out on her branch that it had drooped down level with mine, even though my branch was lower on the trunk of the tree.

"Want to keep going?" she said.

"Keep going where?"

"To the top."

"No!"

"C'mon, we're halfway already."

"The branches aren't strong enough, Beverly."

She stood up, which caused her branch to droop even more. Balancing herself with just her fingertips against the branch above hers, she took a step farther out, and her branch made a noise that sounded like a groan. I was about to tell her to stop, but she stepped off her branch and onto mine, which caused it to droop and groan too. I tightened my grip and pressed my stomach into the bark. It felt cold and damp, but I wasn't letting go. With how much the branch was drooping, my head was actually closer to the ground than my feet were. It was a queasy, terrifying feeling.

"You're going to kill us both!"

"You think so?"

She hopped several times on one foot. Every time she landed, the branch vibrated into my guts.

"Stop it!"

"Say I'm a better climber than you are!"

"What?"

"Admit it," she said. "I'm a better climber than you are."

"All right, I admit it," I said.

"What do you admit?"

"You're a better climber than I am," I said.

"And a faster runner."

"C'mon, Beverly!"

"Just admit it!"

"But it's not true! I'm not going to admit something that's not true!"

She began hopping up and down again.

"Stop doing that!"

She stopped and said, "Then admit it. Admit I'm faster than you. Just say the words, all right?"

"Nothing's going to change if I say it."

"Then why not say it?"

"I told you," I said. "It's not true. *Why is that so hard to understand?*"

"So you're like George Washington?"

"What does that mean?"

"*You cannot tell a lie*, right?"

"This is a stupid conversation," I said.

That made her hop up and down again.

"I'm *not* doing it, Beverly!"

She stopped jumping up and down. "You're really afraid, aren't you?"

"I'm afraid of getting killed, yes."

She stepped over me, then stretched and swung from branch to branch until she was back on the ground. It took her less than a minute. She *was* a better climber than I was. She called back up, "So are you stuck, or what?"

"No!"

"Are you sure?"

"I'm fine, Beverly. Just leave me alone."

"C'mon, Julian. You can do it."

"I know I can do it! I got up here, didn't I?"

"I'm not leaving until you're down."

"All right, I'm coming down," I said.

She was making such a big deal out of it that I had to remind myself that I *wasn't* stuck. Still, I was thinking about falling—which always makes climbing feel harder than it is. You don't want to let go of the thing you're holding on to, and you don't trust the thing you're reaching for. It was only after I got to the last few branches that I relaxed again.

Beverly started to laugh as I hung from the bottom branch and dropped to the ground. "You're the world's slowest climber."

"That's *real* funny."

"It's *kind of* funny."

As we were talking, she walked over to where Quentin's sneakers had landed. She picked them up and slung them over her shoulder.

"Why do you care about those?" I said.

"It was a stupid thing that Lonnie did."

"How is that your business?"

"You came for them too!"

"Lonnie's my friend. I didn't want him to get in trouble. Or Quentin. I didn't want either of them to get in trouble."

"Well, I came for the Quakers," she said. "You know what? I think you did too."

I couldn't think of a good comeback for that. She had me dead to rights. She and I were there for the same reason. There was no use denying it, which meant there was nothing more to say. We were staring at one another, on the lawn behind the Bowne House. It felt weird, like a gunfight in a Western movie, except it also felt different, since now the two of us had a secret, and we had to trust each other to keep it between us.

"You don't have to admit I'm faster than you. . . ."

"C'mon, Beverly!"

"As long as we both know it."

She turned and walked toward the stone wall, then jumped down to the sidewalk below. I wasn't going to follow her, but then she stopped and looked back. We were going in the same direction. If I waved her away and waited until she turned the corner, I'd only wind up walking home half a block behind her.

She rolled her eyes when I hopped down to the sidewalk beside her, but I let it go. I'd had enough of the Bowne House and Quakers for one night. Counting the painting, I'd had enough of them period.

As we started to walk, I said, "What are you going to do with the sneakers?"

"I'll tree them on the block."

"Lonnie's going to be mad. . . ."

"If you're worried about that, you can tell him I did it."

"I'm not going to tell him who did it. I'm just saying he's going to be mad."

We walked another half block without talking. Then, at last, she said, "Do you think they're grateful?"

"Who?"

"The Quakers."

"How can they be grateful? They're dead."

"Didn't you ever hear of the Grateful Dead?"

"That's the worst joke I've ever heard," I said.

But then the two of us cracked up. Hard. We kept cracking up the entire walk back to Thirty-Fourth Avenue.

Rabbi Salzberg and the Apple

It turned out Lonnie's reaction wasn't the one I should've been worried about. He noticed Quentin's sneakers hanging from a tree in front of the Hampshire House, where Quentin lived, a couple of days later. They were real noticeable, swaying back and forth in the breeze. He asked me if I was the one who'd done it, and I told him no—which was the truth, even if it wasn't the *whole* truth.

The two of us stood there, staring up at them, and Lonnie nodded. He had to admit: whoever had done it had done a good job. They were even higher than he'd treed them behind the Bowne House. Plus, the sneakers were back on the block, right below Quentin's fifth-floor window. When Quentin got home from the hospital, he'd be sure to notice them every time he looked outside. It was a good tribute.

Like I said, though, Lonnie wasn't the one I should've been worried about. Rabbi Salzberg was ticked off, and I mean *ticked off,* at how I'd run out of temple the past Saturday. When I showed up for my haftarah lesson on Thursday afternoon, I could almost see puffs of steam leaking out from under the yarmulke on his head.

"You have a problem with your ears, Mr. Twerski—am I correct?"

I sat down in front of his desk and shook my head. "No, Rabbi."

"Because I'm sure the congregation would take up a collection for a hearing aid."

"I don't have a problem with my ears, Rabbi Salzberg."

"No?"

"I'm sorry I rushed out after services," I said. "It was a real rude thing to do."

"There's no need to apologize, Mr. Twerski. You're a busy fellow. I'm sure God understands that. He's busy too. I'm sure he wouldn't want to keep you from your next appointment."

That kind of got under my skin, the way he brought God into it. Maybe I had insulted Rabbi Salzberg by running off, but *no way* did I insult God. Plus, if you stop and think about it, I wouldn't have insulted *anyone* if I hadn't gone to temple in the first place. If I'd just slept late and skipped temple, I wouldn't have wound up standing in front of Rabbi Salzberg, taking his sarcasm.

"Do you really think God cares, Rabbi?"

As soon as the words were out of my mouth, I wanted them back. Not because of what I'd said, but because I knew I'd opened a can of worms.

Rabbi Salzberg arched his shoulders. His eyes got real wide and then, a second later, got real narrow. "The question isn't whether God cares, Mr. Twerski. The question is whether *you* care."

"Why should I care if God doesn't care?"

His eyes narrowed even more, until they were slits. "You're quite a clever boy."

"Thank you," I said.

"But tell me this: When will you become a man?"

"It was *your* idea to push back my bar mitzvah, Rabbi."

"Mr. Twerski, the bar mitzvah does not make the man."

Then I blurted out something without thinking about it . . . which I guess means I must have been thinking about it without realizing it. "If God cares so much, why doesn't he care about Quentin?"

"Ah."

"What did Quentin do to deserve a tumor? Why did he get one and I didn't?"

"You think you deserve a tumor?"

"As much as Quentin does," I said.

"So you want the world to be fair."

"Yes."

"You're sure?"

"Yes," I said.

"You want only good things to happen to good people and only bad things to happen to bad people."

"I want people to get what they deserve."

"That's the world you want to live in?"

"I think it would be much fairer," I said.

"Let's imagine that world, Mr. Twerski. Let's call it Twerski-World, all right?"

That made me smile, even though I knew he was setting me up. "All right."

"So in Twerski-World, if you're a good Jewish boy, and you study your haftarah, and you go to services, and you clean up your room, and you honor your mother and your father, God makes your life perfect. Nothing bad ever happens to you. There are no lumps in your oatmeal. You get lean brisket for dinner and cinnamon rugelach for dessert. Would that be acceptable to you?"

"No, because you'd get sick of it," I answered. "If you have to eat nothing but brisket and rugelach forever, you're definitely going to get sick of it. Sooner or later, it'll feel like a punishment."

"That's a decent point," he said. "So let's say that if you're a good Jewish boy, in Twerski-World, you can eat whatever you want, whenever you want—as long as it's kosher. Is that more acceptable?"

"Yes."

"But, on the other hand, if you're *not* a good Jewish boy, if you *don't* study your haftarah, and you *don't* do those things I mentioned, then a lightning bolt comes out of the sky and strikes you dead."

"Well, it doesn't have to strike you dead—"

"But at least singe you around the edges," he said.

"That would be fair, yes."

"So then here's my question to you: Who would ever be bad in Twerski-World? If good boys get cinnamon rugelach and bad boys get struck by lightning, you'd have to be a fool to be a bad boy."

"Wouldn't that be a better world?" I said.

"Do you know the story of Adam and Eve, Mr. Twerski?"

"Everybody knows that story."

"But do you *know* the story?" he said.

"Adam and Eve eat the apple—"

"The what?"

"The apple," I said. "Adam and Eve eat the apple. . . ."

His eyes got real wide, and I braced for him to yell. You could see he was thinking about yelling. He leaned forward as if he was about to rush out from behind his desk, but then didn't. He sank back down in his chair and reached into the bookcase behind him. He took down a Bible and slid it across the desk.

"Show me the apple, Mr. Twerski."

"It's in the story of Adam and Eve."

"Then show it to me," he said. "I'll wait."

I opened the Bible to the book of Genesis. I knew right where to look, because that was the first thing the rabbis had taught us when I started Hebrew school. I found the story of Adam and Eve in the second chapter of Genesis, and I skimmed through the Garden of Eden stuff. I didn't see the word "apple." So I read the entire thing, line by line. It took about three minutes. Not a word about an apple.

"It isn't here," I said.

"So there's no apple in the Garden of Eden?"

"I guess not."

"What tree did Adam and Eve eat from?" the rabbi asked.

"It says they ate from 'the tree of the knowledge of good and evil.'"

"That makes more sense, doesn't it?"

"But there's no such thing as the tree of the knowledge of good and evil."

"You're missing the point of the story, Mr. Twerski.

Apples are good for you. They're nutritious. This, we all know. Why would God tell Adam and Eve not to eat an apple?"

"He wouldn't," I said.

"As for the tree of the knowledge of good and evil—where was it?"

"In the Garden of Eden."

"But where *exactly*? What does the Torah tell us?"

I glanced down at the page. "It says that the tree was in the middle of the garden."

"In the *middle* of the garden, correct?"

"Yes," I said.

"Not on the edge?"

"No, it says in the middle."

"What does that say to you, Mr. Twerski?"

I thought about it for a second. "He wanted them to see it?"

"Don't *ask* me! *Tell* me!"

"God wanted Adam and Eve to see the tree of the knowledge of good and evil. That's why he put it in the middle of the Garden of Eden."

"Now here's my question: *Why did God want Adam and Eve to see the tree?*"

"How would I know?"

"*Think*, Mr. Twerski! God told them not to eat from the tree, yet he put it right in the middle of the garden.

100

He could have put it where they'd never see—out of sight, out of mind. But he put it where they'd have to walk past it every day. Why would he do such a thing?"

"Because it was a test?"

"Don't *ask* me! *Tell* me!"

"It was a test," I said.

"Exactly!"

"But if he knew they were going to fail—"

He slammed his fist down on the desk. "It's not a test if you can't fail!"

"So you're saying that Quentin got a tumor because he failed a test?"

Rabbi Salzberg slapped his forehead. "Does that sound likely to you?"

"Then I don't get it," I said.

"Figure it out, Mr. Twerski. That's your haftarah lesson for today."

Good Citizenship

Here's the fourth essay on good citizen-ship I wrote for Principal Salvatore:

> The apple isn't an apple. The apple isn't an
> apple. The apple isn't an apple. The apple
> isn't an apple. The apple isn't an apple.
> The apple isn't an apple. The apple isn't an
> apple. The apple isn't an apple. The apple
> isn't an apple. The apple isn't an apple.
> The apple isn't an apple. The apple isn't an
> apple. The apple isn't an apple. The apple
> isn't an apple. The apple isn't an apple.
> The apple isn't an apple. The apple isn't an

apple. The apple isn't an apple. The apple
isn't an apple. The apple isn't an apple.
The apple isn't an apple. The apple isn't an
apple. The apple isn't an apple. The apple
isn't an apple. The apple isn't an apple.
The apple isn't an apple. The apple isn't an
apple. The apple isn't an apple. The apple
isn't an apple. The apple isn't an apple.
The apple isn't an apple. The apple isn't an
apple. The apple isn't an apple. The apple
isn't an apple. The apple isn't an apple.
The apple isn't an apple. The apple isn't
an apple. The apple isn't an apple. The
apple isn't an apple. (It's an inside joke,
Principal Salvatore.)

As usual, I slid the paper under the door of Principal
Salvatore's office as soon as I got to school, and as usual,
Miss Medina handed it back to me an hour later. Principal
Salvatore had written on the back:

Try again. No joke.

The Yankees Cap

Maybe that Garden of Eden talk with Rabbi Salzberg was good luck, because sure enough, Quentin came home from the hospital a week later. I know there's no *logical* connection between the two things, Rabbi Salzberg grilling me and Quentin getting out of the hospital, but somehow they felt connected. I mean, think about it. Last Friday, I was asking the rabbi why the world wasn't fair, why a guy like Quentin would get sick, why God would let that happen, and then, today, Quentin comes home.

It was a big deal for the entire block, Quentin coming home. Even before he got home, there was a big crowd in front of the Hampshire House. The first ones to show up were Quentin's relatives, six cars full of them, grand-parents and uncles and aunts, and more cousins than I could keep track of, who started to arrive around four o'clock. They double-parked and spilled out of their cars, dressed up as if they were going to a fancy party, and then they stood around on the sidewalk, doing nothing. There was one little girl, who must've been Quentin's youngest cousin, running in circles with a pink helium balloon that said WELCOME HOME!

Before long, there were maybe thirty-five people out on the sidewalk. Quentin's relatives, guys from the block, even grown-ups I didn't know who were just passing by and asked what was going on and then decided to stick around.

The whole gang was there, obviously. Even Shlomo Shlomo. He never hangs out with us after school on Fridays, on account of his dad is real serious about the start of Sabbath. But Lonnie figured this was a special thing, so he and I ran over to Shlomo's house and walked right up to the front door and rang the doorbell like it was nothing. Lonnie explained the situation to Shlomo's dad, and sure enough, for the first time I could remember, Mr. Zizner actually cracked a smile. He said Shlomo could skip Sabbath dinner just this once, and not even a minute later, Shlomo had pulled on his overcoat, and the three of us were running back to the Hampshire House.

It was right around five o'clock when Quentin's car came cruising up the street. The sun had just gone down, but there was still enough light to see Mr. and Mrs. Selig's faces in the front seat. Mrs. Selig put her hands over her mouth when she noticed the big crowd in front of the Hampshire House, and Mr. Selig started to laugh. You could see how glad they were that so many of us came out.

Once people realized who was in the car, they started to clap. Then, as the car rolled to a stop, a big cheer went up. It sent shivers down my spine, how loud it was. I felt Lonnie grab me from behind and hug me, which would have felt weird any other time, but which felt like a natural thing to do at that moment. It was a hugging kind of moment.

Quentin's mom got out of the car first, and then Mr. Selig got out and hurried around to the back. I thought he was going to open the back door for Quentin, but instead he popped the trunk. It took me a second to figure out what was going on, but then I realized the two of them were hauling out a wheelchair.

They had a lot of trouble getting the thing out of the trunk, and then even more trouble unfolding it, but every time one of their relatives took a step forward to help them, Mr. Selig waved them away. While they were doing that, I was wrapping my brain around the idea that Quentin was going to be sitting in that wheelchair. As stupid as it sounds, I was thinking he'd just climb out of the backseat, get a good night's rest, and then turn up tomorrow morning in Ponzini. I was thinking nothing would be different, that Quentin would be just like he was before he got sick.

It took maybe half a minute for Mr. and Mrs. Selig to get the wheelchair set up on the sidewalk. That might not sound like a long time, but it sure felt like a long time when I was watching them do it. Then Mr. Selig went back around the car and pulled open the back door, but Quentin didn't come out on his own. His dad had to lean into the car and lift him out. Then Mr. Selig carried him over to the wheelchair and sat him down in it. He was wearing blue pajamas and a Yankees baseball cap, which was pulled down on his forehead so you couldn't even see the look on his face. It was scary how skinny he'd gotten. I'd only seen him in the hospital that one time—the doctors said afterward Lonnie and I had tired him out—and back then he was covered up to his neck with a blanket, so I had no idea what was going on with the rest of him. But now, sitting in that wheelchair, he looked unreal. His arms and legs looked like pipe cleaners. He looked like a Yankees cap stuck on top of a skeleton.

You could tell how shocked people were by how quiet they got, and how sudden the quiet came. I glanced up at Lonnie, and he'd shut his eyes. He couldn't bear to look.

It was the same way with Shlomo and Eric and Howie. They were staring straight down into the sidewalk.

Except then Quentin reached up real slow with his right hand and tilted back the Yankees cap. He had this huge grin on his face, just like he always did back in Ponzini. I mean, he still looked bad. Even without much light, you could see dark circles under his eyes, and his cheeks were kind of caved in. But the grin on his face was pure Quentin.

His dad got behind the wheelchair and pushed Quentin toward the entrance of the Hampshire House. People were kind of leaning in for a closer look and stepping back at the same time, which made it hard for Mr. Selig to steer Quentin in a straight line. But his mom got in front of the wheelchair, and she led them up the path until they got to the lobby door. I figured that was going to be it, that Mr. and Mrs. Selig would take Quentin inside, and probably the relatives would follow them upstairs, and the rest of us would go home. But then, as Mrs. Selig was fishing around inside her purse for the key, out of the crowd stepped Beverly Segal.

Until then, I hadn't even noticed her. But she stepped forward while the rest of us were hanging back. She did what none of us had the nerve to do. She touched him. Just like that. She walked up behind the wheelchair, like it was her right, and she took hold of Quentin's hand. Then she leaned over and kissed him on the cheek. Quentin didn't even realize what she was doing until she'd done it. But once it sank in, he started to crack up.

You could just feel the relief in the crowd when they heard him laugh. People started laughing along with him. Then, one at a time, they came up behind the wheelchair and rubbed his shoulder or patted his arm or squeezed his hand. It was like Beverly broke the ice, and now the rest of us lined up to pay our respects. Mrs. Selig was holding the key in her right hand, but she didn't open the door. She just stood there, smiling, letting it happen.

As Lonnie and I waited our turn, Beverly walked past us. She wasn't going to say a word, but Lonnie caught her by the arm and nodded. That was his way of telling her she did a good thing.

She nodded back and whispered, "It's not like the guy has cooties."

That was all she said. After that, she headed back to her house. It was like . . . she did what she felt like doing, and she didn't think it was a big deal.

You had to give her credit.

The Guy in the Blue Suit

Most Saturdays, Lonnie is the last one to roll out of bed. It's like a running joke, how me and Eric and Howie and Quentin always wind up twiddling our thumbs on the corner of Parsons and Thirty-Fourth until he pokes his head out the door. It's like waiting for that groundhog in Pennsylvania. But this morning he was already downstairs, ringing the doorbell of my house, at eight o'clock. Not that I'd slept much either. How could I? Quentin's mom had said, when we were begging to go upstairs with the relatives, that we could stop by and visit him tomorrow.

I was still in my pajamas when Lonnie showed up. But I hustled downstairs and let him in.

"C'mon, let's get a move on," he said.

"Isn't it too early?"

He put his hand on his chin. "She said 'tomorrow,' right? That was yesterday. Which makes today tomorrow. So let's get this show on the road. Chop chop!"

"She said tomorrow, but I'm sure she didn't mean—"

"*Tomorrow* starts as soon as the sun comes up," he said. "That's a scientific fact, Julian. You can't argue with a scientific fact."

It didn't take a lot to convince me. I was itching to see Quentin too. The more I thought about how bad he'd looked sitting in that wheelchair, the more I realized how much he'd gone through just to get out of the hospital. He had to get unplugged from those beeping hospital machines, then get hauled out of bed, then get cleaned up, then get wheeled out, then get shoved into the backseat of the car, then get rattled around in traffic. . . . I mean, that would suck the life out of anybody. The real test was how Quentin looked after a full night's sleep in his own bed. So I wasn't going to try to talk Lonnie into waiting an hour or two. (As if I'd win that argument!) The worst that could happen, I figured, was Mrs. Selig would answer the door, shake her head, and tell us to come back later.

Lonnie waited downstairs as I ran back up and put on my clothes. Not even three minutes passed before the two of us were walking up the block toward the Hampshire

House. Halfway there, we met up with Eric and Howie—who were on their way to get us. (Only Shlomo was missing, on account of his dad forcing him to go to temple for Sabbath services, but he'd know where to look for us as soon as the sun went down.) Then the four of us walked back to the Hampshire House together.

As we turned up the path toward the front door, Eric the Red mumbled under his breath, "I hope his mom lets us in."

"She'll let us in," Lonnie said. "We've got the right to see him. He's our friend."

"But what if she says—"

Lonnie cut him off. "Look, he's *our* friend."

Right then, there came a shout from high above us. "Hey, guys!"

The four of us looked up at once. Quentin was looking down from his fifth-floor window, waving his Yankees cap.

"Hey, Quent!" Lonnie called up to him. "How do you feel?"

"Okay, I guess. What kept you?"

Lonnie laughed. "What do you mean, *what kept us?*"

"I've been waiting by the window the whole day."

"It's like eight-thirty, Quentin," I called up to him.

"Yeah, well, there's not too much to do up here."

"Are you stuck in the wheelchair?" I said.

"No, I'm walking around."

"Then buzz us in!" Lonnie said.

It took half a minute for the buzzer to go off, which meant Quentin wasn't getting around too quick. While we were waiting, I thought about the nickname Lonnie gave him years ago—Quick Quentin. It was supposed to be ironical, because Quentin always took an extra second to figure things out, like his brain had to haul itself out of mud before it got going. But another reason for it was his eyes. Quentin had big brown eyes and droopy eyelids that hung down, so he looked like he was about to fall asleep even when he was wide awake. Plus, "Quick Quentin" just sounded right—on account of the two Qs.

Right then, however, I didn't care how quick or how slow he was moving. The main thing was he was up and around, on his feet, out of the wheelchair. His voice sounded normal.

Quentin was standing just outside the door of his apartment when the elevator opened on the fifth floor. He had on regular clothes—a brown T-shirt and blue jeans, plus the Yankees cap. He still looked bony, especially his face. His cheekbones were jutting out like a Halloween skull. But he looked about a hundred times better than he did in that wheelchair.

The apartment smelled of pancakes and bacon. Even by the elevator, you got a whiff of it, and the smell got stronger once you walked through the door. It reminded me I hadn't had breakfast, and I was half hoping Mrs. Selig would be in the kitchen and offer us a slice of bacon. But she wasn't. Neither his mom nor his dad was out. Their bedroom door was shut, but I could hear the television playing inside as we filed into Quentin's room.

It was a mess, Quentin's room, which was also normal. I don't think I've ever seen the guy's bed made or his junk not scattered on the floor. He loves to build plastic models, so he always has plane kits that he's gluing together or painting or decaling. He's good at it too. They always look just like the pictures on the boxes. But he never hangs them from the ceiling or sets them up on the windowsill, like you're supposed to do. When he's finished with them, he leaves them on the floor and plays with them, the way a kindergarten kid would play with them. It's kind of dumb, but it's also . . . I don't even know the right word. It's just, well, *Quentin*. He's not embarrassed about it. He likes to sit on the floor and wave the planes around his head and make humming engine noises, and no one thinks less of him because of it. It's just his way.

Another thing about Quentin's room is that he has more records than the rest of us put together, and they're scattered on the floor too. He has every record the Beatles ever put out, right up through *Abbey Road,* plus every one by the Rolling Stones and Creedence Clearwater Revival.

Plus, he likes the Monkees. Lonnie likes to tease him about that, but Quentin likes what he likes. Before he went into the hospital, his favorite song was "Daydream Believer"—he'd just about worn out the grooves on that one. He got me real sick of it. But when I saw the record sitting on his turntable, I asked him to play it. Not because I wanted to hear it, but because it meant things were getting back to how they used to be.

He put on the record, not too loud, just in the background. But I did listen for the word "'neath" in the first line:

Oh, I could hide 'neath the wings
of the bluebird as she sings . . .

That always cracks me up, the way they shorten "underneath" to "'neath." It's the kind of thing you expect in a Shakespeare poem, not in a Monkees song. I listened for that, and then I forgot the song was even playing.

"Did you see your sneakers up in the tree?" Lonnie said.

That made Quentin laugh. "I *thought* those were mine."

"I treed them in that old oak behind the Bowne House. But then *someone* got them down and treed them out there. I would've got them down and treed them back at the Bowne House, but I figured you'd like to see them out your window, so I left them where they were."

"Who got them down at the Bowne House?" Quentin said.

"It's still a mystery. Jules swears up and down it wasn't him, but I got my suspicions."

"It *wasn't* me, Lonnie."

Quentin smiled at me.

"I *swear,* Quent, it wasn't me."

"Well, I like them where they are."

For a couple of seconds after that, no one said a thing—which felt weird.

Then, at last, Eric said, "Shlomo's going to come over as soon as he can."

"Yeah," Lonnie said. "He's busy Jew-ing it up."

"Today's Saturday?" Quentin said.

"Yeah."

He shook his head. "I guess I kind of lost track."

"Are you going to school on Monday?" I asked.

"The doctors said I could. But I don't think my mom's going to let me."

"Why not?" Eric asked.

"She says I'm still too weak. I get out of breath real fast."

"You can take the bus both ways," Lonnie said. "We'll ride with you."

"I don't know if I can make it up and down the stairs at school."

"Then we'll carry you," Lonnie said. "We can take turns doing it."

Quentin smiled in a strange way. "My mom's scared I'll get teased."

"C'mon, why would you get teased?" I said. "It's not your fault you got a tumor. It could happen to anyone. Plus, who's going to know? You've got a thousand kids, and no one's paying attention. For all anyone knows, you moved out of state and then moved back. Or maybe you took a long vacation. The point is, we're the only ones who'll know what happened. No one's going to tease you."

He began shaking his head again. "Jules . . ."

"What is it?"

He started to talk, but his voice cracked. It was just for a half second, or maybe not even that long. But it was noticeable. He swallowed hard and took a deep breath. "I got no hair, guys."

"What do you mean?" Lonnie said. "You got plenty of hair."

"It's a wig."

"It looks just like your hair," Howie said.

"The nurses took a picture when I first got to the hospital. Then, afterward, they got a wig that matched."

"So take it off," Howie said.

"No!"

"C'mon, just do it for a second—"

"He told you no," Lonnie said. "End of discussion."

"Will it grow back?" I asked.

"Except where the scar is," Quentin said. He reached behind his head and up under the Yankees cap and touched the spot right where the bottom of his head joined the back of his neck.

"Can we at least see the scar?" Howie said.

Lonnie shot him a look, but then Quentin said, "Not now with the gauze pads and stuff over it. But I know it's bad, because every time my mom changes the dressing, she starts to bawl."

"How many stitches did you get?" Howie said.

"I'm not sure. But a lot. Maybe forty, at least."

That made the rest of us sit up. I said, *"Forty?"*

"Yeah."

"Does it hurt?" Howie asked.

"Nah, it just feels kind of tight."

"Forty stitches!" Eric said, shaking his head. You could tell he was impressed.

Howie said, "The most I ever got was six."

"When did *you* get six stitches?" Lonnie said.

"Playing tag, two years ago . . . *you* were the one chasing me!"

"You mean that time you grabbed the fence?"

"I dodged you, didn't I?"

"Hey, I just didn't want to touch you because of all the blood."

Then Eric chimed in. "I got four stitches the time Shlomo fell on my head. I got them right under my left eye. When they were sewing me up, I could feel the needle right under my eyeball. Look, I still got the scar. . . ."

Just like that, we were back to normal.

About an hour later, we were still yakking away in Quentin's room when his mom poked her head in to make sure we weren't tiring him out. Quentin told her he was fine, which she didn't seem to believe. She just stood there, not quite in the room but not quite gone, with a suspicious look on her face. But then Quentin said he was hungry, and that perked her up. She asked him what he wanted, and he told her peanut butter and jelly, and then she asked the rest of us who else wanted peanut butter and jelly, and Howie's hand went up, and then Eric's, and then Lonnie's. I raised my hand too, even though I was still kind of hoping for a slice of that bacon I'd smelled when we first walked in.

We were just finishing up the sandwiches when the doorbell rang. Quentin figured it was either one of his doctors or one of his relatives, which meant, either way, his mom was going to make us leave. But when Quentin cracked the door and peeked out into the living room, he saw a guy he didn't know. He motioned me over to the door to take a look. The guy was wearing a dark blue suit and carrying a dark blue briefcase. It didn't seem like the kind of bag a doctor would carry on a house call. It was too flat.

"You're sure he's not a long-lost uncle?" Lonnie asked. He was half sitting, half lying on the edge of Quentin's bed, too comfortable to take a look. But now he was curious.

"No way," Quentin whispered.

"What's he doing now?"

"He's sitting at the dining room table with my mom and dad."

"Here, let me see." Quentin and I made room as Lonnie slid in next to the door. "Wait . . . he's opening the briefcase. He's got papers inside, lots of them."

"What sort of papers?" I asked. "What do they say?"

"Pass me your periscope, and I'll let you know."

That made Howie and Eric crack up, how sarcastic Lonnie sounded. It *was* kind of humorous, but maybe you had to be there.

"Quent, why don't you just walk out there and ask what's going on?" I said.

"I could do that," Quentin said.

Lonnie slid the door shut. "Plan B, we could just sit tight and wait to see what happens. I vote Plan B. For all we know, the guy might be selling vacuum cleaners door-to-door."

"But he doesn't have vacuum cleaners," I said.

"Or encyclopedias. Or whatever. Geez, Jules!"

"Maybe the guy's a Chinese spy," Howie said.

Lonnie looked at him. "Except he's not Chinese."

"Maybe that's what makes him good at his job."

It was about the funniest thing Howie had ever said, and it had us cracking up until we were gasping for air. It even cracked up Quentin—which couldn't have felt too good, since he'd just told us how fast he got out of breath. He staggered back and fell onto the bed, laughing hysterically, holding on to his Yankees cap with one hand and holding his stomach with the other.

We were still laughing hard when a knock came at the door. Quentin's dad pushed the door open a second later. He looked at us like we were out of our minds, which I guess, right then, we kind of were. Slowly, though, we began to calm down. I could feel a stitch in my side from laughing, but at least I could focus my eyes. Mr. Selig, meanwhile, stood at the door and waited.

"When you jokers feel you're up to it," he said, "there's a fella out here that wants to talk to you."

He ducked back out of the room as we caught our breath. Maybe a half minute later, another knock came at the door.

"Come in," Quentin called out, which made Howie sputter. But the rest of us kept straight faces.

The guy in the dark blue suit stepped into the room. He smiled at us in a stiff way, the way grown-ups do when they want you to like them.

"Hey, nice room!" he said. "So, a little birdie tells me one of you boys is a big Bobby Murcer fan."

I stared at him in disbelief. "Yeah, that's me. But how did you know?"

The guy's expression changed when I said that. The smile left his face, and for a second he looked real nervous and confused.

But then Quentin said, "I'm a Bobby Murcer fan too."

Now I stared at *him* in disbelief . . . because I knew he was lying. Quentin's favorite baseball player is Willie Mays. Right before he got sick, he built and painted a plastic model of Mays making that over-the-shoulder catch in the World Series. The thing was sitting on the windowsill, right behind the bed. But the guy in the suit didn't notice it. Instead, he began to smile again.

"Make room for me, will you?"

Lonnie got up to make room for the guy at the edge of the bed. The guy sat down next to Quentin and stuck out his hand. "You're Quentin, right?"

Quentin nodded and shook his hand.

"My name's Jerry Manche," he said. "Sounds like there are two *e*'s at the end of Manche, but there's only one. People mess that up all the time. I'm with the New York Yankees. . . ."

That got our attention real fast.

"What I'm thinking—correct me if I'm wrong—is that you know why I'm here."

Quentin smiled. "You've got an autographed picture of Bobby Murcer?"

"Coming right up!" He popped open his briefcase and pulled out a photo, which he handed to Quentin. There was writing in black Magic Marker at the bottom. "You want to read out loud what Bobby wrote? I'm sure your friends would like to know."

Quentin read: "'To Quentin. From one home run hitter to another. Get well soon, buddy. Bobby Murcer.'"

Jerry Manche said, "What do you think about that?"

"It's great," Quentin said. "But what about Julian?"

"It's okay, Quent," I said.

"He's a Bobby Murcer fan too. Do you think Bobby—"

"Consider it done!" Jerry Manche said.

"Can you get me Mickey Mantle?" Lonnie asked.

"Now hold your horses—"

"C'mon, you work for the Yankees!"

"In case you haven't heard, the Mick's retired."

"Don't you know where he lives?"

Jerry Manche started to laugh. "I'll see what I can do. What's your name?"

"Lonnie Fine. Sounds like there's two *e*'s at the end of Lonnie, but it's *i-e*."

Jerry Manche gave Lonnie a look. "You're quite the wisenheimer, aren't you?"

"No, sir!"

"That's good to hear," Jerry Manche said, "because I don't think Bobby Murcer would've agreed to come out here in April, after the Yankees finish spring training, just to meet up with a bunch of wisenheimers."

My mouth fell open. "Bobby Murcer's coming *here*?"

"What do you wisenheimers think about that?"

"Can we talk to him?" Eric asked. It was a dumb question, but the rest of us were too stunned to razz him about it.

"You're going to hurt his feelings if you don't."

"What day in April?" Lonnie asked.

"We're still working that out," Jerry Manche said. "But don't you worry. He'll be here. You can take it to the bank."

"Thanks, Mr. Manche!" Quentin said.

"There are two conditions, though. The first is that you guys have to call me Jerry. I don't want to hear about Mr. Manche unless you're talking about my dad. Do we have a deal on that?"

"What's the second condition?" Lonnie asked.

Jerry Manche turned again to Quentin. "The second condition is that this guy right here"—he grabbed Quentin by the shoulder and give him a gentle shake—"this guy right here has got to start feeling better. Do you think you can do that? Do you think you can do that for Bobby Murcer and the Yankees?"

"Sure, he can do that!" Lonnie said.

Quentin shrugged. "I'll do my best."

"If you give a hundred percent," Jerry Manche said, "you get a hundred percent."

"What if you give a hundred and ten percent?" Lonnie said in a real sincere voice.

"Now *that's* what I like to hear! How about it, Quentin? Do you think you can give a hundred and ten percent?"

Quentin looked him in the eye and nodded. But even he was struggling to keep a straight face.

"Then we got a deal." Jerry Manche stuck out his hand again. "Put it there."

Again Quentin shook his hand.

"There's just one more thing," Jerry Manche said. He glanced toward the front of the room, near the door, where Howie and Eric were standing. "You boys want to police that area?"

"What do you mean?" Eric said.

"I need you to get that stuff off the floor. Just move it out of the way. Can you do me that favor?"

"Why us?" Howie asked.

"Because you're standing there."

"C'mon, just do it," Lonnie said.

As Eric and Howie started picking up Quentin's model planes and loose clothes, Jerry Manche stood up from the bed and walked to the window. He slid it open, leaned out, and whistled real loud.

After that, he turned back to us. "Bobby Murcer and the Yankees got a little get-well gift for Quentin. We're going to set it up in that corner of the room. Now, if you'll excuse me for a minute, I'm going to head downstairs and oversee the operation."

"What did you get for him?" Lonnie asked.

"Hold your horses, pardner. It'll be here in a minute."

Jerry Manche said that on the way out of the room. As soon as he closed the door behind him, I turned to Quentin. "Why did you tell him you're a Murcer fan? You don't even like the Yankees."

"But you do," Quentin said. "I figured I owed you."

"Owed me for what?"

"You pushed back your bar mitzvah 'cause of me."

"You don't owe me for that—"

"So I got a nurse to write a letter to the Yankees saying how I was sick," Quentin said, cutting me off, "and how I liked Bobby Murcer, and could I please have an autograph. I thought for sure they'd send it, and then you could have it, 'cause he's your favorite. I didn't expect it would get like this. So don't rat me out, okay?"

"I'm not going to rat you out, Quent," I said, "but that's the dumbest thing I've ever heard. You didn't need to do that."

"Yeah, it's dumb, but who cares?" Lonnie said. "What matters is what's coming up in the elevator."

"What do you think it is?" Eric asked.

"It's got to be pretty big," Lonnie said.

"I'll bet it's a fort!" Eric shouted.

"Why would the Yankees give Quentin a fort?" Lonnie said. "That makes no sense whatsoever."

"Maybe it's a baseball bat," Howie said.

Lonnie rolled his eyes. "I guarantee you it's not a baseball bat. If it were a baseball bat, Manche would've brought it up himself. I'm telling you, it's got to be big. It's got to be too big for one guy to carry."

"Maybe it's a TV," I said.

They turned toward me, all at once.

"Now *that* makes sense," Lonnie said.

"Maybe it's a *color* TV," Howie said.

"It could be one of those humongous ones," Eric said, "with a remote control and a built-in stereo."

That set us off.

For the next half minute, we were arguing not so much about *whether* it was a TV but about *what kind* of TV it was. But then I noticed Quentin, sitting up on the bed, waving his hand, trying to get our attention. "Um, guys . . ."

"What is it, Quent?" I said.

"Why don't you just look out the window?"

We stared at one another for a split second, then jumped up, the four of us at once, and rushed to the window. There was already a huge wooden crate on the sidewalk. Two short, stocky guys in tight jackets were unloading another crate, not quite as huge but still plenty big, from a long truck. Jerry Manche was standing on the curb, near the truck, pointing at the two other guys and giving orders. You could see puffs of smoky breath coming from his mouth.

"It's definitely a TV," Howie said.

"No, I don't think so," Lonnie said, leaning to the right for a different angle. "Why would there be two boxes?"

"Maybe it's another TV," Howie said. "Maybe Quentin's getting two TVs."

The rest of us just stared at him.

"All right," Howie snapped, "then *you* tell *me* what it is."

I had a thought at that moment, but I couldn't say it out loud: that first crate, the bigger one, was the size and shape of a coffin. It creeped me out to think that, and I tried not to think it, and afterward I tried to shake the thought out of my head. But it stuck with me.

"Hey, Quent," Lonnie said, "don't you want to see what's going on?"

"Nah, you guys can tell me."

"Are you tired out?" I said.

"Not too bad."

Lonnie stepped away from the window. "Do you want us to go? You can say if you do. We'll clear out in a minute."

"Nah, I want you to stay," Quentin said.

"They got the crates on wheels!" Eric said. "They're rolling them through the front door of the building!"

"C'mon, Quent, let's meet them at the elevator!" Lonnie said.

"You guys go ahead," Quentin said. "I'll meet you out there."

He seemed to mean it, so we ran out of the room like a buffalo stampede, then out past Mr. and Mrs. Selig, who were sitting at the kitchen table, and then out into the hall.

It took a long time for the elevator to get to the fifth floor. When the doors slid open, we couldn't even see the guys. It was just the two wooden crates sitting on dollies. But then the crates lurched forward, and we jumped back out of the way, and the two stocky guys steered the crates out of the elevator and into the hall.

The last to come out was Jerry Manche, who looked

rumpled up. He must have gotten squeezed behind those crates and between those two stocky guys. But he managed to wink at us. Lonnie gave him a real goofy thumbs-up sign, and sure enough, Jerry Manche gave him a thumbs-up sign right back. I almost laughed out loud at that, but I turned my head to the side and held it in.

Quentin was standing at the front door of the apartment, holding it open, and his mom and dad were standing behind him.

"We'll take it from here, folks," Jerry Manche called. "If you'll just step back and give us ten minutes, we'll be out of your hair and gone."

Quentin's mom and dad pulled him back into the apartment and out of the way, and the two stocky guys steered the crates toward the front door. It was a miracle the bigger one fit. Right up until it rolled through, I was thinking, *No way!* It was so tight that the guy had to pull in his fingers from the edges of the crate. Then the second guy got the second crate through, and Jerry Manche led them to Quentin's room. The four of us were trailing behind them, but Mr. Selig held up his hand, as if it were a stop sign, and that was that.

Quentin turned to his dad and asked, "C'mon, what is it?"

"You'll find out soon enough."

Then Quentin turned to his mom, but she made a

motion with her hand as if she was zipping her lips closed.

You wouldn't believe the noises that came out of Quentin's room for the next ten minutes. Hammers thudding, screwdrivers twisting, metal parts clanging onto the floor—it sounded like they were putting together a battleship. We were milling around in the living room the entire time, just kind of rocking back and forth on our heels.

Not Mr. and Mrs. Selig—they were sitting down on the couch. But they were listening to the racket like the rest of us, waiting for it to end. Every so often, when it got real loud, Mrs. Selig would wince. I heard her yell to Mr. Selig, "The neighbors must think we've gone crazy." Mr. Selig didn't answer her, but he gave her a quick hug.

Toward the end, there were other sounds. Not as loud as before, but weirder. Dinging. Buzzing. Clacking. I'd never heard a television make those noises. I glanced at Lonnie, and he glanced back at me, and we both kind of shrugged without shrugging. It was a total mystery.

Then, at last, Jerry Manche came out of the room. The two stocky guys came out right after him, dripping with sweat, and the second guy shut the door behind him. As soon as Mrs. Selig saw them, she jumped up off the couch and asked if they wanted glasses of lemonade. One of them nodded, and then both of them followed her into the kitchen.

Jerry Manche, meanwhile, walked over to Quentin and said, "Now, you remember our deal, right? You're going to give a hundred and ten percent, and you're going to start feeling better. We shook hands on that, and I'm going to hold you to it."

"Right," Quentin said.

"Remember, you didn't just make that deal with me. You made it with Bobby Murcer and the New York Yankees. You live up to your end of the deal, and I promise you, Bobby will swing by for a visit when the Yankees come north in April. That sounds like a pretty good deal to me. What about you?"

"Sounds good to me too," Quentin said.

Jerry Manche gave Quentin a soft jab in the arm, then stepped aside. It took a second for Quentin to realize he was letting him back into his room. As soon as that sank in, Quentin rushed past him, and the rest of us followed one step behind. Quentin flung open the door and stopped in his tracks.

There, in the corner of the room, stood a pinball machine . . . an actual, full-size dinging and buzzing and clacking pinball machine.

The game was called Challenge the Yankees.

January 26, 1970

Good Citizenship

Here's the fifth essay on good citizenship I wrote for Principal Salvatore:

I've been giving a lot of thought to
what it means to write 200 words. For
example, I started that last sentence
with "I've"—does that count as one word
or as two? Since I have to count the
number of words each week, I don't want to
make a mistake and come up a word short
because I thought "I've" should count as
"I have." That's the kind of mistake that
could get a guy in trouble, even if he's

being a good citizen and trying to turn
in a 200-word essay like he's supposed
to do. I guess I could make it easier on
both of us by just writing "I have." That
way, there's no possibility of getting
it wrong. Oops, I just wrote "there's." I
should have written "there is." When you
think about it, why would I ever use a
contraction? And what about numbers?
If you look back over this essay, I
have written the number 200 twice. Does
that count as a word, or does it count
as a number? What if I had written "two
hundred" both times? Then I'd be that
much closer to two hundred words. Hey, I
just got there!

Like I always did, I slid the paper under the door
of Principal Salvatore's office when I got to school,
and, like she always did, Miss Medina handed it back
to me an hour later. Principal Salvatore had written on
the back:

Contractions count as one word. So do numbers.
Try again.

* * *

Quentin's mom kept him home from school today, and when the gang went over to his house after school, Mrs. Selig answered the door and said he needed to rest. That kind of put a damper on things, and I was feeling pretty lousy about it, but then, right after dinner, the phone rang, and it was Quentin. He asked if I could come over, and I said sure, and I was sure Lonnie could come over too. But he said his mom wouldn't let in more than one friend—and besides, he wanted to talk to me.

That sounded odd, but I wasn't going to say no. I put my sneakers back on, grabbed my coat, and headed to Quentin's house. His mom let me in, even though she wasn't smiling, and I don't think she was crazy about me being there. I headed straight for Quentin's bedroom. He was sitting on the edge of his bed in his Yankees cap and pajamas when I walked in.

"What's going on?" I said.

He reached into the pocket of his pajama pants and pulled out a folded-up sheet of loose-leaf paper, then handed it to me. "What do you make of this?"

I unfolded the paper. It was a list of five words, except they weren't words: *zeetoosk, quilby, krestenfireyuk, horgonk,* and *fiffle.* I stared at them for a few seconds, then glanced up at Quentin. He had a big grin on his face. "What are these?"

"Words," he said.

"Did you make them up?"

"No, I discovered them!"

"You didn't *discover* them, Quentin. . . ."

"But they're not in the dictionary," he said. "I wrote them down while I was in the hospital, and my mom looked them up for me. She couldn't find them."

I could see it meant a lot to him. "All right, you discovered them. What do they mean?"

"That's what I can't figure out," he said. "I got the last one, *krestenfireyuk*. That's the gunk that builds up under the cap of a hot-sauce bottle. That's the easy one. The others I can't get."

"That does sound like a pretty good definition for *krestenfireyuk*."

"When I was lying there, I couldn't do much. I couldn't get out of bed. . . ."

"How did you go to the bathroom?"

"You don't have to go at first because of the tubes. After the tubes come out, they give you this metal thing that looks like a toilet seat, but it's got like a pan underneath—"

I waved my hand. "All right, I can figure out the rest."

"Anyway, I was lying there, and the nurses kept coming in and asking me how I felt, but I couldn't talk, because that tube thing was stuck down my throat, and I got mad—"

"C'mon, Quent, you never get mad."

"Well, I did in the hospital," he said. "I got mad because I couldn't talk. So when the doctors took the thing out of my throat, I started talking and talking." He let out a weak laugh. "I didn't even know what I was saying. I just kept going. I like *words*, Jules. I like how they sound. You ever think about words? They come out of your mouth, and right away people know what you're talking about."

"I think about words all the time," I said. "I think about them when I'm writing."

"But also when you're talking, right?"

"Well, talking happens a lot faster than writing. You don't have as much time to think about words when you're talking."

His eyes got a frustrated look in them, like I was missing the point he was making. "But don't you ever get the feeling that there's stuff you want to say, but there's not enough words?"

"Is that why you made up those new ones?"

"I *discovered* them! There's a difference!"

"If you say so."

His voice got low. "Look, I know I'm not so smart as you, Jules—"

"C'mon, Quent!"

"But I'm good at discovering words. I'm just not so good at figuring out what they mean. I thought maybe you could figure out what they mean, and I could keep discovering them. Then, maybe, someday you could make a book out of them, and it could be all the words I discovered."

"Do you mean like a dictionary?"

"It could be that, or else it could be like a story with my words in it."

"If I use your words in a story, we're going to need a dictionary too."

"Then maybe you could write both," he said.

That made me laugh. "You wouldn't believe the things people are telling me to write at school."

"You don't have to do it right away. You could do it when you have time."

"All right," I said. "I'll figure it out as soon as I have time. You just keep coming up with the words."

He put out his hand, and I shook it.

"I've got one more question," I said. "You don't have to answer it if you don't want."

"You want me to take off the wig?"

"No!"

"'Cause I'm not taking off the wig."

"I don't want you to take off the wig, Quent."

"Then what's your question?"

"It's just that . . . when I first heard how sick you were, I thought . . . even though I didn't want to think it—"

"You thought I might die?"

"Yeah," I said.

"Me too."

"You thought about it too?"

"Yeah," he said.

"I guess what I want to know is, when you were in the hospital, were you scared?"

"Not all the time," he said.

"But you *were* scared, right?"

"It really wasn't so bad. It didn't hurt that much, not even the needles. I guess I got scared sometimes just because—" He cut himself off and took a breath. "Just because I had so much time to think about it. Like a couple of times, I got scared to close my eyes, so I tried not to fall asleep. That was the worst thing."

He looked up at me like he'd said enough, like he wanted me to let it go.

Right then Mrs. Selig knocked on the door. She didn't come in, but she said through the door, "Quent-Quent, it's getting pretty late. Don't you think your friend should be heading home?"

I smiled at Quentin. *"Quent-Quent?"*

"She says stuff like that," he said.

"I guess I'll be heading home."

He nodded. "Yeah, I guess."

"You think you'll go back to school this week?" I asked.

"I don't think so. My mom says next Monday."

"Oh."

"But I can go out before then. Maybe tomorrow."

"Then we'll come by tomorrow, after school."

I slipped the paper with Quentin's words into my pocket and stood up.

"You're not going to forget about them, right?" he said.

"No."

"You can wait until you have more time. Just don't forget about them."

"I won't forget them, Quent. I'll give them a hundred and ten percent."

That cracked both of us up, because it sounded like Jerry Manche. Quentin was still laughing as I shut the door to his room, said goodbye to his mom and dad, and left.

January 31, 1970

Shlomo and the Machine

Thirty-Fourth Avenue is starting to feel like Thirty-Fourth Avenue again. It's like the time Quentin was in the hospital was a bad dream, and the entire block is waking up from it. I mean, it *wasn't* a dream. For one thing, Quentin's got a pinball machine in his bedroom. For another, he's not back to how he was. He gets winded real fast, so there's a lot of stuff we used to do—even just walking-around kind of stuff, let alone playing wolf tag—that we can't do for now.

To be truthful, it would be easier if he'd let us push him in the wheelchair. But he shot down that idea the first time I suggested it, and no one's brought it up since. So we've been hanging out mostly in Quentin's room, and the few times we did get him out of the house, we had to take it real slow and stop for him to catch his breath every couple of minutes. He's getting stronger, though. The plan is still for him to go back to school on Monday, but I'll believe that when I see it. I don't know how it's going to work.

As for the pinball machine, it was fun for maybe three days, but after that we got pretty sick of it. That sounds ungrateful, for sure, but . . . well, *it's a pinball machine.* It gets old fast. You want to know the weird part? The fact that it's free, that we don't have to drop in a dime to start a new game, makes it *less* fun. Lonnie shakes the thing until it tilts every time. I'm not sure he's ever actually finished a game. It's like a joke with him. He starts up a new game and then tilts just for the heck of it.

The last time I took a turn was on Thursday, after school. I don't even know why I bothered. After the first five minutes, I got bored, but I kept hitting the bonus flag, which kept making the center post come up between the flippers, which meant the ball couldn't roll down the center chute to end the game. It just went on and on. I tripled my highest score, but I felt like a prisoner. Finally, I just waited for the post to go down and let the ball slide between the flippers on purpose.

The only one who stuck with it was Shlomo Shlomo. Mr. Selkirk, my sixth-grade teacher, used to say that writing was my "thing." Turns out pinball is Shlomo's "thing." What I mean is he took to that machine like a woodpecker to a tall tree. (Or like Beverly Segal to a tall tree.) The look on his face when he turned and noticed the pinball machine was love at first sight. Like one of those cartoons where the boy cat sees the girl cat, and his eyeballs go *boi-yoing-yoing*. It was comical to watch.

Except how can you hold it against him? Challenge the Yankees is the first thing Shlomo's been better at than the rest of us.

Lonnie's always had basketball. The guy can dribble between his legs like it's nothing. Eric's got baseball, on account of his dad coached Little League and taught him to switch-hit, even though Eric's still afraid of getting beaned. Howie's got football, or at least defense in football, because he loves to tackle people. He'll tackle you even if you're just playing tag. Not in a mean way, he just gets carried away.

On the other hand, Quentin, before he got sick, was a great wide receiver, because he had soft hands. I don't think I ever saw that guy drop a pass. Plus, he even started to get faster in the last year. Before he got sick, I mean. It used to be that the only guy he could catch in tag was Shlomo. But then he started to catch Eric, and once he even caught Howie. So I guess, in a way, he *was* Quick Quentin, or at least he was getting to be Quick Quentin before he got sick. So let's say Quentin gets the edge on offense in football, and Howie gets the edge on defense. Plus, you should see Quentin with a yo-yo! It might not count as a sport, but he can make that thing walk the dog and rock the cradle and go 'round the world.

Challenge the Yankees isn't a real sport either, of course. But it's Shlomo's thing, so you've got to respect it. That doesn't mean it's not annoying. The rest of us will be yakking it up at one end of Quentin's room, but we can't even hear one another because Shlomo's at the other end grunting and moaning, and meanwhile the machine is buzzing and dinging and clacking. He's in his own world . . . challenging the Yankees. Lonnie joked that from now on, when Shlomo rings the doorbell, he should forget about Quentin and ask Mrs. Selig if the pinball machine is home.

You want to know how carried away Shlomo got with Challenge the Yankees? On Friday afternoon, he almost forgot about Sabbath! He *did* forget, actually. It was Lonnie who remembered. He slid up behind Shlomo just as the sun was going down, and tapped him on the shoulder. Shlomo hunched over the machine as if he was protecting his lunch. "C'mon, lay off!"

Lonnie said, "I just thought—"

"I got a good score going!"

"Yeah, it looks like you do."

Shlomo still hadn't taken his eyes off the game. "What do you want?"

"Isn't there something you're supposed to be doing?"

"No . . ."

"All right, let me put it another way," Lonnie said. "Isn't there something you're supposed to be . . . *Jew-ing?*"

"What?"

"Do you know what today is?"

"Of course I know what today is. Today is—"

That was when it hit him, the fact that the sun was going down. It was like all of a sudden, he could *feel* the shadow across his face. His neck got real stiff, and his shoulders went up. He took a half step backward, but even then he couldn't quite let go of the flippers. I don't know what would've happened if, right at that moment, the telephone hadn't rung. Even before Mrs. Selig picked it up in the kitchen, Shlomo knew it was his mom.

We all knew.

Shlomo let go of the flippers, grabbed his coat, and ran home.

The one other thing that happened last week was that my autographed picture of Bobby Murcer came in the mail, just like Jerry Manche had promised. It was signed, "For Julian. Looking forward to meeting you in April. Sincerely, Bobby Murcer." As soon as I read that, I started to feel bad. What I mean is I feel bad the guy's going to make a trip out to Flushing even though he's not Quentin's favorite player. (He sure as heck wouldn't be making the trip just because he's *my* favorite player.) But whose fault is that? Quentin was only trying to do something nice for me. He had no way of knowing that the Yankees would do what they did, that he'd wind up with a pinball machine and a visit from Bobby Murcer.

What makes it worse is that Murcer seems like such a nice guy. Last year, he got into a fight with Ray Oyler of the Seattle Pilots because of a hard slide at second base, which caused both teams to run out onto the field and start fighting, but the *Post* said that at the bottom of the pile, Murcer was already apologizing to Oyler for slugging him. That's the kind of guy he is. So you just know he's going to come out here and be real sincere and make a big deal out of Quentin—not realizing that Quentin's favorite player is Willie Mays. The whole thing just feels wrong.

But what can you do?

February 2, 1970

The King of Egypt

Well, I was wrong. Quentin did wind up going back to McMasters today. How it worked was his dad told him he *had* to go back to school, and he *had* to go in the wheelchair. End of discussion. It never crossed my mind that he'd go in the wheelchair, that he'd bring the wheelchair on the bus.

I decided, right off, that getting Quentin on and off the school bus was more important than rushing to Principal Salvatore's office first thing in the morning and turning in another stupid essay on good citizenship. If you think about it, getting Quentin on and off the bus, and back to school, *is* good citizenship. So I decided to skip a week and see what happened. If Principal Salvatore wanted to punish me for doing the right thing, let him. It made as much sense as him punishing me for *not* doing the wrong thing.

Shlomo and I headed over to Quentin's house at seven-thirty to help out with the wheelchair. Lonnie was supposed to lend a hand too, but as usual he overslept. Except it didn't matter, since there wasn't much for us to do except stand around and wait for Quentin to get ready. Shlomo killed time with a couple of games of Challenge the Yankees—which, come to think of it, might've been the main reason he was so quick to volunteer.

It *was* kind of weird, how Quentin was hustling around the apartment, yanking his clothes out of the closet, chugging a glass of orange juice in the kitchen, doing what he had to do in the bathroom . . . and then, after all that rushing back and forth, putting on his overcoat and settling down into the wheelchair so Shlomo and I could push him out the door. He kept saying how sorry he was to make us do it. But it was nothing to us. Really, we were glad to do it.

The hard part turned out to be getting Quentin on the school bus. Actually, getting *him* on the bus was no problem. He just got out of the wheelchair and walked up the three steps. Getting the chair folded and then hoisting it up the steps—*that* was a problem. The bus driver, who's like ninety years old, didn't lift a finger to help. He just sat behind the wheel and watched Lonnie, Howie, Eric, Shlomo, and me wrestle with the thing until we got it on board. It was only half folded, but we held it in place in the center aisle for the ride to McMasters.

Getting the wheelchair off the bus was just as hard, which was bad because a crowd of kids gathered to watch us. They saw Quentin climb down the steps and stand on the sidewalk as we got the chair unfolded again. They were pointing at it, wondering who it was for . . . and then, when Quentin sat down in it, there was like a group moan.

"Hey, that guy's not crippled!" someone called out.

Lonnie yelled, "Shut up!"

The rest of us glanced around to see who'd said it, but no one stepped forward.

The crowd followed us as we started to push Quentin toward the main entrance of McMasters. Except there were three stairs that led up to the double doors. I'd never even noticed the stairs. It's the kind of thing you don't notice—how many stairs you climb in a regular day. You don't notice it because you don't have to notice it. But with Quentin in the chair, now we noticed it. Quentin had to hop out of the chair, again, to let us carry it up the stairs. Then he had to sit down again.

The kids behind us roared with laughter when he stood up and laughed even louder when he sat back down.

"Who made him the king of Egypt?"

It was the same voice as before. Except this time, I recognized who said it: Devlin. I wanted to tell him to shut up, but I knew if he hadn't listened to Lonnie, he sure wasn't going to listen to me.

We rushed Quentin through the front door and rolled him to the elevator. Since the school only has four floors, students aren't allowed to use the elevator unless they've got broken legs, or at least sprained ankles, but we figured a wheelchair was better than crutches, so we rang for the elevator and waited. Three teachers got off the elevator when it came, and none of them said a word.

Lonnie and Howie were in the same homeroom as Quentin, so the two of them took him up in the elevator. I knew I wouldn't see them again until three o'clock, because their lunch period was an hour later than mine, so I forced myself to smile. But it was real sad, watching the elevator doors close. Quentin didn't even look up. You could tell it was killing him, sitting in that chair. But what could he do? His dad had laid down the law, and Quentin wasn't the kind of guy who'd shrug that off.

After the elevator was gone, Shlomo, Eric, and I went our separate ways.

I was maybe ten feet from my homeroom when I heard, "Hey, Twerp-ski!"

I turned around.

Devlin was standing behind me, grinning. Until you're looking right at him, you forget how bony the guy is. It's almost painful. It's not just his arms and legs—it's even his face. His jaw and cheekbones jut out. You could make a portrait of him out of origami.

"Yeah?"

"How come your friend's in that chair?"

"I don't know, Devlin."

"What do you mean, you don't know?"

"He just is," I said. "That's all I know."

He stepped forward and grabbed me by the chin. He turned my head to the left and then to the right. He didn't do it fast. He wanted to see if I'd make a big deal out of it. I just relaxed my neck and went with it. He turned my face forward and looked me in the eye. "What you mean is, you know why he's in that chair, but you're not going to tell me. Is that it?"

I tried to smile, even though he still had a pretty tight grip on my face. "I guess so."

"You want to fight?"

"No," I said.

"Why not?"

"Because you're bigger than me, and you'll beat me up."

He let go of my chin. "You're not as stupid as you look, Twerp-ski."

After that, he turned and walked off. There were maybe a half dozen kids who saw what had happened, who stuck around to see if there would be a fight. Now they were looking at me as if I'd ruined their fun. I just shrugged at them. Really, I didn't know what else to do.

There's a guy named Hector who sits in the back row of homeroom and plays a trick on old Mrs. Griff a couple of times a week. He does it at the end of the day, when she's writing her afternoon announcements on the board and the class is sitting around, twiddling their thumbs, waiting for the three o'clock bell. Hector's got a miniature Chinese gong that sounds just like the classroom bell. He says he got it in Chinatown, but I think that's baloney—like his parents would let him go into Manhattan alone! More likely, he bought the thing at Gertz department store on Main Street. It's not as loud as the actual classroom bell, of course, but Mrs. Griff's hearing is so bad that she can't tell the difference. So a couple of times a week, Hector hits the gong a minute or so before three o'clock, and Mrs. Griff lets the class go home.

He's been doing it for a month now, and Mrs. Griff still hasn't caught on—which amazes me, since she must hear the actual bell go off a minute or so later. Maybe she hasn't figured it out because she doesn't want to figure it out. At her age, she's got to be pretty tired by three o'clock.

During lunch, I asked Hector to hit the gong extra early, and I even gave him my peach cobbler (which is pretty awful, but he loves it) so he'd do it. Sure enough, the gong sounded at 2:56. I grabbed my books, snatched my jacket from the hook on the wall, flew out of homeroom, and ran down the two flights of stairs. I wanted to be right outside the main entrance when Lonnie and Howie wheeled Quentin through the double doors.

I was standing outside in the cold air, catching my breath and pulling my jacket tighter—I mean, the air was *ice* cold—when someone grabbed my elbow from behind. For a split second, I thought it might be Devlin, but then I spun around and saw Beverly Segal.

She smiled at me. "What kept you?"

"How'd you get down here so fast?" I asked.

"Race me and find out," she said.

"You went out the side door."

"Bingo."

She stood with her hands on her hips, as if she'd made her point.

"What?" I said.

"I went out the side door, which means I had to go farther than you did. Plus, you got out of homeroom before I did. I was still packing up my books when Hector hit the gong. I saw you running out the door. You had a head start, and I went farther, and I still got here first."

"I'm not going to race you, Beverly."

"Bawk, bawk, bawk, bawk, bawk!"

"If that makes me a chicken, fine."

"C'mon, it doesn't have to be in front of lots of people. We can do it back on the block. It'll just be the two of us by ourselves."

"Then what's the point?" I said.

"To find out who's faster."

"But I *know* who's faster—and if you don't know, it's because you don't want to know."

"But I *do* want to know," she said. "Maybe it's you who doesn't want to know."

"Can we just drop it? It's freezing out here."

Right then, the actual three o'clock bell sounded. Seconds later, there was a sound, a low rumble, that came from inside the double doors. It got closer and closer until the doors crashed open and kids started to pour out. You don't realize how loud that is, the rush of kids going through the double doors, down the stairs, and out onto the sidewalk, until you're standing on the outside and not part of it. I mean, it's like a tidal wave of noise.

Meanwhile, the cold was starting to get to me. Every gust of wind felt like needles against my face. I began rocking back and forth on my heels, trying to stay warm. It was a dumb thing to do, running outside like I did. Watching the kids pour out of McMasters, I realized it was going to take a while before Lonnie and Howie came out with Quentin. They were smart enough to wait until the rush was over. I turned back to Beverly. The look on her face was different than before, more serious. "Why didn't you tell me that today was Quent's first day back?"

"I didn't *not* tell you," I said. "It wasn't a secret."

"I wouldn't have walked. I would've ridden the bus with the rest of you. I would've helped."

"We had enough—"

"I *know* you had enough help, Julian. You're missing the point."

"Then what *is* the point?"

"The point is you don't think of me as one of your friends."

"That's not true," I said. "I think of you as my friend."

"Yeah, but you don't think of me as part of your group."

"C'mon, you're part of the group. You live on the block."

"You know *exactly* what I mean," she said.

"I would've told you about Quentin if I knew it meant so much to you."

"It's not just today, Julian."

"Then I don't get it," I said.

"If Eric the Red asked to race you, I'll bet you'd race him."

"But he *wouldn't* ask, because he knows who'd win."

"But if he *did* ask, you'd race him. Wouldn't you?" she said.

"I don't know, Beverly. You're talking about something that would never happen."

Eric picked that exact moment to come out the double doors. He noticed us off to the side and jogged over. Shlomo turned up about three seconds afterward. He looked annoyed. He shoved Eric in the back and said, "Why didn't you wait for me? Didn't you hear me calling your name?"

"No," Eric said.

"Then you must be as deaf as Danley Dimmel, 'cause I was right behind you."

"I didn't hear a thing," Eric said.

I cut them off. "Did you guys have lunch with Quentin?" They both nodded.

"How did he seem?"

"He seemed fine," Shlomo said. "That stupid wheelchair's the problem."

"Plus, he doesn't even need it," Eric said. "It's stupid he had to bring it. It makes no sense. Kids are laughing at him. I mean, they're not laughing at *him*. But they're laughing at how he gets up and sits back down. Maybe Lonnie can talk to Quentin's dad—"

"Julian is chicken to race me," Beverly blurted out.

"Will you please just let it go?" I said.

"He's not chicken to race you," Shlomo said.

Eric grinned at her. "He could give you a head start and still beat you by a mile."

She looked straight at Eric. "Well, then, what about you?"

"He'd beat me by a mile too."

"You think *you* can beat me?"

"*Of course* I can beat you," Eric said. But there was a wobble in his voice. You could tell he wasn't so sure. "I can beat you any day of the week, and twice on Sundays."

"What about today?" she said. "What about right now?"

"I'm not going to race you now."

"Why not?" she asked.

"Because we don't have time. We've got to get Quentin back on the bus."

"Then we can race afterwards . . . when we get off the bus," she said.

"When we get off the bus," Eric said, "we have to take Quentin back to his house."

"You don't think Lonnie and Howie can manage without you?"

"Sure they can. Anyway, it's too cold to take off our jackets."

"Then we can race with them on," she said.

"That's stupid. I'm not going to race you with my jacket on."

"Bawk, bawk, bawk, bawk, bawk!"

Eric turned to me. "Why don't you just race her and get it over with?"

But Beverly shook her head. "No, I want to race *you*. I'll race Julian later."

As they were talking back and forth, I noticed Devlin come out the double doors. He didn't notice me, but he also didn't head down the block toward the buses. He turned and stood about ten yards from the doors. He had on a green snorkel parka, zipped to his throat. He looked as though he wasn't going anywhere anytime soon. That wasn't a good sign.

Lonnie and Howie wheeled Quentin through the doors a couple of minutes later. The rest of us—me, Shlomo, Eric, and Beverly—hurried over to meet them. As soon as he saw us, Quentin stood up from the wheelchair, and then Lonnie and Howie carried it down the three stairs. When they got to the bottom, Quentin walked down the stairs and sat back in the chair.

That was when Devlin called out, "Look who's back . . . it's the king of Egypt!"

Lonnie stepped forward, clenching his fists. But then, without warning, Beverly jumped in front of him. She called back, "Hey, Mouth, why don't you mind your own business?"

There were maybe thirty kids still hanging around the

front of McMasters who heard her. They were stunned at first, but then about half of them let out a loud, "Ooooh!" It was directed at Devlin. It was pretty obvious what they meant: *Are you going to take that from a girl?*

Devlin looked stunned too. "What's *your* beef?"

Beverly took another step forward. "What's yours?"

"You friends with the king of Egypt?"

"Yeah, I am. You got a problem with that, Mouth?"

Devlin grinned at her. "Why don't you go play with your Barbies?"

"Only if you bring over Midge and Skipper."

"Shut up!"

"C'mon, Mouth, we'll have a big old tea party!"

"Stop calling me that!"

"Then shut your mouth, Mouth!"

"If you weren't a girl . . ."

"Yeah, and if you weren't a girl . . ."

"I'm not a girl," Lonnie said, stepping in front of Beverly.

Devlin looked him up and down, then shook his head. "I don't have time for this."

"Yeah," Lonnie said, "I think your bus is leaving."

Devlin turned and started to walk away.

Beverly called after him, "Tell Ken I said hello, Mouth!"

Devlin's shoulders hunched up, but he kept going.

The Other Shoe Drops

The announcement that I had to report to Principal Salvatore's office came five minutes before the end of third period this morning. I'd kind of been expecting it for the two days since Monday, when I didn't turn in another good citizenship essay. It was almost a relief when the crackle came over the intercom and I heard my name. I grabbed my books and coat and headed downstairs.

Miss Medina was sitting in the office, off to the side. She had a real worried look on her face. Principal Salvatore's expression was harder to read. I figured I owed him an explanation, so I spoke first. "I'm sorry I didn't turn in a citizenship paper on Monday. I'll do two next week. But the thing is, my friend Quentin—"

"I know why you didn't turn in the paper, Julian," he said. "I don't fault you for your decision."

"Oh."

"What I do fault you for is the tone of your responses until now."

"Oh."

"Is that all you're going to say?"

"I know it's kind of disrespectful, turning in stuff like that. But I really and truly didn't scratch up that painting, and I don't think I should get punished for something I didn't do."

"I'm glad you used that word, 'disrespectful.' It *is* disrespectful, the way you've gone about your business. Even if you're as innocent as you claim, you were given a specific assignment by the principal of your school, and you've treated that assignment with disrespect. You're a student at McMasters Junior High School. I'm your *principal*, Julian. When you disrespect me, you disrespect McMasters."

"But that's not what I meant to do. It's just that—"

"I'm afraid this isn't working out."

"Am I suspended?"

"That would serve no purpose because you don't have a discipline problem. You have an *attitude* problem. Do you understand the distinction?"

"I think so," I said.

"You either did or did not vandalize the painting.

There is a dispute over that. But there is no dispute over the contempt with which you've responded. Contempt is an ugly response, Julian. It is a childish response, wholly misplaced here. You need to grow up."

I bowed my head. I didn't know what else to do.

"You're in our Fast Track Program, if I'm not mistaken."

"Yes."

"Which means you plan to skip eighth grade, correct?"

"Yes."

"I'm not sure if you're a good match for that program. . . ."

My heart sank. "But I get good grades—"

"I'm sure you can do the work," he said. "But we're not discussing your intellect. We're discussing your maturity. You were suspended from sixth grade for participating in an attack on a handicapped boy—"

"But I told you—we apologized to him. He's our friend now."

"I don't doubt that you have good intentions," he said. "I doubt that you have good judgment. I doubt that you will be emotionally prepared to start ninth grade in September."

"Please!"

Miss Medina jumped in at that point. "I'm sure Julian understands how wrong he was—"

"I'm not so sure," Principal Salvatore said. Then he looked me square in the eye. "Do you?"

"Yes."

He leaned back in his chair. "All right, on Miss Medina's recommendation, I'm going to act against my better judgment. You have exactly one more chance, Julian. You can write one more essay on good citizenship. But I want you to think about it, long and hard, before you write it. You can turn it in anytime before the end of the school year in June. If the tone and the content of it are appropriate, you can remain in the Fast Track Program. But you have zero margin for error. Is that clear?"

"Yes."

"You may go."

My knees were wobbling as I walked out. The only thing that kept me upright was the thought that I had until June to figure out what to do. Right then, that sounded like a long way off.

Cheerleaders in Ponzini

Quentin got through his first week back at school in pretty good shape. It would've gone smoother if not for the wheelchair. But his dad said he had to use the chair for the entire week—since that was what Quentin's doctors said. End of discussion. Truthfully, though, the first day was by far the worst, on account of the king of Egypt stuff. After that, the kids at school got used to Quentin standing up and sitting back down. For sure, they snickered about it, but no one hung around to watch him do it. Even Devlin laid off, maybe because of how bad Beverly had ranked him out.

Beverly, meanwhile, kept after Eric the Red to race her.

She did that chicken-clucking thing at the bus stop every morning until he said yes.

The big race came this afternoon in Ponzini. Pretty much the entire block showed up. The only guy missing was Shlomo, who ran straight from the bus stop to Quentin's house to squeeze in a couple of hours of Challenge the Yankees before the start of Sabbath—which must have seemed weird to Mrs. Selig, since we took Quentin with us to Ponzini.

The place was more crowded than I'd ever seen it. Even guys who don't hang around with us, like Beverly's brother Bernard and Mike the Bike and Victor Ponzini himself, came out for the race. Even a couple of high school girls who live on Beverly's floor in the Dorado House were there. I don't know if they were actual cheerleaders, but they sure acted like they were. They were hooting and hollering and shouting out Beverly's name. They got the crowd revved up. I felt bad for Eric. It seemed like no one was rooting for him except Lonnie, Howie, Quentin, and me.

As bad as I felt for Eric before the race, I felt even worse for him after. It wasn't close. She slaughtered him. It was kind of mean, almost, how bad she beat him. She had him whipped after the first few steps, but she didn't ease up. It wasn't quite forty yards that they raced, maybe thirty-five, and she must've beaten him by ten.

What made it more painful to watch was that Eric didn't even know how bad he was losing. He runs with his arms thrashing and his head down, so he had no clue until he crossed the finish line that Beverly had already gotten there, turned around, and waved to her cheerleader friends, who were hooting and hollering even louder than before. She and Eric shook hands afterward, but you could tell how ashamed he was.

He walked over to us, and we told him it was no big deal, but he looked like he might bawl, so we stopped talking and hustled him away.

Before we got to the hole in the fence that led out of Ponzini, Beverly called after us, "You're next, Twerski!"

"It's not going to happen!" I called back to her, and kept going.

Lonnie was pushing Quentin in the wheelchair, and I was next to them, and Eric and Howie were a couple of steps ahead of us. As soon as we got through the alley and out to the sidewalk on Parsons, Eric turned back to me and said, "This whole stupid thing is your fault."

"How do you get that?" I said.

He didn't answer. He started to walk faster, and Howie kept up with him. I took a step to catch them, but Lonnie caught me by the shoulder and said, "Let him go. He's just sore now. He'll get over it."

"But it's *not* my fault."

"Let it go, Jules. He'll be fine by tomorrow."

So I hung back with Lonnie and Quentin. When we got to the corner, Lonnie peeled off to his house, which left me to push Quentin home in the wheelchair.

"You don't think it's my fault, do you, Quent?"

He glanced up at me and smiled. "Beverly's faster than Eric. How could that be your fault?"

"Exactly!"

"You didn't make him race her."

I pushed him another few steps and thought about it. "Well, I *kind of* made him race her."

"You did?"

"I mean, if I'd raced her, she wouldn't have bothered to race him."

We went half the block without talking again, just making our way along Thirty-Fourth Avenue. Then, as the Hampshire House came into sight, Quentin said, "I guess maybe it is your fault."

He started to laugh, and I jostled his wheelchair.

"Dope!" I said, which made him laugh harder.

Shlomo Tilts

Quentin left the wheelchair home on Monday, after his dad said he could, and the rest of us were grateful for that. He really and truly is getting back to normal, except that we have to take things extra slow because he gets tired and can't catch his breath. But compared with folding and unfolding that chair, and hauling it up and down stairs, that's nothing.

Quentin's biggest headache this week turned out to be Shlomo. Him and that stupid pinball game. Remember how I said it was love at first sight? That was kind of a joke when I said it, but it got less and less humorous. I mean, the way he hunched forward and leaned over the machine while he was playing, it looked like he was about to kiss the thing. Like Romeo and Juliet, except Romeo had horn-rimmed glasses and a yarmulke, and Juliet dinged and buzzed and clacked instead of saying, "Wherefore art thou?"

The reason it got to be a headache for Quentin was that he couldn't get Shlomo out of his room. Shlomo came over before breakfast every morning, faking like he was there to walk Quentin to the bus stop, and he played pinball while Quentin got dressed. Then he walked Quentin home after school, and it was the same thing. It was like Howie Wartnose and his crush on Beverly Segal, except it was even worse, because Challenge the Yankees liked Shlomo back. What I mean is he got real good at it. No, he got *great* at it. He had the five highest scores on the machine. Lonnie started calling him Pinball Wizard Pinball Wizard instead of Shlomo Shlomo.

You want an idea of how crazy it got? After school on Wednesday, the six of us were hanging out in Quentin's room, and Shlomo was bent over the pinball machine, and Howie decided to pull a prank on him. He strolled over to the machine like nothing was going on, and then, without warning, he kicked out the plug.

Shlomo didn't even realize what had happened at first. He kept hitting the flippers and staring down at the game, trying to figure out why it went dark. Then he mumbled, maybe to himself, or maybe to the machine, but definitely not to any of us, "C'mon, I didn't tilt!"

It was only after he heard the rest of us cracking up that he noticed Howie standing next to the plug, and then he noticed the plug hanging out of the wall socket. We figured he'd crack up too at that point. But instead his eyes got real wide, and his head started to shake, and then he charged at Howie.

It was scary. I mean, Howie could take Shlomo no problem in a normal wrestling kind of fight, but the way Shlomo charged at him was different. It was like he wasn't even Shlomo. He was a bull charging at a red cape.

Howie seemed as scared as the rest of us. He jumped out of Shlomo's way, and Shlomo hit the wall so hard you could hear the windows rattle. But he bounced off the wall and came after Howie again. Except he tripped over one of Quentin's model planes and fell forward onto the bed. His glasses went flying, but his yarmulke stuck to his head—it was kind of a miracle how it stuck there. Then Lonnie jumped on Shlomo's back, and Eric and Howie grabbed his arms, and the three of them held him down. That was when Mrs. Selig poked her head into the room and said, "No roughhousing, all right?"

You'd think the sound of her voice would've snapped Shlomo out of it, but even after she slid the door shut, he was still twisting and straining to get off the bed. His eyes were bugging out, and you could see the veins in his neck bulging and pulsing. That was what scared me the most, the veins. I thought the guy was going to have a stroke right on the bed. It took the three of them to keep him there. I don't think Lonnie could've done it on his own. Lonnie, meanwhile, was talking to him in a soft voice, almost a whisper, telling him to calm down.

Quentin got Shlomo's glasses off the floor and put them back on his head. They were crooked, but Shlomo's eyes at least started to focus. It was the glasses, maybe, that started to bring him back. He took deep breaths. Lonnie leaned down and said into his ear, "C'mon, buddy, you're all right."

"I'm real sorry," Howie said, also in a soft voice. "I didn't know . . ."

After another half minute, Shlomo had simmered down. His eyes were back to where it was Shlomo looking out from behind them, and his breaths were normal speed, and you couldn't see the veins in his neck anymore. Lonnie let him roll over onto his side, but he didn't quite let go of him, and the rest of us waited to see how Shlomo would react.

We got our answer a couple of seconds later, when Shlomo started to laugh. It was a quiet laugh at first, but it kept getting louder. He wound up hysterical, which made the rest of us start to laugh too. Lonnie let go of him, but by then it didn't matter. All Shlomo could do was curl up like a baby, with his hands holding his stomach, and laugh.

Then, at last, Lonnie said, "What the heck was *that*?"

"I don't know," Shlomo said, coughing out the words more than saying them.

"Never mess with a guy's pinball," Lonnie said, but in a deep, grown-up voice, as if that was the lesson we were supposed to learn. That cracked up Shlomo again, and by then, the rest of us were hysterical too.

But we didn't talk about it afterward.

Still, as weird as that was, it was nowhere near as weird as what happened today. I was lying on my bed around five o'clock, not sleeping, not even shutting my eyes, just resting up and thinking about the weekend, when the phone rang. I thought for sure the call was for Amelia, since it's Friday, and she gets like a dozen calls every Friday, but then my mom picked up the phone and yelled that it was for me. I figured it had to be Lonnie—maybe he was lying around thinking about the weekend too.

I hustled into the kitchen and took the phone. But it was Quentin on the other end, not Lonnie. He was talking, except his voice was more like a whisper, before I got the thing to my ear. ". . . you got to help me. You got to get this guy out of here."

"Who?"

"Shlomo," he whispered.

"He's still there?"

"He's been going at it for like two hours. I think he broke the machine, but he's still playing."

"How could he be playing if he broke the machine?"

"I don't know," Quentin said. "But he won't leave."

"Well, he *has* to leave soon. It's almost sundown. He has to go home for Sabbath."

"I'm telling you, Jules, the guy's not going to leave."

"Why don't you get your dad to kick him out?" I said.

"He's not home yet. Plus, I don't want to do that to him."

"You don't want to do it to Shlomo or to your dad?"

"Either one," he said.

"What about your mom?"

"I don't want to kick him out. He can't help himself."

"Then what do you want?" I asked.

"I want him to go home," he said.

"Should I call Lonnie?"

"No, Lonnie's just going to kick him out."

"Then tell me what you want me to do," I said.

"Maybe you can talk to him."

"What can I say to him that you can't?"

"If I knew that, I'd say it to him. C'mon, Jules. I'm *really* tired."

That got to me, the fact that Shlomo wasn't letting Quentin rest. So I said goodbye and hung up the phone and headed over to Quentin's house. I had to walk past Shlomo's house on the way, and I could see through the front window. There was no sign of anything unusual. Mrs. Zizner was setting the table for Sabbath dinner. Mr. Zizner was already sitting at the head of the table, flipping through the pages of the newspaper. Shlomo's older brother, Hiram, was sitting on the couch, getting in a last half hour of TV before sundown. I'm sure they were expecting Shlomo to walk through the front door any second.

I kept going until I got to the Hampshire House, and Quentin must've been watching out the window, because he buzzed me in about a second after I rang the bell. He was standing at the front door when the elevator opened on the fifth floor, and he led me back to his room. Mrs. Selig had a sour look on her face as I walked past her. The last thing she wanted, you could tell, was another guy in Quentin's room.

"Look who's here, Shlomo," Quentin said, opening the door to his room.

Shlomo didn't even turn around. He just said, suspiciously, "Who is it?"

"It's me," I said.

"Julian?" Shlomo asked.

"Yeah."

"It's *just* you?"

"It's just me."

"Lonnie's not with you?"

"No, it's just me."

"That's good," Shlomo said. "You've *got* to see this."

"See what?"

"I got the most amazing game going." His voice was so high it sounded like a girl's, and I could see trickles of sweat behind his ears. "You won't believe this game. No one's going to believe it, so I need witnesses. Look at the score!"

I glanced at the score in the top right corner of the machine. It was ninety thousand and change.

"What's the big deal, Shlomo?" I said. "Heck, I got a hundred thousand the last time I played—"

"You don't get it!"

"What don't I get?"

"It's the third time around. It's gone back to zero twice."

"C'mon!"

"I swear to God!"

"It goes up to a million, Shlomo. That's not possible."

He hit the flippers and smashed the pinball up toward the bumpers again. "Look at the post!"

The center post had come up between the flippers.

"So you hit the bonus flag."

"You're still not getting it," he said. *It's stuck like that.*

"What do you mean?"

"The post. It came up, and it didn't go down. It's stuck."

"Then why don't you stop playing?" I said.

"Because I'm at two million ninety thousand!"

"But the machine's broken!"

"It's not broken!" he said. "It's still working!"

"But the post is stuck—"

"Because I hit the bonus flag over and over!"

"What difference does that make?"

"I *earned* it," he said. "It's like as if I broke the bank in Las Vegas!"

"Then you admit it's broken," I said.

"It's not *broken* broken," he said. "Look, the score's still going up!"

"Shlomo, the ball can't go down the chute while the post is up. If the post is stuck, that means the game can't end. You can't lose."

"So what's your point?"

"If you can't lose, the score doesn't matter," I said. "It could be a million times a million, and it wouldn't matter, because you have to be able to lose. That's how you know you're still playing."

"I don't see it like that."

"If the ball can't go down the chute, it's not even a game anymore. Think about it. Right now, what's the difference between Shlomo Zizner playing Challenge the Yankees and a chimpanzee playing Challenge the Yankees?"

"The chimp wouldn't know when to hit the flippers."

"Shlomo, you *have* to be able to lose, or else there's no challenge. Get it? You're not really *challenging* the Yankees if you can't lose. You play the game to test your skill. But it's not a test if you can't . . ."

"If I can't what?"

"It doesn't matter," I said. "Look, Shlomo, the sun's going down. It's Sabbath. You're going to get in trouble if you don't go home. You know that as well as I do. What if you just walk away from the machine, and we'll leave it exactly how it is until Sunday night? No one will touch it—"

"No!"

"Shlomo, it's the only way. Your mom's going to call any minute."

"What if the post goes down?" he said.

"But it's stuck. You said so yourself."

He shook his head. "What if it gets unstuck?"

"Shlomo!"

"I've got to finish it, Jules."

"But you *can't* finish it. That's the point."

The phone rang in the kitchen. The sound came just

after Shlomo rocketed the ball through the left tunnel and up into the cluster of bumpers—it was like *clack-whoosh-bibidi-bang-bang-bang,* and then the sound of the phone. Shlomo reacted to it like he'd been punched in the jaw. His head rocked backward and then rolled to the right. But he recovered and focused again on the game.

Half a minute later, Mrs. Selig knocked on the door. "Shlomo, your mom's on the phone. She says the dinner table is set."

"Tell her I'm on my way," Shlomo called back to her.

Quentin and I watched him keep going for another half minute. We were expecting him to step away from the machine—or at least I was. But he kept playing. His head was bowed, and his shoulders were loose, but he kept hitting the flippers and sending the ball back up toward the bumpers.

"Shlomo . . ."

He heard me say his name, but he didn't turn around. Instead, he let go of the right flipper button, reached up, and took off his yarmulke. He folded it around his thumb and pushed it into the back pocket of his pants. Then he brought his hand back to the flipper button.

"C'mon, Shlomo . . ."

He let out a loud sob, just one, and he kept playing.

Then, at last, Quentin said, "Why don't you tilt it?"

Shlomo choked down a second sob. "What?"

"You could tilt it, and the game would be over."

Shlomo glanced over his shoulder, and I nodded at him.

"There's no other way," I said. "You have to go home."

He turned back to the machine and gave it a quick shove. Nothing happened. Then he hit the left flipper and sent the ball up through the tunnel again. He was still playing, even though he was also trying to tilt.

"You have to do it harder," Quentin said.

Shlomo gave the machine another shove, slightly harder. Again, it didn't tilt—and, again, he kept playing.

"C'mon, Shlomo," I said. "Just tilt it."

He took a deep breath and slammed into the machine with his hips. He hit it so hard that it actually moved an inch closer to the wall.

But it still didn't tilt.

He moaned and let out a deep sob. Then, suddenly, he bent over and smashed his forehead against the glass top of the machine. It was ferocious. I thought for a second he was going to put his head right through the glass. But he came back up with no damage to his head or to the glass. He looked down at the machine and hit the right flipper, which sent the ball back up to the bumpers. As soon as the ball hit the first bumper, the machine went dark.

The tilt sign came up, and the center post slipped down.

Shlomo snatched the yarmulke out of his back pocket

and slapped it back onto his head. He was still holding it there as he grabbed his coat from the chair and ran out of the room.

Quentin and I just kind of stared at the door for a couple of seconds after he was gone.

"You think he'll get home by sundown?" he said.

"Not unless he invents a time machine."

"You think his dad will kill him?"

"I doubt it. He's not allowed to kill him on the Sabbath."

"I figured out another word, Jules."

"You did?"

"Yeah, are you writing them down?"

"Yes," I said.

"Did you figure out the meanings yet?"

"Not yet. But I'll get to it. I promise."

"You're not going to forget, are you?"

"C'mon, Quentin. I'm not going to forget. What's your new word?"

"Addleeooonee."

"How do you spell it?"

"I'm not sure. I just know how to say it: *ah-duh-lee-oon-ee.*"

"Don't worry," I said. "I'll figure out how to spell it."

"And you'll figure out what it means?"

"I promise, Quent. I'll figure out what it means."

February 18, 1970

The Dying Pen

Rabbi Salzberg didn't notice I was standing at the entrance to his office for at least half a minute. I waited for him to look up. I didn't want to barge in on him—even though his secretary, Mrs. Klein, told me I could. I think that's a joke Mrs. Klein plays on him sometimes, telling guys to walk right in and not giving him a heads-up.

He was writing in a spiral notebook, and the ballpoint pen he was using kept running out of ink. He was pressing down real hard. You could see the strain in his wrist. Plus, he kept turning the pen upside down, licking the tip, and trying it again. Then he gave up. He stared at the pen in a real disgusted way and dropped it into the wastebasket beside the desk.

He caught sight of me as he did that. "Yes, Mr. Twerski?"

"Are you busy?"

"That depends upon why you're here. Why are you here?"

"I don't want to bother you, Rabbi. You look pretty busy."

"I'm writing a letter to the Beatles," he said. "I'm asking them to grow their hair longer. That way, no one will know if they're boys or girls. Do you agree that the Beatles should grow their hair longer, Mr. Twerski?"

"I think it's long enough," I said.

"How can I help you, Mr. Twerski?"

"The thing you said last time—"

"You'll have to remind me."

"You know . . . about what the world would be like if only good things happened to good people and only bad things happened to bad people. You asked me if I'd want to live in that kind of world, and I said I would. Remember?"

"Yes, Mr. Twerski."

"Well, I changed my mind," I said. "I wouldn't want to live in that kind of world."

"Why not?" he asked.

"Because there would be no point. It wouldn't be a test."

He leaned forward. "Yes?"

"It would be like a pinball game where the post gets stuck between the flippers."

"What are you talking about, Mr. Twerski?"

"If the post gets stuck between the flippers, the ball can't go down the chute. You can't lose. That means there's no challenge. It's not a game anymore. It's only a game if you can lose."

"Are you saying that life is a game?"

"No, but it's *like* a game," I said.

"I think you should explain your theory to Mrs. Fine. She'll be relieved to hear that those four years in the concentration camp were a game."

"That's not what I mean, Rabbi."

"Then tell me what you mean. But don't tell me pinball."

"What I mean is, if people who did good things always got good stuff, and people who did bad things always got zapped by lightning, and that was how life worked every single time, then no one would ever do bad things. Because who wants to get zapped by lightning, right?"

"And?"

"But if people who do good things are only doing good things because they don't want to get zapped by lightning, then they're doing good things for the wrong reason. They're doing good things because it would be stupid of them to do bad things. It's not a real test."

"How would you make it a real test?"

"I'd mix it up," I said. "I'd sometimes make bad things happen to good people, and sometimes make good things happen to bad people. That way, people have to decide for themselves if they're going to be good or bad. It's a much harder choice if you don't know for sure what's going to happen."

He leaned back in his chair and crossed his arms over his chest. "Haftarah is a miraculous thing, isn't it, Mr. Twerski?"

"What do you mean?"

"What do you *think* I mean?"

"I don't know, Rabbi."

"Maybe that's what you should study."

"If I don't know what you mean, how can I study it?"

"That's your problem, Mr. Twerski. Not mine."

He pulled open the middle drawer of his desk and began scrounging for another pen. I turned and left his office.

Showdown in Ponzini

The thing with Beverly Segal wanting to race me was kind of humorous the first few times. I didn't mind, because I figured she knew, deep down, what the result would be, and it was just kind of a humorous thing between us. But after the way she slaughtered Eric the Red, I'm not so sure. I mean, *I* know what the result would be. But I'm not so sure she does.

It's not humorous anymore because she's not letting it go. She stands at the bus stop every morning with her hands on her hips, looking real smug, with her head tilting downward to the left, and with her grin tilting upward to the right, and she stares me down. I'd walk to school just to avoid that look on her face, but Quentin still doesn't have the breath for it, so there's nothing to do except ignore her.

But now even ignoring her isn't working. The bus was running a few minutes late this morning, and I was huddled with the rest of the guys, trying to stay warm, and she came up behind me and tapped me on the shoulder. "So how about it, Twerski?"

"No, Beverly. I'm not racing you."

The guys started laughing, since they knew she was getting on my nerves.

"C'mon, Julian, you look real cold. You need a quick run to warm you up."

But then Lonnie spoke up for me. "He's got no reason to race you, Segal."

That caught her by surprise, I think, the fact that Lonnie got involved. She stepped back, and I thought that was the end of it. But then, a few seconds later, she said, "What about you, Fine?"

"What about me?" he said.

"Do you want to race?" she asked.

"Don't make me laugh."

"You think it's funny?"

"Yeah," he said. "I do."

"Bawk, bawk, bawk, bawk, bawk!"

Lonnie's eyes got narrow, but a second later he cracked up—which was a relief, because no one had ever called him a chicken before, and I didn't know how he'd react. If you think about it, though, how could he *not* crack up? Calling Lonnie chicken is like calling Wilt Chamberlain peewee.

"Okay, Segal," he said, "I'll race you. . . ."

"Finally!"

"The day after you beat Julian."

That made the rest of us laugh.

"Psych!" Eric yelled, which must've felt good after his race with her.

But then Beverly glared at him, and he clammed up real fast.

"What about you, Shlomo?" she said.

Shlomo waved his hands in front of his face. "Uh-uh. No way. You're faster."

That made the rest of us laugh harder, and it even made Beverly smile, so I thought *for sure* that would be the end of it and we could just get on with our morning. But then Howie stopped laughing and said, "I'll race you."

It was kind of stunning to hear Howie say that, on account of how long he'd been sweet on Beverly. I mean, that crush lasted from the start of third grade until the end of sixth grade. Even now, a half year after I'd told him to forget about it, that she didn't want to be his girlfriend— which the entire block, except for him, knew—he still couldn't look her in the eye. Except here he was, standing at the bus stop, looking her in the eye, looking her *right* in the eye, and telling her he'd race her.

It definitely caught Beverly off guard. The expression on her face changed. The sarcasm went away, and her nose wrinkled as if to say, *You* want to race *me*? She didn't say the words, but you could tell she hadn't figured on Howie being the guy to step up. Plus, Howie was pretty fast. It was always close between him and Lonnie about who was the second-fastest guy on the block. Lonnie was shiftier and harder to catch, but Howie had beaten him by a hair the two times they'd raced.

"Are you sure you want to, Howie?" she said.

"What's the matter, Segal? Are you chicken?"

"I'm not chicken! I want to race Jul—"

"Bawk, bawk, bawk, bawk, bawk!"

She shook her head. "All right! You're on!"

Howie said, "See you in Ponzini after school."

I admit it: I was curious to see Howie race Beverly. I wouldn't have given Beverly a chance until I saw her race Eric. But with how bad she beat Eric, I honestly didn't know who'd win between her and Howie. Of course I knew if Beverly won, she'd nag me even more to race her. Which I wasn't going to do. Which I'm *not* going to do. What I mean is even if she wasn't a girl, I wouldn't race her, because it's not close. I've played tag with her a hundred times, and I can catch her from behind without breaking a sweat, and she's *never* caught me, not even once—except maybe in wolf tag, when she had three or four guys helping her chase me down.

None of us talked to Howie about the race beforehand. You could tell it was on his mind during the bus ride home. Beverly was sitting near the front of the bus, by herself, in the third row of seats, and we were sitting in the back, and Howie kept glancing up at her when he thought none of us was watching, even though all of us were watching every move he made.

She got off the bus first at the corner of Parsons and waited for us. As I hopped down the last step and onto the sidewalk, she shot me a look that said what Eric had said to me after their race: *This whole stupid thing is your fault.* That ticked me off, because, yeah, you could say it was my fault for not racing her, but it's not like she *had* to keep bugging me to race her. So I was rooting for Howie even more after she shot me that look.

The walk to Ponzini was real quiet. It felt mechanical, like we were robots doing what we were supposed to do, what we *had* to do, and there was nothing else to say about it. No one knew about the race except the six of us and Beverly. She didn't have time to bring out her cheerleaders. Or else she didn't want to bring them out, maybe because she knew how emotional the thing was for

Howie. Three years is a long time to stay sweet on a girl, especially if you don't have the nerve to talk to her, and then to find out that she's known you were sweet on her the entire time, and that the entire block has known the entire time—I mean, it's just hard.

Without even looking at one another, Beverly and Howie took off their coats and walked side by side to the far end of Ponzini. That was where the starting line was— the first fence post. The rest of us waited at the finish line, which was the end of the fence, by the garage door.

Then Lonnie shouted, "On your mark . . . get set . . . go!"

The race wasn't as close as I thought it would be.

Howie got off to a good start. He definitely reacted quicker to Lonnie's voice, and he might have been ahead for the first couple of steps—it was hard to tell because they were running toward us—but Beverly passed him after that, and when Howie caught sight of her, his arms started to flail, which is never a good sign. She had him by six steps at the finish line . . . and she was coasting. Not that she was rubbing it in. She wasn't waving at us or making a show of winning. She just wasn't running full speed.

By the time Howie crossed the finish line, he looked killed. He shrugged as he walked over to us, but his eyes were blank, like there was no one home in his head. It was painful to see, how blank his eyes were, how glazed over and flat they looked. It made me mad, and for a second I thought maybe I *would* race Beverly, then and there, and I'd beat her worse than she'd beaten Howie, even worse than she'd beaten Eric. But then I noticed the look on *her* face, and I realized she felt bad too. She was standing ten feet past the finish line, alone, staring up at the brick wall of the apartment building. She couldn't bear to look at Howie. She couldn't bear to look at any of us.

Then, out of nowhere, Quentin said, "I got next."

The rest of us stared at him in disbelief.

"C'mon, Quent," Lonnie said. "You know you can't—"

"No, I can do it," Quentin said. "I want to race her."

Beverly had turned around and was shaking her head. "I won't do it, Quentin."

"You want to race everybody else. Why not me?"

"Because . . ."

"Because what?"

Her mouth opened, but no words came out. She couldn't answer him.

"Because you're still sick," Lonnie said.

"But I'm not sick anymore! Why doesn't anyone believe me?"

"Because it's too soon," I said. "You still can't walk from your house to the bus stop without catching your breath. Maybe in a month or so—"

"I'm not a baby, all right? I know what I can do." He turned to Beverly. "I want to race you. I want to race you *right now.*"

"No, Quentin, I'm not doing it," she said.

He lowered his head and said in a soft voice, "I'm *begging* you, Beverly."

The way he said that, the way he said the word "begging," he put her in a real tough situation. How could she say no? On the other hand, how could she say yes? She looked at me, like I might have an answer, but I had nothing. I looked straight down at the ground.

"You really think you can do it?" she asked.

He nodded at her. "I'm sure of it."

"And you swear you'll stop if you start to feel sick?"

"I swear."

Beverly took a deep breath, then said, "Let's race."

As soon as she said that, Quentin peeled off his coat and dropped it to the ground. He kept on his ski cap, though, because of the wig, and I was thankful he kept it on, since it was real cold out. But I still had a bad feeling watching the two of them walk together toward the far end of Ponzini. Except if you didn't know Quentin was sick, there was no way to tell anything was wrong. He'd been home for four weeks. He looked skinny, but not skeleton-skinny like that first day back from the hospital. He was walking all right too, keeping up with Beverly, and she wasn't slowing down on his account.

Lonnie started to inch forward as they were walking. It took me a couple of seconds to realize what he was doing. He was changing the finish line, bringing it closer, shortening the race.

He turned to me and said under his breath, "Jules, why don't you make sure it's a fair start."

I nodded and began to trot after them. Beverly heard my footsteps coming up behind them, and she turned around. She looked real relieved. "If you tell me you want to race too, I'm going to slug you."

"I'm just making sure no one cheats."

She laughed. "You think I have to cheat to beat this guy?"

"I know *you* won't cheat. I'm not so sure about Quentin."

That made Quentin laugh.

They got to the starting line and turned around.

I said, "On your mark . . ."

But Quentin held up his left hand. "Hold on a minute."

"Are you out of breath?" I said.

"I'm just revving myself up."

Then Beverly said, "Quentin—"

"I'm fine!"

Nothing happened for maybe ten seconds.

Then Quentin said, "Okay, I'm ready."

I said, "On your mark . . ."

The two of them crouched over.

"Get set . . ."

Beverly shot me one last, desperate look.

"Go!"

It was a fair start. Beverly reacted quicker, but Quentin's first step was longer, and for the first few steps, the two of them were dead even. Then, though it didn't seem possible, Quentin started to pull in front. His head was down, and his arms and legs were churning, and maybe ten steps into the race, he had Beverly by a full step—and not because she wasn't trying. Her head was down too, and she was leaning forward, running as hard as she could.

Then, without warning, Quentin stopped running.

Except *stopped running* doesn't get across how sudden it was. One second his legs were working, and the next second they were buckling under him. I've never seen a guy go down like that. It was as if he'd been hit across the chest with a baseball bat as he was going full speed. That was where he grabbed too—his chest. He seized up in the middle of a stride, grabbed his chest, and stumbled forward until he dropped to his hands and knees. Beverly caught sight of him out of the corner of her eye, and she stopped running too, and the rest of us ran toward the two of them.

By the time I got there, Beverly was kneeling alongside Quentin, who was lying facedown and not moving. Tears were rolling down her face, and she was screaming, "What happened? What happened?"

But she was getting nothing back. He was breathing, but he was just lying there. She reached down to grab his shoulder, but then she didn't touch him. You could tell she was afraid to lay a hand on him. I was too. I slid down next to her, but I had no idea what to do.

Lonnie ran up behind us and yelled, "Get his face out of the dirt!"

I leaned forward, but I couldn't roll him over. I couldn't make myself do it.

"All right, get out of the way!" Lonnie yelled, and he knelt down on the other side of Beverly. He grabbed the back of Quentin's shirt and rolled him over onto his back. You could see Quentin's eyes fluttering even though his eyelids were still closed. Then Lonnie got down on his stomach and said into his ear, "Quentin? Hey! C'mon, wake up! Do you know who I am?"

Quentin's eyes slid open, and he took a deep breath. "Are you God?"

As soon as he said that, he started to laugh, but then the laugh turned into a cough, and the rest of us sat there and listened to him cough for the next half minute.

It was an awful cough. It came from his guts, not from his throat. On the other hand, when he wasn't coughing, he was smiling. Not just smiling, he was grinning like a fool. Not even Lonnie knew what to make of it.

As the coughing died down, Lonnie slipped his hand behind Quentin's head and helped him sit up. When Quentin had caught his breath, he looked up at Beverly and said, "I was winning."

She stared at him in disbelief. "Did you fake that?"

"No!"

"What happened?"

"I ran out of gas . . . but I was winning."

"What difference does it make, who was winning? I thought you were dead!"

"That was great. It was just . . . great. . . ."

Beverly jumped to her feet. "You're an idiot! You're all idiots!" Then she turned to me and said, "And it's *your* fault!"

"That's right!" Eric said.

"It's *not* my fault," I said.

Beverly rubbed the tears from her eyes and stormed out of Ponzini.

Sluppy

Here's the thing about writing stuff down, and the reason I recommend it: when you read back what you wrote, stuff makes more sense. When I first started to write about what happened last week in Ponzini with Beverly and Howie and Quentin, I felt like the whole thing was Beverly's fault—maybe because she said the whole thing was my fault. But after I wrote it down and read it back, I got a different feeling about it. It *wasn't* Beverly's fault, what happened. Not really. I'm not saying it was my fault, but it wasn't hers.

She took it real hard, though. She didn't hang out with us over the weekend, not for a minute. Then, on

Monday and Tuesday, she wouldn't ride the bus with us—which she'd been doing ever since Quentin came back to school. She walked to school, even though it was pouring rain both mornings. She walked right past us at the bus stop. She didn't even nod in our direction.

But you know who took it even harder than Beverly? Quentin.

I don't think he'd ever had anyone get mad at him, let alone *stay* mad at him. He couldn't take it. He kept asking me how long it would be until Beverly wasn't mad anymore, and I kept telling him I didn't know. That didn't sit well with him. After she walked past us on Tuesday morning, he followed her halfway down the block, trying to apologize, but she wouldn't even turn around. If Lonnie hadn't chased him down and brought him back to the bus stop, he likely would've missed the bus.

Last night, he showed up at my house with a note. He wanted me to copy it over so that he could give it to Beverly. (If you'd ever seen Quentin's handwriting, you'd know why he needed me to copy it over.) Here's what the note said:

Dear Beverly,
    I feel real sluppy since the race we had, which is a word I discovered

that means "sorry" and "unhappy."
I really thought I could do it.
I didn't mean to scare you so
bad. Please don't be mad at me
no more.

Sincerely,
Quentin

I copied over the note while he sat on my bed and waited. I fixed up the punctuation, but I kept the words the way he wrote them. So even if Beverly recognized my handwriting—which she likely would because of how many classes we had together—she'd know it was really and truly Quentin's note.

He read it after I was done and nodded.

"How are you going to get it to her?" I said.

"I'll slide it under her door," he said. "I got an envelope."

"Can I see it?"

He unfolded the envelope from his back pocket and showed it to me. On the front he'd written "FOR BEVERLY," which you could just about make out, because he'd written it in capital letters. His print capitals weren't as bad as his cursive.

"How are you going to get into her building?"

"I'll wait for somebody to come out," he said.

"You want me to go with you?"

He shook his head. "You did enough already."

This morning Beverly walked past us again at the bus stop.

But she said hello to Quentin.

What Was in the Box

After a week, Beverly's freeze-out started to get to me too. If it was just the thing at the bus stop, I could've taken it a lot longer. But I also had to deal with her in homeroom and then in half of my regular classes. That was the worst of it, because none of the other guys were there, so the icicles were pointed straight at me. I'd stop by her desk and start talking, just to see if I could get something back, and she'd stare straight ahead. She wouldn't even look me in the eye.

"Let her cool off," Lonnie told me. Which was kind of an ironical choice of words.

But another weekend came and went, and she didn't come around, and even though—if you think about it—I *hadn't* done anything wrong, I started to feel like I had. I decided to make things right. I didn't have a plan, just a gut feeling that if I could talk to her for couple of minutes, with no one around, she'd at least hear me out.

I finally got my chance yesterday, after school. I was standing in line for the bus outside McMasters with the rest of the guys, and I noticed Beverly at the end of the block, about to turn the corner. I nudged Lonnie and pointed her out. He understood what I meant. As the bus pulled up, I trotted off to catch up with her.

She carried her textbooks and school supplies in a blue backpack, which always looked big enough to flip her backward, but she also had a brown cardboard box tucked under her right arm. It was the size and shape of a pizza box, but she was holding it sideways, against her body, so I knew there was no pizza inside. She heard my footsteps coming up behind her and glanced over her shoulder. When she saw it was me, she turned back around.

"I just missed the bus," I said. "Can I walk home with you?"

"Not if you're going to lie to me."

"I didn't miss the bus. I was thinking maybe we could talk."

"What do you want to talk about?" she asked.

"I don't care," I said. "Whatever you want to talk about."

"I'm not the one following you home."

"I'm *not* following you home."

"Then what would you call it?" she said.

"We live on the same block. We're going in the same direction."

"So what's your point?"

I took a deep breath, but I didn't answer her. I let maybe ten seconds go by. Then, at last, I said, "What's in the box?"

"None of your business," she answered.

"C'mon, Beverly. . . ."

"C'mon, what?"

"I'm just trying to have a conversation."

"I don't want to talk about what's in the box," she said.

"Then what *do* you want to talk about? We can talk about anything."

She looked me in the eye for the first time. "Why won't you race me?"

"I already told you—"

"Why won't you race me *really*?"

It was a tough question to answer, because the real answer was the one she thought was fake: I didn't want to race her because I knew who'd win, and I knew it wouldn't be close. It was like when Principal Salvatore first called me into his office about the painting. You keep telling people the truth, but they don't want to hear it because it's not deep enough.

"What do you want me to say, Beverly?"

She took a deep breath. "Did you ever race a girl—even once?"

"Not that I can remember," I said.

"Do you know what that makes you?"

"No."

"That makes you a male chauvinist," she said. "It means you think boys are better than girls."

"I know what it means . . . and, for your information, I don't think boys are *better* than girls. I just think they're *faster* than girls."

"Tell that to Eric and Howie," she said.

"Do you honestly think that racing Eric and Howie is the same as racing me?"

"Here's what I think, Julian. I think that you think I'm not *worth* racing. You don't care how hard I worked to get faster, how many times I ran around the track at Memorial Field, how many blisters I got on my feet. The only thing that matters to you is that I'm a girl, so I'm not worth racing."

The way she said that, you could hear the hurt in her voice. She *had* gotten faster. I mean, maybe she could've beaten Eric a year ago, but there was no way she could've beaten Howie. She'd gotten a lot faster, for sure . . . it just never crossed my mind that she'd *worked* at it. I figured it just kind of happened, like she woke up one morning faster than Howie.

"All right," I said.

She stopped and looked at me. "All right, what?"

"Let's race," I said. "Here to the end of the block."

"I don't want to race you *now*."

"You're kidding, right?"

"No one will believe it if I win."

"You're not going to win, Beverly."

"I need witnesses," she said.

"Fine, when *do* you want to race?" I asked.

"Friday, after school, in Ponzini."

"Are you going to bring your cheerleader friends?"

She smiled. "Maybe."

"They're going to be disappointed."

"We'll see," she said.

I started to walk again, but she didn't. Instead, she knelt down on the sidewalk and started to pick at the tape on the edges of the pizza box.

"What are you doing?"

She looked up at me. Her mouth crinkled at the edges. "Do you want to know what's in the box or not?"

"Can't you just tell me?"

"No, I want to show you."

I waited for her to pick through the tape on the second

corner. After she did that, she slid open the box and pulled out a canvas painting. It was wrapped in layers of brown paper, but you could see the edges of it, where the paint had dripped over. She was real careful unwrapping it. She was also careful not to let me see the picture until she got the brown paper completely off.

"Ready?" she said.

"C'mon, I'm cold."

"Ta-da!"

She held the painting out in front of her, and I gasped: it was the painting of the Bowne House.

"Beverly, where . . . *how* did you get that?"

"How do you think?"

"You *stole* it?"

"Yeah, that's right," she said. "I'm actually Catwoman, and I steal art from junior high schools. I'm going to add this to my collection. You have to pinkie-swear to keep my secret."

"I'm serious, Beverly. Where did you get it?"

"I painted it, you idiot! It's mine!"

"C'mon!" I said.

"You don't even know I paint, do you? We've known each other since third grade, and you don't know a thing about me."

"How would I know you paint? You've never talked about it."

"You've never asked about it," she said.

"How would I know to ask about it if you've never talked about it?"

"Fair point," she said, then held up the painting again. "So, do you like it?"

"Do you know how much trouble I got into because of that painting?"

"Why would you get into trouble because of a painting?"

"Principal Salvatore thinks I'm the one who scratched it up," I said.

"You mean the *JF*?"

"He thinks it's *JT*."

"Well, it looked like *JF* to me. I don't know why anyone would want to do that. I figured it was just some idiot ninth grader, but I didn't know anyone whose initials were *JF*. I guess it *could've* been *JT*. Anyway, it's no big deal. I fixed it, so your troubles are over." She pushed the canvas closer to my face, and I looked in the lower right corner. The scratches were gone. The signature, now that I knew what to look for, clearly read "bsegal." "Do you want me to tell Principal Salvatore I fixed the painting, so he can forget about it?"

"It's not that simple," I said. "He's going to kick me out of Fast Track unless I write him an essay on good citizenship."

"Then write the essay!"

"But that would be like admitting I scratched up the painting—which I didn't do."

"So you'd rather get kicked out of Fast Track?"

"I don't know," I said. "I need time to think about it."

"Let me talk to Principal Salvatore—"

"No!"

"Why not?" she said. "I know you, Julian. I know you didn't scratch up the painting."

"This is between him and me!"

"But he doesn't know you—I do. Plus, it's my painting, so I'm already involved."

"Promise me you won't talk to him."

"But—"

"Please, Beverly, promise me you won't."

She shook her head. "All right, I promise."

"Thank you."

She smiled in an odd way. "You never told me whether you liked it."

I didn't know how to answer. "It's all right."

"That's it?"

"What do you want me to say? It's nice. It looks like the real thing."

"You used to stand in front of it and stare."

"I did not."

"C'mon, Julian. I saw you doing it."

"I look at lots of paintings," I said.

"Yeah, but you don't stand and stare at them."

"Why did you paint the Bowne House?"

"I like Quakers," she said. "I did a book report on them. Did you ever hear of Mary Dyer?"

"No."

"I thought you knew about Quakers."

"Not as much as you do," I said.

"She was a Quaker who got hanged," Beverly said.

"Did she live in the Bowne House?"

"No one lived in the Bowne House except the Bowne family," she said. "But John Bowne let a group of Quakers meet there. They were being persecuted by Peter Stuyvesant, who was the governor of New Amsterdam. He had a wooden leg."

"Why are you telling me all of this?"

"Because it's *interesting*," she said. "Don't you like knowing stuff?"

"Yeah, but—"

"Don't you want to know why Mary Dyer got hanged?"

"All right," I said. "Why did Peter Stuyvesant hang Mary Dyer?"

"*Peter Stuyvesant* didn't hang her," she said. "Mary Dyer had nothing to do with the Bowne House. She got hanged in Massachusetts. John Winthrop was the guy who hanged her. He didn't want Quakers in his colony, so he kept kicking her out. But she kept coming back and preaching. She stuck with what she believed, no matter what. She kept coming back and coming back, so in the end he hanged her. He also dug up her dead baby."

"Why would he do that?"

"I just told you. She kept coming back—"

"No, why would he dig up her dead baby?"

"Because it was deformed," she said. "He wanted to prove that she was working with the devil, so he dug up the baby and showed it to the people of Massachusetts, and it had a face but no head. Also, it had two mouths, and four horns, and it had claws and scales."

"C'mon, you're making that up."

"I swear it's true, Julian. Cross my heart. It's in the encyclopedia."

"What encyclopedia?"

"The *World Book*," she said. "I can show you if you don't trust me."

"No, I trust you."

Which was the truth. I did trust her. She knew I trusted her too, because her smile got bigger. Then she started to rewrap the painting in the brown paper. As I watched her doing it, kneeling on the sidewalk and wrapping the painting, I had a weird feeling that started in the pit of my stomach and rose into my chest. It was like a gust of wind, except it was warm instead of cold.

I was still trying to figure out what it was when I heard myself say, "It's a great painting, Beverly. You should be an artist."

"Do you want it?"

"The painting?"

"You can have it," she said. She looked up at me when she said that, but then she looked back down. Then, a second later, she looked back up. She looked straight at me. "I *want* you to have it."

"But it's *your* painting," I said. "Why would you give it away?"

"I've got lots of paintings. I don't have room to hang them all."

"But—"

"It's not a big deal, Julian. You like it, so I want you to have it."

"I *do* like it. . . ."

She stood up and handed it to me. "You have to carry it home."

We started to walk again, except now I had the pizza box under my arm. Neither of us spoke, but I kept peeking over at Beverly. She looked real pleased with herself— I didn't know if it was because I'd liked her painting or because I'd agreed to race her. But I couldn't peek at her for more than a split second, because she kept peeking over at me. After the third time our eyes met, I stopped doing it.

I stared straight ahead and tried to think of a conversation starter. But nothing came to mind, which makes no sense, since she's real easy to talk to. What I noticed, though, was that we weren't walking as fast as before.

Then, at last, she said, "I know you're probably going to win."

"But you still want to race?"

"Yeah."

March 5, 1970

Weird Conversations

When Rabbi Salzberg suggested putting off my bar mitzvah until the end of May, he kind of left it up to me how often I'd come in for haftarah lessons. You're supposed to go once a week, which I was doing every Thursday up until January, but when the date got moved back, there didn't seem much point. He and I both knew I had the thing down cold. It wasn't like there was a big decision. What happened was one week the lesson came to an end, and he didn't say, "I'll see you next Thursday, Mr. Twerski," so I took that to mean we were done, and that was that. Except I know the guy. If I stopped going altogether, he'd think I was taking stuff for granted . . . and make it a regular thing again. That's the way he operates. So I stopped by his office every so often just to show him that I wasn't taking stuff for granted.

That was the reason I headed over to Gates of Prayer this afternoon. Mrs. Klein, as usual, waved me right through without giving Rabbi Salzberg a heads-up. I pushed open the door to his office real slow. Except as soon as the door started to move, he called out, "Come in, Mr. Haft."

I poked my head around the door. "It's me, Rabbi."

"Mr. Twerski?"

"Yes."

"To what do I owe this honor?"

"I just wanted to tell you I'm working on my haftarah."

"Maybe you should be helping your friend Mr. Haft."

"Eric will do fine," I said. "He's studying like crazy."

"He has very little time left."

"That's why he's not slacking off one bit. I mean, you should see how he's going at it. I've never seen him hit the books like that in regular school." I almost slipped and said *real school,* which would've made Rabbi Salzberg blow a gasket. "Trust me, Rabbi. Eric's going to come through with flying colors."

Rabbi Salzberg slid his glasses down his nose and peered over them. "Things come easily to you, Mr. Twerski. That's a blessing you shouldn't take for granted. Not everyone is as fortunate."

"Do you want me to tutor Eric?"

"No," he said. "We don't want to put more pressure on him at this point."

"I'm really sure he'll be all right, Rabbi."

"How is your sick friend, Mr. Twerski?"

"Quentin? He's doing much better. It's like night and day from when he first came home. He ran a race last week. You should've seen him, Rabbi. He was ahead until he stopped—"

"You're not worried he's going to die anymore?"

"No!" I said. "The doctors said he's going to be fine!"

"Do the doctors consult with you on a regular basis?"

"No, but—"

"You're a man now, Mr. Twerski. You must be prepared."

"Prepared for what?"

"Do I have to answer that question?" he said.

"But I just told you. The doctors said—"

"God has the final word. Not the doctors."

"I'm telling you, Rabbi, he's getting better."

"You should be like Jacob, Mr. Twerski."

"All right . . ."

"Do you remember what happens to Jacob? Do you remember what happens when he wrestles the stranger?"

"Yes," I lied.

"*Do* you remember it, Mr. Twerski?"

"No."

"Do you know who Jacob is?"

"Jacob is Isaac's son," I answered. "Abraham, then Isaac, and then Jacob."

"When Jacob wrestles the stranger, he loses. But he doesn't let go. That's the key, Mr. Twerski. You need to be like Jacob. You need to hold on, even when it's difficult."

"Do you mean Quentin? I'm not going to let go of him, Rabbi."

"I don't *just* mean Quentin."

"Then I don't get it," I said.

"You should thank God for the time you've had with your friend."

"Why are you talking like that, Rabbi? If you'd seen the guy run—"

He shook his head. "Go and study your haftarah, Mr. Twerski."

I shut my eyes. I shut them real tight and felt like I was going to bawl, but I fought it off. I wasn't going to let him make me bawl. I opened my eyes and said, "You're wrong, Rabbi Salzberg."

"Am I?"

"You're wrong about Quentin, and you're wrong to talk like that."

"You may be right, Mr. Twerski. But only in one of your opinions."

The conversation with Rabbi Salzberg would've ruined my day by itself, but when I got home, Howie was pacing back and forth in front of my house. I noticed him as I turned the corner at Parsons, and I slowed down. It wasn't something he'd do for no reason—hang around in front of my house. Don't get me wrong. Howie's a great guy, but he and I have always been kind of at the opposite ends of our group. We're friends because of the group, not because we'd be friends no matter what. Plus, things between us have never gotten back to normal since I told him Beverly didn't want to be his girlfriend. I knew he might be sore because I'd walked her home on Monday. And if he knew she'd given me that Bowne House painting, he might be more than just sore.

I wanted to figure out what kind of mood he was in while there was still distance between us, so I called out, "Hey, Howie!"

He looked up and said, "Hi, Jules!"

I knew right away, from the sound of his voice, he wasn't sore. The look in his eyes proved it even more. He still had the same killed look from when Beverly outran him in Ponzini.

I walked over and leaned against the iron rail in front of the driveway. "I just got back from temple."

"Yeah, your mom told me," he said. "I didn't think you still had to do that."

"I show my face every so often. It keeps Magoo happy."

The name Magoo made Howie smile. As hard as Rabbi Salzberg rides me, he rides Howie even harder. Back in our third year of Hebrew school, he once knocked on Howie's forehead with his knuckle for half a minute, yelling, "Hello? Is anybody home?" just because Howie screwed up a vowel sound. That's half a minute of the class pointing at you and cracking up. You don't forget something like that.

"The old guy's always telling me I should study like how you do," Howie said. "But the joke's on him 'cause you don't even study."

"Well, at least you've got until September," I said. "Eric's the one on the hot seat."

"Yeah, that's going to be painful to watch."

"You think so?" I asked.

"He's going to crash and burn for sure."

"I think he'll come through all right. What's the worst that could happen?"

"You know Eric," Howie said. "He could piss his pants."

"C'mon, even if he's a little shaky, I'm sure Magoo will help him out. He's not going let the guy stand on the stage and choke. Eric's family is shelling out a lot of money for the thing."

"I hope you're right, Jules."

"So did you want to talk?"

He started to rub the side of his face with his right hand. "I heard you're going to race Beverly tomorrow."

"Yeah, but it wasn't my idea."

"I was thinking maybe you should take it easy on her."

"She didn't take it easy on you," I said.

"Yeah, but that was different."

"It's different, but it's not *that* different."

"I don't mean you should let her win. You should *definitely* win. But I don't think you should slaughter her. It just . . . it just wouldn't be right."

He looked down right after he'd said that, like it was a relief, like he'd been saying it over and over to himself, and now that it was said, he could let it go. He didn't have to remember it anymore.

"I'm not going to slaughter her. . . ."

"I know she gave you that Quaker painting. I know she's sweet on you, Julian."

"Howie, I don't think—"

"No, it's okay to admit it," Howie said. "I talked to Lonnie. I know you didn't plan nothing. You and her got more in common than me and her. That's what Lonnie said, on account of you're both such brainiacs."

"Lonnie said that? I'm real sorry, Howie."

"It's just that . . . sometimes things don't go how you

want them to go. They go how they're going to go, and you wind up looking like the bad guy. But you're not the bad guy, even if you did a bad thing. Do you know what I mean?"

"No," I said. Which was the truth.

"I'm not saying it's a bad thing, what you did with Beverly. It could happen to anyone. That's all I'm saying."

I had no idea what he was talking about. But when a guy gets killed the way he got killed, you can't expect him to make sense right away.

I patted his shoulder and said, "Don't worry about it, Howie."

He turned and headed back to his house. As he was walking away, I got a low-down feeling that was hard to describe. But then, suddenly, I knew the exact word to describe it: I felt *sluppy.*

The Big Race

Right up until the last minute, I was hoping Beverly would change her mind about the race. Not that I thought she would. I knew she was dead set on it, but I was still kind of thinking, in an unthinking way, she might come to her senses.

It's like when you're watching a baseball game on TV and your guy strikes out, and then the replay comes up and you kind of hope he'll foul off the pitch—even though you just saw him strike out. Your brain tells you that it's stupid to think like that, that it's not going to happen, that it *can't* happen. But your heart still holds out hope.

Beverly wouldn't talk to me during morning or

afternoon homeroom. She waved me off the couple of times I tried to make conversation. Then she walked home alone while the rest of us took the bus with Quentin, who was having one of his bad-breathing days. (Lonnie called them BBDs.) It was a strange thing. He had a much easier time on miserable, overcast days when the air was thick and wet. The days when the air was crisp and cold were harder.

He wouldn't gripe about it, but you could tell he had to focus on inhaling. He'd be standing next to you, and then, without warning, he'd get this panicky look in his eyes, like he was choking, and he'd take like ten breaths in five seconds. But afterward he'd be all right.

Quentin was sitting in the back row of the bus, next to Howie, who was keeping an eye on him. We rotated doing that, keeping an eye on Quentin—even though he didn't know that was what we were doing. It wasn't something we sat down and worked out. It was more like a habit we fell into. Eric and Shlomo were in the next-to-last row, right behind Lonnie and me. As the bus turned the corner at Twenty-Sixth Avenue and Parsons, Lonnie jabbed me with his elbow and said, "You're going to teach her a lesson, right?"

"I'm just going to beat her. That's it."

"I think you should teach her a lesson."

"Why would I do that?" I asked.

"Because if you don't, she'll want to race again. Maybe not today, and maybe not tomorrow, but down the line. Then where does it end? You've got to nip this thing in the bud."

"Yeah, but it's *Beverly*."

He shook his head. "I know you like her—"

"I don't *like* her."

"What I mean is, we *all* like her," he said. "I didn't mean, you know, *you* like her. Which would be fine if you did. I'm not saying it's good or bad. That's not what I meant. What I meant was, this whole girls-racing-guys thing, you've got to put a stop to it. You've got to teach her a lesson, or else you're just going to make things worse."

"How about this?" I said. "I'll beat her bad for the first half of the race, and then I'll let her catch up a little. That way she'll know I could've beaten her by more, but I won't embarrass her."

"Just one problem," he said. "How will she know you're *letting* her catch up? To her, it's going to feel like she's catching up on her own. She's going to come away from it thinking, 'Maybe, if the race was longer, I could've caught him.' Then you're back to square one. I'm telling you, Jules, you have to wipe her out. There's no other way to end it once and for all."

That was as much strategizing as we could squeeze in before the bus pulled up at the corner of Thirty-Fourth

Avenue. The six of us walked back to Ponzini and waited. It was maybe three minutes until Beverly showed up with her cheerleader friends from the Dorado House. But that was it, just the two cheerleaders. She didn't even bring out her brother, Bernard.

She nodded at me from across Ponzini. Then she hung her coat over the fence and began to walk toward the starting line. I handed my coat to Lonnie and followed her, still unsure what I was going to do.

Once we were out of earshot of the rest of them, I came up behind her and said, "We really and truly don't have to do this. We can call it off. You can even say I chickened out if you want."

"You said you'd race me, Julian. I want to race."

So that was that.

We took our places at the starting line and leaned forward. Beverly had her hair tied back, her head up, her eyes straight ahead. The way she was balanced, it was just so *earnest*. I don't know if I've ever used that word before, or ever *thought* that word before. But you should have seen her. There was a steady breeze behind us, but nothing on her was ruffling. She was just dead still and determined. Meanwhile, I was in a half stance, more like the way you'd lead off first base than the way you'd start a sprint. I felt ashamed, even before the race started, about winning.

"On your mark . . . ," Lonnie yelled.

I took a deep breath and held it.

"Get set . . ."

I shook my head.

"Go!"

Between the time Lonnie yelled "get set" and the time he yelled "go," here's what I decided: I wasn't going to teach Beverly a lesson. There was no logical reason I decided that. I didn't get smarter in that one second. But sometimes, even when you're not sure what you *should* do, you get a gut feeling what you *shouldn't* do. Slaughtering her in front of her cheerleader friends wasn't the way to go, even if it meant I had to race her over and over for the next ten years. That much, I knew in my gut. As weird as it sounds, Howie was right and Lonnie was wrong.

Beverly took off, and I took off a step behind. You know the poem "Casey at the Bat," where the guy gets overconfident and then strikes out? This was nothing like that.

After the first half dozen steps, Beverly was running full speed, and I was running next to her—and I was coasting. It really *wasn't* a close race. Well, it *was* a close race, but only because I was hanging back and running next to her, thinking about how earnest she looked. The way she kept her head down, the way she kept her eyes forward! She was putting everything she had into the race, every ounce of strength, every drop of concentration. If you had stuck a brick wall in front of her, she'd have crashed into it like Wile E. Coyote in a Road Runner cartoon. Except not in a funny way. In an earnest way. What I mean is it was just a total effort.

But then the weirdest thing happened, the weirdest thing in an entire week of weird things. The sun started to come through the clouds, and about halfway into the race, a glint of it flashed across Beverly's face. It came from behind her and caught her cheek. I was running right beside her, watching her, watching her face, how earnest she looked, and then the sunlight hit her left cheek, and it was just the most perfect pink cheek, the most perfect pink *thing*, I'd ever seen. She was straining to run as fast as she could, with her legs churning, and with her arms cutting the air, but her left cheek was pink and peaceful.

As I stared at her cheek, I got that feeling again in the pit of my stomach, that warm gust of wind that came up inside me and whirled into my throat. You know that feeling you get when you shove pieces of Bazooka gum into your mouth? How the first piece tastes good and the third piece tastes good, but around the sixth piece, even though it tastes the same, it's kind of bad? What I mean is it's still sweet, and you still want it, but you gag on it. It felt like that, running next to Beverly, staring at her left cheek.

I'm not quite sure what happened next. I've thought about it over and over, and there are only two possible explanations. Either I slowed down, which is highly likely, given the sick feeling I had in my guts, or else Beverly sped up, which is highly unlikely, given how hard she was running the entire race. But who knows? Really, it could've been either one. For whatever reason, I blinked hard, and when I opened my eyes, she'd crossed the finish line a step ahead of me . . . which I guess means it *was* like "Casey at the Bat," if you stop and think about it.

There was dead silence in Ponzini.

It was the first race I'd ever lost. Ever. Not that I was upset—I mean, it wasn't like I was running hard. I figured that had to be pretty obvious. You *couldn't* watch that race and think I was running hard. Not even Beverly's cheerleaders were cheering, which meant even they knew what had happened. Or at least what *hadn't* happened, which was that Beverly had beaten me fair and square.

I looked at her, and her eyes were like grapes.

"I won," she said. Her voice was shaking.

That was when it hit me: *she* didn't know.

"Well, yeah . . ."

"I didn't think I had a chance. But I *won*."

She rushed over and hugged me, but only for a second. Then she let go of me and stepped back. "I'm sorry. I mean, I actually *won*. I'm so sorry, Julian. I swear I didn't think . . . I mean, I wouldn't have made such a big deal out of it. We could've raced when no one was around—"

"Beverly . . ."

"I actually *beat* you!"

"Well, you did win."

She started to speak again but stuttered and gave up. She turned around and ran over to her cheerleader friends. She was running as fast as she did during the race. I noticed, as she got close, that the cheerleaders were looking past her. They were looking straight at me, and they were ticked off.

Meanwhile, the guys were walking slowly in my direction.

"Why'd you do that?" Lonnie said. "That was just stupid."

"I don't know. It just happened."

Howie was shaking his head. "I said you shouldn't slaughter her. You didn't have to let her *win*."

"I didn't let her win, exactly. . . ."

"That's what it looked like," Quentin said.

"I was going to beat her by a couple of steps. I don't know what happened. I think maybe I got distracted."

"You think too much," Lonnie said. "You need to turn it off."

"What distracted you?" Eric said.

"I just had a bad feeling," I said. "I wasn't paying attention."

"Are you going to race her again?" Shlomo said.

"Of course he's going to race her again!" Lonnie said. "He *has* to race her again!"

"What's the point?" I said.

"What's the point? The point is—"

He didn't get to finish the sentence. Beverly came running back. I heard her footsteps and turned. There were tears streaming down her face as she pushed through the other guys and came right up to me. "How could you do that?"

"I didn't plan it. I got distracted—"

"I hope you got a good laugh out of it!"

"No!"

She brushed away the tears with both of her palms and stared at me. It was the hardest, iciest stare I've ever gotten. Then, suddenly, she tried to kick me in the shin with her left foot. If I'd had even a second to think about it, I would've stood there and taken it. But instead I jumped backward, and she missed. She stumbled to the side and almost fell, but then she caught herself.

Beverly stared me down again. Her eyes were freezing cold, but also scalding hot. As I looked at her, that stupid wind gusted up inside me again. It felt like when your mom opens the door to the oven and you get caught by a rush of hot air. That's what it felt like inside my chest.

"I hate you," she said.

She didn't scream it. She said it under her breath so that only the two of us could hear. That made it a hundred times worse.

"C'mon, Beverly! We can race again. . . ."

But she turned and ran out of Ponzini.

The Stomach Versus the Heart

Quentin called after dinner to ask if he could come over. He wouldn't tell me over the phone what it was about, but I said sure. Looking back, I should've gone to his house, because it took him a half hour to walk the half block from the Hampshire House and then another five minutes to get up the two flights of stairs. That's the bad thing about living upstairs in a two-family house: no elevator. But it's only a bad thing if you're toting a couple of bags of groceries for your mom . . . or if you're waiting for Quentin on one of his bad-breathing days.

He was still breathing hard when he got to the front door. My mom handed him a glass of iced tea, but his grip was so shaky that you could hear the ice cubes clinking, so I carried it back to my room for him. He sat down on the edge of my bed, and I handed him the glass of tea. Then I closed the door and sat down across from him, on my desk chair.

He didn't talk at first. He gulped down the tea, which seemed to make him steadier. I didn't want to stare at him, but there wasn't much else to do while he caught his breath. The way he was gripping the glass with both hands made his hands look real small. He was always the smallest of us. He was shorter than I was by a couple of inches—and I was pretty short—and even before he got sick, he was the skinniest of us.

He finished the tea and handed me the glass, and I put it down on a coaster on the windowsill.

"Did you figure out a new word?" I asked.

He shook his head. "It's nothing like that."

"Then what's on your mind?"

"I got kind of a weird question," he said.

"Yeah?"

"The thing is . . ."

"Whatever you want to ask, just ask it."

"Lonnie said you let Beverly win because you're in love with her."

I started to laugh. "I'm not in love with Beverly, Quentin."

"Then why'd you let her win?"

"I told you. I got distracted."

"Lonnie said you got distracted because you're in love with her."

"I got distracted because . . . I don't know why I got distracted. But—"

"Then how do you know you're not in love with her?" he asked.

"Let's look at it logically," I said. "Howie's been in love with Beverly since third grade, right? Think about how Howie acts when he's around her. Now think about how I act when I'm around her. Do I act like Howie?"

"Maybe different guys act different when they're in love."

"C'mon, Quent . . ."

I didn't know what else to say to him. But he kept looking at me, leaning forward, expecting me to say something.

"Look," I said, "I guess I did feel something weird during the race."

"Yeah?"

"That's it," I said. "I was looking at her, and I felt something weird."

"You think it was love?"

"You can call it that, but I don't think that's the right word."

"Lonnie was pretty sure—"

"If you want to believe Lonnie, believe Lonnie. Who knows? Maybe he's right. Maybe I'm in love with Beverly and just too stupid to know it. All I'm saying is that's not what it feels like."

"What does it feel like?"

"Quentin!"

"C'mon, I just want to know what it feels like."

"Why?"

"I just . . . I just want to know."

I shook my head. "Here's why I don't think it's love. You're supposed to feel love in your heart, right?"

"Yeah?"

"The thing with Beverly, it's more stomach-y."

"How do you mean?"

I had to think for a few seconds to find the right words. "Do you remember when you were a little kid, and you'd spin yourself around and around on a swing until you felt sick to your stomach? That's the closest thing I can compare to it. I mean, it was kind of what you were trying to do, but you still felt queasy afterward."

As soon as I said that, his face got real pink. He let out a weak laugh, but he looked straight down at the floor.

"What is it, Quent?"

"When I was in the hospital," he said, "there was this nurse with red hair. She was younger than the rest of them, like maybe twenty years old . . ."

"Yeah?"

He started to laugh. "No, I can't talk about it."

"C'mon, you can't leave me hanging like that."

"The thing is, I was stuck in the bed, so she used to come in and wash me. You know? She would wash my arms and legs, and then she'd roll me over and wash my back. But while she was doing it . . ." His voice broke off, and he stared down at the floor again.

"You're not going to tell me you're in love with her, are you?"

"No, nothing like that," he said. "But after the first few times, whenever she walked into the room, I got a feeling in my stomach, like what you said. That kind of feeling."

"So what do you make of it?" I asked.

"I don't know."

"You think it's a wrong feeling?"

"Maybe," he said.

"You think it's a right feeling?"

"Maybe it's both."

"Did you ask Lonnie?" I said.

"Please don't ask Lonnie about it, Jules."

"Why not?"

"Because he's not going to understand."

"All right," I said. "It stays between us."

Eric's Bar Mitzvah

The talk with Quentin got me thinking even more about what's going on with Beverly, about the wind that gusts up when I'm around her. It bugs me that Lonnie thinks I let her win the race because I'm in love with her. It's like saying I can't control myself. Except, if you think about it, I didn't intend to let her win, but I did let her win. Doesn't that prove I *can't* control myself? Maybe looking at it from the outside, Lonnie can see stuff that I can't see because I'm the one going through it.

I mean, isn't that what happened with Howie for three years? Everybody knew except him that he was in love with Beverly, and everybody knew except him that he had no chance . . . *because he was the one going through it.*

Beverly, meanwhile, hasn't spoken a word to me since the race, which I guess isn't a shock. Every time I've tried to apologize, she's turned her head (if we were in school) or walked off (if we were outside). Plus, that wind keeps coming back. It's gotten to the point where I expect it. As soon as I get near her, I feel it whirling around in my guts. It's always the same, but always slightly different. Sometimes it stays down in my guts and feels warm. But other times it dances around inside me, and I feel chills running back and forth between my shoulder blades.

But the worst thing about it is—and it's a shameful thing to say—I kind of *like* it. Right now, writing about the thing with Beverly, I can feel that wind rising up, and I've got a warm, glowy feeling. It's like sitting by a campfire as it's dying down, except the yellow embers are inside me, and I'm poking at them with a stick, thinking about her, and they're warming me from the inside out. I mean, I know she's hurting on account of what I did, and I feel bad on account of what I did, but every time I think about her, about the hurt look on her face, I feel good in a way that's hard to explain.

Reading back those last two paragraphs, I almost want to rip out the page and start over. But I've never done that, not even once, going back to when I was writing for Mr. Selkirk last year. Don't get me wrong. I've crossed out stuff and erased like crazy because I came up with better

words. But I've never written something and afterward decided to get rid of it because it was too stupid or too embarrassing or too weird. What's the point of writing stuff down if you're not going to tell the truth?

But to get back to Beverly, the best chance I had to say what I had to say to her came yesterday, at Eric the Red's bar mitzvah. (Now *there's* a guy who had a tough week.) I thought maybe, with the two of us being in temple, and dressed up in nice clothes, she'd at least hear me out. So while I was hanging around with the guys before the start of the service, I kept an eye on the back door.

It was hard to do, because we kept getting rushed by neighborhood moms. They came at us in clusters. Most of them were from the Hampshire House or Dorado House, and they were wearing big flowery dresses, and they all wanted a piece of Quentin. You'd have thought it was *his* bar mitzvah with how big a deal they were making over him. They were real weepy too, telling him what a fighter he was, and how good he looked, and how brave he'd been. You know how moms get.

The worst part was they were hugging the life out of the guy. There's this one lady who lives at the end of the block, across the street from Danley Dimmel—she must weigh three hundred pounds, and she squeezed poor Quentin so tight I thought he was going to come out the other side of her. I mean, he'd just gotten through a week

of BBDs, when he had to fight for every breath, and he was finally having a good-breathing day, but the last thing he needed was a date with the Purple People Eaters.

It was right after the three-hundred-pound lady got done with Quentin that I saw Beverly and Bernard show up, and I made a beeline for them. She didn't see me until I was right next to her.

"Look," I said, "I just want to explain—"

She put up her hand. "Go away."

"But I just want to apologize. . . ."

"Julian, I don't want to talk to you."

That was when Bernard, who's a fifth grader and a total dingus, stepped between us. He folded his arms across his chest, like he was her bodyguard. It was kind of comical, the way he did it, sticking out his chin as if to say, *Wanna make something of it?*

"C'mon, Beverly—"

Her brother took another step forward. He was right in front of me. "Get lost, Twerp."

"Bernard," I said, "what are you doing?"

He poked his finger into my chest. "I said *get lost.*"

I looked past him to Beverly, and for a split second our eyes met. Even though she didn't want to do it, she cracked a smile. It was only for that split second, and then she turned her head, but it was enough.

"All right, Bernard," I said. "You win."

I turned and walked back to the guys.

That smile made the rest of the morning bearable. It also let me concentrate on Eric, and on his haftarah—though, looking back, I wish I'd been distracted, on account of it was the most painful bar mitzvah ever.

Rabbi Salzberg was right. Howie was right too. The guy wasn't ready.

He looked nervous from the start, even when he was sitting off to the side and Rabbi Salzberg was at the podium, plowing through the morning service. I was sitting with the rest of the guys in the fourth row, with Lonnie to my right and Quentin to my left. We were at the end of the row, as out of the way as we could get, but still with a good angle to keep an eye on Eric. He was real pale, which you'd kind of expect, but you could also see droplets of sweat trickling down his forehead and into the corners of his eyes, which kept making him blink and rub them. He even used his tallit shawl to wipe his forehead. But it was no use. The trickles came back, and you could see sweat spots staining the cotton.

The main problem, I think, was his red tie. His mom had made the knot too tight. His throat was as red as his tie. Since his face was as white as a marshmallow, he looked like he was strangling. I mean, he *wasn't* strangling, but that was what it looked like.

It was a half hour into the service when Rabbi Salzberg

waved him up to the podium. Every step he took had a wobble in it. He stumbled at the edge of the podium, but he made it. The rabbi whispered into Eric's ear, and Eric glanced over his right shoulder at the Torah, which sat on a ledge at the back of the stage and was wrapped up in decorative blue cloth. He gave the thing a good long look.

After that, he faced forward again and stared down at the huge open Hebrew Bible in a real serious way. Then, at last, he reached into his suit pocket and took out five pages of notes—where he'd written out the sounds of the Hebrew words in English letters. It was no big deal. Lots of guys did it if their bar mitzvah came around and they still couldn't figure out the Hebrew letters. Even Rabbi Salzberg didn't seem to mind. The sight of the crib sheet seemed to calm down Eric. He started to smile but caught himself and glanced from side to side as Rabbi Salzberg lowered the microphone. Then the rabbi stepped back from the podium. Eric the Red was on his own. He took a deep breath.

Nothing happened.

Not a sound came out of his mouth. The trickles of sweat became rivers, and he was blinking like crazy, and nodding up and down, but he couldn't get out that first line. The thing is, he *knew* the first line. I knew he knew it. I'd heard him practice it a hundred times. Heck, even *I* knew the first line of Eric's haftarah. But he was stuck.

He was dead stuck. I leaned forward, mouthing that first line, trying to push the words into his head. But I couldn't make eye contact.

He was standing there, alone, with nothing coming out of his mouth, for at least a half minute before Rabbi Salzberg slid across the stage and whispered a couple of words into his ear. Then, as if he'd gotten a jolt of electricity, Eric sang out, *"Vayosef od-daveed ut-kol-bachuul beh-yisrahel . . ."*

Which means: "Something-something-something of Israel . . ."

Rabbi Salzberg slid back across the stage.

Except as soon as the rabbi stepped away, Eric stopped again.

There was another half minute of nothing, of torture. You could hear people in the rows behind us murmuring and coughing. When it was about to get unbearable, Rabbi Salzberg came forward again and whispered again into Eric's ear. Again, it was like when Frankenstein gets shocked into life. Eric's eyes jumped open, and he sang a few more Hebrew words: *"shlosheem alef vayacohm vayellech daveed . . ."*

But as soon as Rabbi Salzberg stepped away, again Eric stopped.

More torture.

Rabbi Salzberg didn't wait as long this time, maybe ten seconds. He came forward and was about to whisper into Eric's ear for the third time. But before he could, Eric blurted out, *"Vehchol ha-ahm asher eetoh . . ."*

Just like that, he was off. Rabbi Salzberg stepped away, but Eric the Red kept going. You could feel relief spread through the entire temple. The congregation settled in, and Eric's face started to go back to its normal color, and even the knot in his tie didn't seem as tight.

It was about five minutes later when Lonnie nudged me with his elbow. He didn't turn his head but said under his breath, "Kill me now."

"Yeah," I said. "You forget how boring it is."

"Maybe we can liven things up."

"No!"

"Oops, too late!"

By the time I looked over at him, he'd already reached forward and grabbed a copy of the Gates of Prayer monthly newsletter from the book sleeve on the back of the seat in front of him. Slowly, quietly, he began to tear off the back page.

"No, Lonnie!"

But he was smiling the way he does when he's about to do something really bad—or really good, depending on how you look at it. I knew the fact that I'd told him to stop would only make him more determined to keep going.

"Lonnie, c'mon. . . ."

There's this thing that Lonnie does with a sheet of paper that you have to see to believe. He tears off a narrow strip at the end and rolls it around his thumb, then pulls on the tip until it forms a perfect missile. I mean, it's like a work of art, the way he does it. He gets the paper to come to a point, and then he licks his fingertips and squeezes the point so that it stays that way. I've seen other guys do it, but their missiles always unravel or come out too fat or too dull. Lonnie's are like doctor's needles.

Then comes step two: he takes the leftover paper and rolls it into a peashooter—except it's a missile shooter, because Lonnie wouldn't bother with a pea. Again, I've seen other guys do it, or try to do it, and blow the missile out of the shooter, and the thing just falls out the other side or goes a couple of inches. But Lonnie always gets the shooter the exact right size so that the missile slides in with no room to spare and comes out like, well, a missile. Plus, the thing's dead accurate. I've seen him spear a Twinkie some guy was about to put in his mouth . . . and the guy was three cafeteria tables away.

Once he had the missile and shooter made, he nudged me again. "All right, you pick the target."

"I'm begging you, Lonnie. Don't."

"You know you want me to do it."

"Look, just wait for the reception," I said. "Not the service. It's the wrong time."

"That's what makes it the right time."

Quentin overheard us at that point and nudged my left arm. "What are you guys doing?"

"Hunting for wabbit," Lonnie said.

That cracked up Quentin, but then Howie, who was sitting to Quentin's left, shushed him, and then Shlomo, who was sitting to Howie's left, shushed both of them. Then a gray-haired old lady sitting in the first row—three rows in front of us—turned around and shushed all of us. She was wearing a tall black hat with spidery-looking loops on it.

"Target acquired," Lonnie whispered to me.

"Are you *nuts?*" I said.

Lonnie slipped the missile into the shooter.

"I think that's his grandmother!"

"Do you see the top curlicue?"

"Lonnie!"

But by then he had the shooter in his mouth, and he was taking aim.

"Don't do it!"

The only answer I got was the sound of his breath: "*Pwah.*"

The missile zoomed right through the loop of the top curlicue on Eric's grandmother's hat and landed next to the emergency exit on the side of the stage. I watched it, then braced myself for the reaction. But there was no reaction. Nothing happened. No one in the congregation, except for the five of us, noticed. Not even Eric's grandmother, though she brushed the top of her hat with her right hand, so she must have felt something zip past her. It was a miracle. Lonnie got away with it. The thing must have shot forty feet, but people were either staring down at their prayer books or looking at Eric, and they missed it.

But *Eric* saw it.

He must have noticed it out of the corner of his eye, because an instant later, he stopped singing. He looked up from his crib sheet and down at us, and for half a second, he cracked a smile. But when he looked back down at his crib sheet, he was lost. His momentum was gone. Even from the fourth row, you could see the panic come back into his eyes. His face went pale again. Then, in about three seconds, the skin of his throat changed four shades—from pink, to dark pink, to red, to dark red.

Maybe it wouldn't have been as bad if Rabbi Salzberg had been paying attention, if he'd slid back across the stage and whispered into Eric's ear again. But I think even he got caught off guard. He was standing off to the side, like before, except his eyes were shut, and he was rocking back and forth on his heels, saying the words to himself. You could see his lips moving. I don't think he even heard Eric grind to a stop.

Eric glanced up from the crib sheet again and then down at the five of us, and he got a weird, surrender kind of look on his face. It was like he was saying, *All right, I'm done.* Except he wasn't done, not by a long shot. Even without knowing the Hebrew, you could tell he was still in the middle of his haftarah. He began to sway behind the podium. You know that thing that happens when a boxer gets knocked down to the canvas and then stands up too fast? That was what it looked like.

He grabbed the front of the podium to settle himself, which caused the microphone to rattle. That, at last, got Rabbi Salzberg's attention. He rushed across the stage and put his hands on Eric's shoulders to steady him, but he was too late. Eric pulled out of his grasp and ran off the stage, and a couple of seconds later you could hear him throwing up in the hall.

Rabbi Salzberg followed Eric, and for the next half minute there wasn't much to do except stare at the wrapped-up Torah at the back of the stage. You could hear Eric the Red retching his guts out, but you couldn't see him or the rabbi. Eric's mom stood up in the front row, but Eric's dad got hold of her and kept her from rushing backstage. I glanced over at Lonnie, and he looked back at me and shrugged. I'm sure he felt bad about shooting the missile. But there was no way to know *this* was going to happen.

Quentin leaned over and whispered, in a low John Wayne kind of voice, "You shouldn't oughtn't have done it."

That cracked up Lonnie and me, especially since it came from Quentin, which got the three of us another round of shushes.

Eric's retching stopped, like I said, after half a minute. It was maybe a half minute after that that he stepped back onto the stage. Rabbi Salzberg was right behind him, his hands on Eric's shoulders, steering him back toward the podium. After he got there, he looked up and muttered into the microphone, "I threw up in the garbage can. I'm real sorry."

"That's okay, honey!" his mom shouted, which made the rest of the congregation laugh.

There was a loud round of applause, and Eric began to smile. Rabbi Salzberg must have loosened the knot in his tie, because his throat had gone back to its normal color, and there was no sweat running down his forehead.

He looked down at his crib sheet, and Rabbi Salzberg pointed to a spot on it, and just like that Eric was off again, as if nothing had happened.

Lonnie's Invention

No one is razzing Eric about his bar mitzvah. Sooner or later, of course, we'll razz him until his ears bleed. I mean, *he threw up at his bar mitzvah!* That's the kind of thing you put on a guy's tombstone. But for the time being we're laying off. It's still too soon. Even so, Shlomo did get in a zinger after school on Wednesday, when Eric accidentally let go of the school bus doors while Shlomo was climbing down the steps behind him, and the doors slammed in Shlomo's face. After Shlomo pushed open the doors again, Eric said he was sorry, and Shlomo shot back, just like Eric's mom, "That's okay, honey."

Even Eric had to smile.

It was right after that, right after we got home from school on Wednesday, that we found out Quentin was back in the hospital. It wasn't a total shock. He'd been sucking air for over a week, and then on Tuesday he got a hacking cough at school, and the nurse sent him home, and then he stayed home on Wednesday—so we knew something was up.

We went straight from the bus stop to his house after school. When his grandmother, who knows maybe nine words of English, answered the door and started to jabber in Yiddish, the look on her face told us where he was.

The good news is that the doctors got Quentin fixed up quick this time. They put him on a couple of new pills, cleaned out his carburetor, changed his oil, and just like that they were done. He came home Friday morning. Really, when you think about it, he only missed four days of school. Not even that much, since he got in two classes on Tuesday morning before he went to the nurse.

The bad news is that he's back in the wheelchair. No ifs, ands, or buts this time around. He's not talking his way out of it again until the doctors give him the thumbs-up, and he said they're not even going to discuss it for a month . . . which means Quentin's dad isn't going to discuss it for a month, which means, starting tomorrow, we're back to hoisting the chair on and off the bus, and up and down the steps in front of the school. That's just how it's got to be.

No one feels worse about it than Quentin. He knows how much that chair screws things up for the rest of us. Don't get me wrong. It's not like any of us are complaining. If Quentin can put up with sitting in the wheelchair, then we can put up with hauling it around. Except you can see how it gnaws at him. The guy's champing at the bit, and he's only been out of the hospital a couple of days.

I'm kind of amazed, to be honest, that his mom even let him go outside so soon. But Quentin can be pretty stubborn—like the time, a couple of years ago, when he was teaching himself to make a yo-yo go around the world. It took him a week to learn that stupid trick, and he wound up with a black eye and a bloody lip from smacking himself in the face with the thing. But you know what? He got it.

He came out this morning like nothing was wrong—unless you count the fact that he was rolling up Thirty-Fourth Avenue in a wheelchair. Eric was the first to notice him. We were hanging around on the corner of Parsons, the five of us, arguing about whether it was too early to ring Quentin's doorbell, and then there he was, rolling up the block toward us. If you'd snapped a photo at that second, you'd have gotten five jaws hitting the pavement.

But once the shock wore off, what were we supposed

to do? For the next couple of hours, we just hung around on the corner of Parsons, yakking and arguing and flipping baseball cards. I mean, it's a decent way to kill an afternoon, but like the song goes, it's not "hot fun in the summertime." Or even in March, for that matter. What made it worse was that the sun came out for the first time in a week, and the temperature warmed up to like sixty degrees, so it almost *felt* like summertime, and Quentin knew, even though no one said a word, that we were dying to head back to Ponzini. So he finally said, "C'mon, let's *do* something."

The rest of us just kind of stared at him.

But he wouldn't let it go. "C'mon, guys, I'm sick of this corner."

Except what was the difference whether we stood around doing nothing on the corner or in Ponzini? Plus, doing nothing in Ponzini would feel worse, because Ponzini was where we did stuff.

But Quentin kept after us, and when we wouldn't listen, he got fed up and started to roll himself down the block in the direction of Ponzini. As he made the turn into the alley that led to the torn-down fence, he glanced back at us and shouted, "You guys coming or not?"

So we followed him back to Ponzini. There was a game of tag going on when we got there. Victor Ponzini was running around, slow as molasses, and behind him was Mike the Bike, who'd left his bike at home for once, and behind him was Bernard Segal, who was doing something that you couldn't even call running. He would've had to speed up to come to a stop.

The three of them, at that moment, were chasing Beverly Segal.

She was the first to notice us as we stood next to the torn-down fence. She stopped running, and then Victor caught up and tagged her, and then Mike crashed into his back, and then Bernard crashed into Mike's back. It was comical to watch.

"Hey, Quentin!" she called.

He waved to her from the wheelchair.

"I heard you got sick."

"Yeah," he called back.

"You feel better now?"

"Yeah."

The second "yeah" made him cough.

She looked straight at me. "Any of you clowns want to stretch your legs?"

Lonnie shook his head. "Nah, we're just going to watch."

"Have it your way," she said, and then tore out. It took a couple of seconds for the other three to react, but then, slow as molasses, they started chasing her again. For the next minute, we stood by the torn-down fence and watched them.

Then Quentin said, "Why don't you guys get out there?"

"C'mon," I said. "They're little kids."

"Beverly's not."

"Yeah, but she's still ticked off at us—at *me*."

"Then why'd she ask you to join in?" he said.

"She asked *all* of us," I said.

"Then why don't you do it?"

"I don't feel like it," I said. "None of us do."

"C'mon, I'll hold your jackets."

"Quent—"

"Will you just go and do it!"

I glanced at Lonnie, and Lonnie nodded, and then the two of us pulled off our jackets, handed them to Quentin, and trotted over to join the game. Howie, Shlomo, and Eric followed a few steps behind. I felt real guilty leaving Quentin in the wheelchair with a pile of jackets in his lap—I'm sure the rest of them did too. But if you think about it, either we were going to feel guilty, or Quentin was going to feel guilty. That was the choice we had.

Plus, I'm not going to lie: it felt good to be running around, even if we were running around with a bunch of little kids. The sun was shining in my face and on the back of my neck, and my skin felt warm, and my clothes felt loose, and my heart was pumping. I even let myself get tagged a couple of times to keep the game interesting. But I didn't chase Beverly, and she didn't chase me. We steered clear of one another the entire time.

It was maybe ten minutes later that Howie tackled Bernard Segal. Why he did it, who knows? Maybe he was sticking up for me because he'd seen Bernard poking his finger into my chest at Eric's bar mitzvah, or maybe he was taking out years of frustration with Beverly on her kid brother. Or maybe he did it just because that's what he does. Like I said, Howie's a tackler. Whatever the reason, he'd just gotten tagged by Shlomo, and he turned and sprinted toward Bernard. Except instead of tagging him, he slammed into him and rode him to the ground.

Then he rolled off Bernard and said, "You're it!"

Bernard sat up and crossed his arms over his chest. He wasn't hurt, but you could see the shock on his face. I walked over to him and stuck out my hand. He looked up at me. His eyes had that wet look—when you're not quite crying, but not quite not-crying either. I felt bad for him, so I said, in a low voice, "It doesn't mean anything. Don't worry about it."

"I'm not scared," he said, then forced himself to smile.

"Here, why don't you tag me?"

He reached up and tagged my hand.

I turned and looked for someone to chase, but the game had ground to a sudden halt. Quentin had gotten out of his wheelchair and was jogging over to us. He jogged the entire distance, but he was out of breath. He coughed a few times. Not hacking coughs, just out-of-breath coughs.

Lonnie sighed real loud, like he knew this would happen. He said, "What are you doing, Quent?"

"C'mon, let's go. I'm it."

But he started coughing again. These coughs were deeper and louder.

"Quentin—"

"I'm okay!" he shouted.

Lonnie said, "Your dad said you have to use the wheelchair."

"You never cared what my dad said before," Quentin shot back.

"Well, I care now."

"He only said I have to *use* the wheelchair. Well, I used it to get here. You saw me do it. He never said I couldn't get out of it."

"Look, you're *not* playing—"

"You're not the boss of me!"

"Put it this way," Lonnie said. "If you play, *we're* not playing."

"Fine with me," Quentin said.

"Have a good time, Quent."

Lonnie started walking away. He headed toward the wheelchair, which was where Quentin had put our jackets. The rest of us followed a couple of seconds later. That left Beverly, Bernard, Mike the Bike, and Victor Ponzini. I heard Quentin say, "All right, I'm it. . . . C'mon, where are you going?"

I glanced over my shoulder. Beverly was walking away, and the sixth graders were following her. Quentin was standing at the far end of Ponzini, alone.

"C'mon!" he yelled. "It's just a game of tag!"

Lonnie stopped walking and turned around. "That's right. It's just a game of tag. It's just a stupid game of tag. It doesn't mean anything."

"It means something to me!" Quentin called back.

"You got out of the hospital two days ago. Give it a week, all right? We can meet back here next Sunday, same Bat-time, same Bat-channel. We can pick right up where we left off."

"Please, Lonnie!"

"No!"

"Please."

The sound of his voice went right through me. It was like his entire life was riding on one stupid game of tag.

Lonnie stared him down. "You want to play tag?"

"Yeah."

"You want to play right now?"

"Yeah."

Lonnie started to walk back, and the rest of us just kind of stood where we were. It was hard to know if he was serious, or if he was going to grab Quentin and drag him back to the wheelchair. He walked past us and over to Quentin.

"All right," he said. "Hop on my back."

Quentin looked confused. "How come?"

"We're going to play tag," Lonnie said.

"C'mon—"

"Will you just hop on my back?"

"You can't run with me on your back."

"Sure I can."

"Not fast enough to catch anybody."

Lonnie waved for the rest of us to come back. "Eric, you get on Shlomo's back. Bernard, you get on Howie's back. Mike, you get on Ponzini's back. And Beverly, you get on Julian's back."

For a couple of seconds, we weren't quite sure if he actually meant it. We were glancing around at one another but not moving.

"Just do it!" Lonnie yelled.

So that's what we did. You could tell Bernard didn't want any part of Howie, but what could he say? The only one who grumbled was Shlomo, who thought he should be on top of Eric, but Lonnie said we'd switch off after a few minutes.

It felt weird having Beverly climb on my back, especially since she wouldn't look me in the eye beforehand. She just came up behind me, and I pulled my arms back, and then I felt her weight, and I grabbed the undersides of her legs. As soon as she was on my back, her hair fell across my face, and I got a whiff of her strawberry shampoo. I was going to tell her how nice it smelled, but I didn't. It didn't feel like the right time. Neither of us said a word.

It was only after he saw the rest of us going along that Quentin climbed onto Lonnie's back. Then Lonnie walked over to me, with Quentin riding him, and stopped about a foot away. He said, "Well, Quent?"

"Well, what?" Quentin said.

"Don't you have something you want to say?"

The light went on in Quentin's eyes. He reached out and tagged Beverly's shoulder. "You're it!"

Lonnie turned and ran off. I just stood there, getting used to the extra weight, until Beverly grabbed me by the hair and gave a soft tug. "Are you going to giddyup, Seabiscuit?"

I started to run, and the rest of them started to scatter, and just like that, Lonnie had invented piggyback tag.

It was more fun than you'd think. For one thing, Beverly had her arms wrapped around my neck, and she was holding on tight, and even if she was still mad at me, which I was guessing she was, she seemed to forget about it. For another thing, for once, I *wasn't* the fastest guy in Ponzini. That was Lonnie, by far, because he was bigger and stronger than the rest of us, and because Quentin was still real skinny on account of being sick. You should've heard that guy laughing—Quentin, I mean. He was just about squealing, which makes sense, if you think about it, given that we were playing piggyback tag.

After the first few minutes, we rested up and switched off, and Quentin got on my back, because he said he wanted to know what it felt like to be fast instead of just quick. I told him not to expect too much, but the thing was, I was warmed up by then, and Quentin felt like a feather, and he kept saying into my ear that he wanted to go faster, even when no one was chasing us, so I was running as fast as I could, and the wind was swirling around us, rushing by our faces, and then it got in right behind us, and it was like getting a hard push, and then, for a few seconds, it felt like I wasn't carrying him, and I was almost running full speed, and he was laughing and squealing, and I could feel his heart beating into my back.

It was the greatest game of tag I ever played.

Getting Beaten Up

Quentin was itching to skip the bus ride home this afternoon. You couldn't blame him, since the temperature was about sixty-five degrees and the sun was out for the fourth day in a row.

If Quentin hadn't been stuck in the wheelchair, we'd have walked home without thinking about it. But we *did* have to think about it, because he *was* stuck in the chair. Except then Quentin pointed out that if we walked home, we wouldn't have to haul the chair onto and off the bus. That clinched it. So at three o'clock, the six of us gathered in front of the school, as usual, and then we walked right past the bus stop and kept going down Twenty-Sixth Avenue. Eric started off pushing

Quentin, and Howie called, "Next!" and Shlomo called, "Next next!"

The going was pretty slow for the first couple of blocks. Even without a wheelchair, the going is always slow at three o'clock. Twenty-Sixth Avenue gets jammed up, because both schools, P.S. 23 and McMasters, let out at the same time, and kids from kindergarten to ninth grade spill out onto the sidewalk, and they hang around in groups, or they wander toward their buses, or else they start walking home, and meanwhile the crossing guards are blowing their whistles, trying to keep them out of the street, and it's just chaos.

We'd gotten two blocks down Twenty-Sixth Avenue, to the corner of 146th Street, when we heard a shout behind us. I recognized Devlin's voice even before I turned around. "Where are you guys going?"

Then I turned around.

He had about a half dozen of his ninth-grade friends with him, staring us down. Tagging along with them were at least another dozen kids, with more hurrying down the block toward us. They were coming in waves, from both McMasters and P.S. 23. The looks on *their* faces, the late arrivers, even more than the looks on the faces of Devlin and his friends, were the giveaway. They were waiting for something big to happen.

Lonnie stepped out in front of us. "You guys got a problem?"

"Nah," Devlin said. "We just want to see the freak show."

"Then why don't you look in the mirror?"

"Don't be like that, man. We came to make friends. Hey, look, it's Barf Boy and the king of Egypt. . . ."

"C'mon, Devlin, why don't you go home?" I said.

"Who said you could use my name, Twerpski?"

"Okay, what do you want me to call you?" I said.

That seemed to confuse him.

Lonnie picked up on it right away. "How about knucklehead?"

But Devlin ignored him. "How about you and me, Twerpski?"

"He's not a fighter, knucklehead," Lonnie said. "How about you and *me*?"

"Oh yeah, I forgot," Devlin said. "Twerpski's not a fighter . . . he's a *writer*."

That got to me, the way he said "writer," and I stepped out from behind Lonnie. "You're right, Devlin. I'm a writer. Too bad you're not a reader. Then maybe we could pass notes."

"That's real funny—not!"

"Wow, nice comeback. Did you make it up yourself?"

"Shut up, Twerpski!"

"See Devlin think," I said in a flat Dick-and-Jane voice. "Think, Devlin, think."

"I said shut up!"

"Hear Devlin yell. Yell, Devlin, yell."

"You're dead!"

He charged at me, but I dodged him.

"See Devlin miss. Miss, Devlin, miss."

He charged me again and dove at my legs, but I jumped to the right, and he landed on his stomach on the front lawn of the house behind us.

"See Devlin fall. Fall, Devlin, fall."

He scrambled to his feet. His face was beet red, and his hands were balled into fists. He charged me a third time. I dodged him again, and he tripped and fell onto the sidewalk. This time, he came up with two skinned palms, and his right pant leg was torn at the knee. The tear was a perfect flap, and you could see the first traces of blood starting to gather in the hole. The sight of the blood was like a jolt. It reminded me of when we egged Danley Dimmel, of how bad I felt afterward.

"Devlin, this is stupid. I don't want to fight you—"

That was as far as I'd gotten when one of Devlin's friends hit me from behind and knocked me to the ground. I fell on my stomach, with my legs on the sidewalk and the rest of me on the lawn. The next second, I felt Devlin jump onto my back. I could tell it was him because no other human being is that bony. After that, there was total confusion.

Out of the corner of my eye, I saw Lonnie rush over, but at least three of Devlin's friends jumped him, and then I saw Howie, Shlomo, and Eric jump them, and then the rest of Devlin's friends piled on, and that was when I started to feel Devlin's fists hitting me in the back of the head and neck and shoulders. I turtled up as tight as I could, with my face in the grass, my hands cupped behind my neck, and my forearms over my ears, and waited for Devlin to get tired.

Getting beaten up doesn't hurt as much as you'd think. Once you get past the first shock, it kind of feels like a hard massage. I'm sure it would've been much worse if I'd landed on my back and Devlin was whaling away on my face. But to be honest, after the first few seconds, I was lying there thinking, *Okay, he's beating me up. So when is this thing going to be over?*

It was maybe ten seconds later that someone tackled Devlin and knocked him off me. The two of them rolled away, and I jumped up and backpedaled several steps.

As I was doing that, I heard Devlin yell, "Whoa!" and right afterward, there was a sudden hush as the fighting stopped, and Devlin and everyone else were staring in the same direction.

Quentin was kneeling on the lawn, about three feet

from Devlin, trying to catch his breath. His wig had come off and was lying on the grass between the two of them. He didn't have a single hair on his head.

"Holy crap!" Devlin said. Before Quentin or anyone else could react, he snatched up the wig and flung it over his shoulder into the next yard. "The king of Egypt is a cue ball!"

There was a roar of laughter.

Quentin's eyes were raging. He caught his breath enough to climb to his feet, and he took a step toward Devlin. "C'mon, fight me!"

But Devlin was standing with his hands on his hips, laughing at him. "No way, Cue Ball."

"Fight me!" Quentin cried.

"Where's my pool stick?"

Another roar of laughter, even louder than before.

Quentin rushed him, and Devlin caught him and shoved him back to the ground. He tried to get back up again but started coughing.

That was when the look on Devlin's face changed. His eyes narrowed, then got wide. I don't know how much he figured out at that moment, but you could tell he figured out something.

He glanced around at his friends. "C'mon, let's get out of here."

He started to walk away, and the entire group followed him. They walked down Twenty-Sixth Avenue without saying another word. The rest of the crowd started to drift away too.

Then it was just us.

"Everybody okay?" Lonnie said.

Eric said, "Is my lip bleeding?"

It wasn't.

My neck was a little stiff, but otherwise I felt fine . . . like I'd just gotten a hard massage.

Quentin had stopped coughing. We watched him stand up, but none of us helped him. You could tell he didn't want to be helped. He took a couple of steps to the left, stopped, then took a couple more to the right. He was looking side to side. "Anyone see where my hair went?"

That cracked up the rest of us, how casual he said it after what had just happened. We started glancing around, and Shlomo noticed the wig between two bushes in the next yard. He ran and got it, brushed the dirt off, and handed it back to Quentin, who pulled it onto his head, even though it looked slightly off.

Quentin wanted to walk the rest of the way home, but Lonnie made him sit back down in the wheelchair. "I think you had plenty of exercise for today, Sugar Ray."

* * *

It's three o'clock in the morning, and I'm wide awake. I've been awake at three o'clock in the morning before, when I was sick with the flu, or when I had to get up and pee, or when I rolled over in bed and opened my eyes and happened to notice the clock on my desk. But I've never been *wide* awake at three o'clock in the morning. For sure, I've never been sitting at my desk, writing, at three o'clock in the morning.

I started writing at eight o'clock last night, and I got into bed at ten, and the entire thing was written down, and then I woke up at one o'clock and couldn't fall back asleep.

What do you expect?

If you'd seen the way Quentin looked without his hair, you'd be up at three in the morning too. You know what else? You'd spend an hour standing outside your parents' bedroom, staring at them while they were sleeping. What I mean is . . . I don't even know what I mean. It's three o'clock in the morning! If I knew what I meant, I'd write it down and get back into bed.

You want the world to make sense. But it just doesn't. I'm sure if I said that to Rabbi Salzberg, he'd tell me to stop thinking about it and concentrate on my bar mitzvah. If you translate that out of rabbi-talk into plain English, here's what you get: *You're thirteen years old, and there's stuff you can't understand, so stick with what you can understand.*

Except what Quentin's going through, the fact that he's

bald, the fact that he got a tumor in the first place, how can you understand that? You can't. Not if you're thirteen. Not if you're a hundred and thirteen. There's no way to understand it, *because it doesn't make sense.* It's like the square root of negative nine. You know the answer's got something to do with three or negative three, but you can't make either of them work.

There is no answer.

The Terrible Truth

Rabbi Salzberg didn't cut me off as I was telling him what happened with the big fight. He was itching to do it. He leaned forward twice and was about to cut me off, but then he leaned back and let me get the whole thing out.

I was standing up when I started, but I sat down on the creaky wooden chair in front of his desk halfway through. I got pretty worked up by the end, when I was talking about Quentin's wig. Afterward, he waited while I caught my breath.

He said, "It's very brave, how your friend came to your defense."

"Yes."

"But—"

"Please don't tell me to worry about my bar mitzvah," I said.

"Ah."

"I know that bad things have to happen to good people. Really and truly, I get that. I know it's not a test if you can't fail. But if God wanted to test Quentin, couldn't he have come up with something a little less drastic than a brain tumor?"

"Ah."

"Plus, doesn't God know in advance how the test is going to come out? I mean, doesn't he already know Quentin is going to be brave?"

"God knows what each of us can bear."

"So what you're saying is God looked down at Quentin and at me, and God said, 'Well, that guy over there is brave, so let's give him a brain tumor, and that guy over there is not so brave, so let's have him write two hundred words each week on why he scratched up a painting, even though he didn't do it.' That can't be what you're saying, is it?"

"Two hundred words? I don't understand, Mr. Twerski. . . ."

"Why do I have my life, Rabbi? What did I do to deserve it? That's what I want to know."

"We don't question the will of God."

"How can you *not* question it? Am I that much weaker

than Quentin? Why did God put so much on his plate, and so little on mine? Let's tell the truth, Rabbi. You and I both know Quentin's not going to be back to normal for a year, maybe more. . . ."

As the words came out of my mouth, the look on Rabbi Salzberg's face darkened. It only lasted for a second—like if you were playing with the dimmer switch on a light, turning it down and then right back up—but it was noticeable.

"There are things we can't run away from, Mr. Twerski."

I felt a chill in my chest and began shaking my head. "No."

"I'm very sorry."

"His bar mitzvah is in November."

"No, it isn't, Mr. Twerski," he said.

"I can help him study for it. I know he's behind—"

"Mr. Twerski, there will be no bar mitzvah."

"How do you know? You're not a doctor!"

"The Seligs are part of this congregation. . . ."

By then I was crying. "You jinxed him!"

"You have to prepare yourself, Mr. Twerski."

"That stuff you said last time, you jinxed him!"

"There is no jinx. There is only God's will."

I slammed my fist down on the desk. "You killed him!"

But then I looked up, and he was wiping away tears. *Rabbi Salzberg was crying.*

"You must keep the truth to yourself, Mr. Twerski."

"But how?"

"You're not a boy anymore."

"It's too much," I sobbed.

"God knows what each of us can bear."

I jumped up from the chair and ran out of his office. What I mean is I *ran* out of his office. I was running full speed down the hall between his office and the temple, and I crashed through the front door and then jumped down the six concrete stairs. My legs kept churning while I was in the air, and when I finally hit the ground, I hit it running.

I ran down Roosevelt Avenue in the direction of Bowne Street, and then I turned right on Bowne, and I ran past the Bowne House. I thought about the Quakers, and how dead they were, and then I thought about Quentin, and how alive he was, and I could barely breathe.

So I tried not to think. I tried to run without thinking. I tried to focus on how hard and loud my heart was beating, how I could feel it in my chest, and how I could hear it in my head. My heart seemed to be beating in my ears, making them throb from the inside.

I caught the light at Northern Boulevard and sprinted across, then turned left in front of Flushing High School. It looked like a huge medieval fort, with thick stone walls and a high stone tower, and even though I didn't want to think the thought, and I tried to push the thought out of my brain, I thought about how Quentin would never see the inside of Flushing High School, and how, in three years, when the rest of us were rushing to classes inside those walls and climbing the stairs into that tower, Quentin would be buried in the ground. How was that possible? How was it thinkable?

How was it bearable?

By the time I got back to Thirty-Fourth Avenue, I was gasping for breath. I slowed down to a trot and then to a walk. There was a soft, damp breeze in my face as I headed up the block. The first person I saw was Beverly Segal.

"You want to race?" I called to her.

She eyed me suspiciously. "You going to run hard this time?"

I nodded.

So the two of us headed around the corner and back to Ponzini.

As we turned into the alley, she said, "Where'd you come from?"

"The Bowne House," I said.

"What were you doing there?"

"Nothing."

"You sure you want to race?" she asked.

"Yeah," I said. "I'm sure."

"What's wrong?"

"I just want to race, Beverly."

She must have seen that I meant it since she clammed up at that point. We hung our jackets over the fence and walked to the far end of Ponzini. My heart had just slowed down to its normal speed, but it began to beat faster again as we got to the starting line.

I turned to her. "Remember, this is what you wanted."

"Are you mad at me?"

I shook my head. "No."

"Do you want to say, 'On your mark, get set—'"

"On your mark," I said.

She took her mark.

"Get set," I said. "Go!"

It was the fastest I've ever run.

I think Beverly stopped running after the first ten yards. Either that, or I was so far ahead that I couldn't hear her footsteps. But I kept going faster.

My heart got real loud again, but not just loud. It felt like it was swelling up, like it was banging away at the front of my chest, straining to get out. Still, I kept pushing and pushing, going faster and faster. Because I wanted it to happen. I wanted my heart to blow up, to blow a hole in the front of my chest, and to land on the ground in Ponzini and flip-flop like a dying fish until it was dead and I was dead. I know that sounds stupid and gross.

But I also had poetical thoughts. I thought about my soul rushing out of my body, rushing out through the hole in my chest, swimming up to heaven, and then just hanging out, waiting around for Quentin's soul, and then the two of us yakking it up for however long it took for Lonnie and Howie and Eric and Shlomo to show up. After that, things would be all right again.

I was just a few steps from the finish line. I closed my eyes and bore down.

That was when the thing happened. There was a sudden spasm of pain in the back of my right leg, about three inches above my knee. It felt like someone had reached underneath my skin, grabbed a hunk of flesh and twisted it to the side. I started hopping as soon as I felt it. I hopped the last three steps, then crumpled to the ground, holding the back of my leg.

"Julian!" Beverly yelled.

I couldn't have answered her even if I'd tried. The only sound I could get out was a moan. I heard her running toward me a few seconds later. But there was nothing I could do except lie on my stomach and clutch the back of my leg.

Her voice was frantic. "What happened?"

I bit my tongue and said, "Don't know."

"Should I get help?"

"No!"

"What should I do?"

I took a deep breath and winced. "Let me rest for a minute."

"Are you sure?"

"I'll be all right," I said, even though I knew I was hurt.

"Did you break something?"

"I think maybe I pulled a muscle," I said.

"Where?"

"The back of my leg." I rolled over onto my side but couldn't make myself let go of the back of my leg. The muscle still felt like someone's fist was clenched around it, about to twist it again. "Ouch. Ouch. *Ouch!*"

"What are you doing?"

"I'm trying to sit up."

She knelt down next to me and took hold of my right shoulder. Then she rolled me onto my back, stepped around behind me, and pushed me upright. As soon as I switched positions, the muscle in my leg unclenched. I let go of it and braced my arms against the ground.

"First Quent, and now you," she said. "I'm not racing you guys anymore."

"I'm going to be fine, Beverly. It's just a pulled a muscle."

"It's called your hamstring," she said.

"What is?"

"The muscle you pulled."

"How do you know that?"

"That's the main injury that fast guys get," she said. "I did a book report on Jesse Owens last year. There was a guy named Peacock who was probably faster than him, but he never made it to the Olympics because he pulled his hamstring. It's the big muscle in the back of your leg, between your knee and your butt."

"I guess that's what I pulled," I said.

Neither of us spoke for a couple of seconds.

"How many book reports do you do?" I asked.

"What do you mean?"

"I mean, you know about Jesse Owens, and you know about Mary Dyer."

"I like doing book reports," she said. "I do them on my own sometimes, for extra credit. I like reading the *World Book* and knowing stuff."

I forced a smile. "I guess that's why you're in Fast Track."

She sat down next to me. "Why did you keep going?"

"What?"

"You made your point. Why did you keep running?"

I shook my head. "I don't know. I felt like it."

She was staring at me in a weird way. I stared back at her, trying to figure out why she was staring at me, and suddenly I felt the wind gusting up inside me warmer and stronger than it had ever gusted up before. She leaned forward and kissed me.

She kissed me right on the lips. That would've been weird enough, but here's the weirder thing: *I kissed her back.* It wasn't something I thought about doing. It just happened. It must have lasted for five seconds, her kissing me and me kissing her back. Then, at last, she leaned back and looked at me.

"Why did you do that?" I asked.

"I don't know. I felt like it," she said.

"Does that mean you're my girlfriend?"

"Do you *want* me to be your girlfriend?"

I thought it over. "What would I tell the guys?"

"You can tell them whatever you want," she said. "I don't care who knows or who doesn't know. The only thing that matters is *we* know."

"But if no one knows, then what's the difference between your being my girlfriend and your being my friend?"

She leaned forward and kissed me again.

"Oh," I said.

"So am I your girlfriend?"

"I guess so."

"You don't sound too happy about it."

I reached for her face, leaned forward, and kissed her. It only lasted a half second, because my leg seized up, but I did it. *I kissed her.* "There."

She smiled at me and then stood up. "Can you walk?"

"I think so," I said.

"Do you need help getting off the ground?"

"Yeah."

She put out her right hand, and I grabbed it. As soon as she began to pull, I felt my leg start to spasm again, but I didn't let go. I held on, and she pulled me to my feet. The first thing I felt was the chill of the air against my back.

"I'll get our jackets," she said.

She jogged off toward the end of the fence, where we'd hung our jackets, and I watched her, and I began to smile. But as soon as I realized what I was doing, as soon as I felt the shape of my mouth, I remembered about Quentin, and the sadness came back in a wave. My heart was still in my chest, and it was drowning.

Beverly came jogging back with our jackets.

"Why are you looking at me like that?" she said.

"Like what?"

"Like you're sorry about what just happened."

"I'm not sorry," I said. "I'm glad it happened."

"Are you crying?"

"I've got a pulled hamstring, all right?"

"It's nothing to be ashamed of," she said. "It must hurt a lot."

"Yeah, it does."

Limp

Lonnie knows there's something wrong. He got to the bus stop before I did yesterday morning, and when he saw me limping toward him, the first words out of his mouth were "What's eating you?"

"I hurt my leg," I said.

"*That* I can see."

"I pulled my hamstring."

"Your what?"

"It's a leg muscle. I pulled it."

"How'd you do that?"

"Racing Beverly," I said.

"Did you beat her this time?"

"Yeah," I said.

"Bad?"

"I beat her by a lot."

"Well, that's a relief," Lonnie said.

"I guess."

"Now you want to tell me what's eating you?"

"What do you mean?"

"Something's eating you, and it ain't your hamstring."

I glanced behind Lonnie at the rest of the guys. They were yakking it up, razzing one another, paying no attention to the two of us. Quentin was sitting in his wheelchair, between Shlomo and Howie, giving as good as he got.

I looked Lonnie straight in the eye. "You've got to keep it a secret, all right?"

"How long have we known each other?"

"Yeah, but this is different. . . ."

"C'mon, Jules," he said. "You're hurting my feelings even saying that. You *know* I can keep a secret. You could stick bamboo shoots under my nails, and I wouldn't say a thing."

"Beverly's my girlfriend."

"When did that happen?"

"Right after I raced her."

"Did you kiss her?"

"Three times," I said. "Don't say anything to the guys!"

"Bamboo shoots under the nails, remember?"

"Because I don't think Howie's going to be too happy about it," I said.

"He'll get over it," Lonnie said. "But he won't hear about it from me."

"It feels good to tell someone."

Neither of us spoke for the next couple of seconds.

Then Lonnie said, "Now you want to tell me what's *really* eating you?"

"I just did."

"All right," he said. "Whenever you're ready to tell me, I'm all ears."

It was between third and fourth periods, as I pushed open the door to the stairwell, that I heard footsteps rush up behind me. "Wait up, Twerski!"

I turned around. "What do you want, Devlin?"

"Just to talk for a minute."

I sighed. "I'm running late."

"Did you hurt your leg? I saw you limping."

"I pulled my hamstring."

"Ouch!" he said. But his eyes were blank. He had no idea what I was talking about.

"The nurse told me I just have to rest it for a week."

"That's good news then, right?"

"I guess."

"The thing is, I got something I want to say to you."

"Does it have to be right now?" I asked.

"I was talking to my brother Duane about the thing that happened—he works the Music Express at Adventurers Inn. You met him last year when you showed up with that girl Jillian."

"I remember, Devlin. Can you get to the point?"

"I just . . . I didn't know your friend was sick with cancer," he said. "I mean, I kind of figured it out when the wig came off. Except I didn't figure it out quick enough. The thing is, I shouldn't have done what I did. With the wig, I mean. I shouldn't have grabbed it and thrown it. He can't help it that he's got cancer."

"Who said he does?"

"Duane said a bald kid in a wheelchair equals cancer."

"Well, that's Duane's opinion," I said.

"They have parties for 'em when the park's closed. He gives 'em free rides because . . . well, you know."

"Quentin is sick," I said. "But he's going to be okay. He's going to be just fine. You can ask Miss Medina if you don't believe me. He doesn't even need the wheelchair. His dad makes him use it."

"The thing is, I wouldn't have teased him so bad if I knew. I mean, I got an aunt who died last year. . . . I saw your friend getting in and out of the chair, and it looked kind of funny, and I just didn't know."

"I'm sure he understands," I said.

"Tell him I'm sorry, would you?"

I turned and started toward the stairs, but he caught me by the shoulder.

"What do you want, Devlin?"

"I just didn't get it. You know?"

I was tempted to ask him about the painting, about whether he'd scratched my initials into it. But I didn't since I wanted the conversation to end. Besides, it didn't matter who'd done what at that point. What mattered was that Principal Salvatore *thought* I'd scratched up the painting, so I had to write a two-hundred-word essay.

Even so, it was pretty decent of Devlin to say that stuff. I've had a full day to think it over, and I could've at least shaken his hand. I *should've* shaken his hand. I should've let him off the hook. I mean, he was trying to do the right thing. Even if he was trying to do the right thing only because he was feeling guilty and low, it was still the right thing. You can't expect a guy to be better than he is.

What I don't get is why Rabbi Salzberg expects *me* to be better than I am. There's no reason I should know what I know. There's no reason he should've told me. Why couldn't he keep it to himself? It's too much to carry around.

It's like I had a life, and maybe it wasn't perfect, but it was good enough for me, and now my life is knowing what I know. I wake up knowing it, and I walk around knowing it, and I go to sleep knowing it. I even dream about it, but in a backward way. I go to sleep knowing it, but then I wake up, and I realize Quentin's going to be all right—except I only woke up in my dream, and then I wake up again, for real, and I know the truth again, and it weighs down on me like it did the moment I first found out.

But the worst part of it is I can't look Quentin in the eye. If Rabbi Salzberg told me because he thought I'd spend more time with Quentin, or he thought I'd be thankful for the time we had left, he couldn't have been more wrong. I can hardly bear to look at the guy. There, I said it! I love him, I really and truly love him, but I can hardly bear to look at him. The sight of him in that wheelchair . . . it makes me sick, knowing what I know, knowing he's not going to be all right, knowing he's never—

But what's the point of talking about it?

Sherlock Amelia

Today is April Fool's Day, so of course today was the day we got the news about Bobby Murcer's visit to Thirty-Fourth Avenue. Quentin's dad was still on the phone with the Yankees when Eric and I showed up in the morning to take Quentin to the bus stop.

"Thanks a million, Jerry," was what Mr. Selig said before he hung up.

Then he told us the news: Bobby Murcer will be here next Wednesday at four o'clock.

I almost wish it were a joke. But Bobby Murcer, my favorite baseball player, *will* be here a week from today, and of course he'll act real cheerful, on account of he thinks he's Quentin's favorite player, except he's not, and on account of he thinks Quentin is getting better, except he's not. So if you stop and think about it, the whole thing *is* just one big joke.

Except it's not.

That was as far as I'd gotten when Amelia knocked on my bedroom door. I wasn't planning to write anything else tonight. What else is there to say? Right or wrong, I'm going to meet Bobby Murcer next week. The cards are dealt. There's nothing to do except play out the hand.

When Amelia knocked on the door, I closed my notebook and shoved it under a pile of schoolwork on my desk. I told her to come in since I knew, from the way she'd knocked, she wasn't going to go away. Usually, she just bangs a couple of times with the underside of her fist. But this time she gave the door six quick raps with her knuckle. It was her *I'm-not-going-away-so-you-might-as-well-let-me-in* knock.

She pushed open the door and said, "You want to tell me what's bugging you?"

I spun around in my desk chair. "Nothing's bugging me. What's bugging you?"

"Something's definitely bugging you, Jules. Even Mom and Dad have noticed."

"So you're their spy?" I asked.

"No, I'm your sister."

"I never knew that. What a coincidence!"

"Jules—"

"I'm glad we got that straightened out."

She came into the room and sat down on the bed. I spun the rest of the way around in my chair to keep eye contact.

"Look, Jules, if you don't want to talk to me, that's fine. I know you've got your own life, and you've got your own way of looking at things, and if you tell me to butt out, I'll butt out—"

"Then butt out."

"I knew you were going to say that," she said. "But before I butt out, I just want to let you know that it doesn't have to be this way. It doesn't have to be any way. You can talk to me, and I'll think about what you tell me—and, if you want, I'll tell you what I think. I'll take it seriously, and it'll stay between the two of us. Mom and Dad don't have to know."

"Is that it?"

"Look," she said, "whatever's going on, it'll pass."

"You're real sure about that?"

"Yes, I am. If Lonnie's giving you a hard time—"

I started to shake my head. "You figured it out."

"Whether it's Lonnie or not is irrelevant. All I'm saying is that it's going to pass."

"How do you know?"

"Because you're thirteen years old," she said. "I know you don't want to hear that, and I know it sounds like an insult. But it happens to be true. The things that seem like life and death when you're thirteen—sooner or later, you'll realize they're not life and death."

"You're right."

"What?"

"I'm thirteen years old," I said. "Whatever it is, how bad could it be?"

"That's right," she said.

"That's a huge relief, Amelia. I'm real glad we had this conversation."

She looked at me in a weird way. "So am I."

With that, she stood up and walked out of the room.

I turned back to the desk, pulled out my notebook, and read back the last couple of paragraphs I'd written. Nothing else came to me, so for five minutes straight I just stared at the last three words: "Except it's not."

Then Amelia knocked on the door again and pushed it open. Her face was pale and her mouth was half open. She said in a low voice, almost a whisper, "Unless it *is* life and death."

I just stared at her. I didn't speak.

"Oh no," she muttered. "Oh God."

I was close to bawling, but I fought it off. "I'm just thirteen, right?"

"Julian—"

"Don't make me say anything else."

"But how do you—"

"Please," I said. "Just let it go."

"But Mom and Dad—"

"I'm begging you, Amelia. . . ."

There were tears running down her face. She swallowed hard, then wiped her eyes. Then she turned and left. She closed the door real soft behind her, and I went back to my notebook.

Finding the Worm

I found a note in my coat pocket when I got to school. It was from Howie. He must have slipped it in there during the bus ride this morning.

> Dear Julian,
> So here's the thing I wanted to say before except I couldn't say it when we were talking in front of your house on account of I'm so ashamed because I did you dirt even though you didn't do nothing to me except hurt my feelings which you did even though you didn't do it on purpose. It's been eating at me for

a long time, but I wasn't ever going to
tell you except ever since I saw how you
stuck up for Quentin a couple of weeks
ago and got beat up, it's been eating
at me even more, and I can't take it
anymore, so I got to tell you that I'm the
one who messed up Beverly's painting
and got you in trouble. I thought you
were sweet on her on account of how
you always stopped to look at it, which
it turned out maybe you were, but then
it turned out she was sweet on you, so
maybe it's not your fault. But anyway
Lonnie says I got no right to be sore
because that's just how life is. Even
though I think it's wrong. So anyway if
you want to tell Principal Salvatore and
get me in trouble, you can. I won't be
mad. I know I've got it coming.

Your friend,
Howie

I read the note a couple of times, then tore it up and
threw it out. What else could I do? Telling on Howie
wasn't going to get me off the hook with Principal Salvatore. That much I knew for sure.

When I saw Howie over lunch, I walked around the table and whispered in his ear that I wasn't mad. He looked up at me in a grateful way. Then he gave me a soft punch in the shoulder, which was his way of saying things were back to normal between us.

The rest of the guys gave us a quick look. It must've seemed like a strange thing, with me whispering to Howie and then Howie punching me. But a second later, they went back to their lunches, and I walked back around to my usual side of the table and sat down next to Lonnie.

April 6, 1970

Good Citizenship

Here's the last essay, the first real essay, on good citizenship I wrote for Principal Salvatore:

The truth is, I'm not sure what good citizenship is, exactly. I've thought about it a lot over the last week. What I mean is, I've really and truly thought about it, not in a sarcastic way. I think it has something to do with treating people and things the way you're supposed to treat them, and not making a big deal out of it, but it's got to be more than that. It's also got to be taking your medicine—even when you don't deserve the medicine. I didn't scratch my initials into the painting of the Bowne House. I wanted to say that one more time, Principal Salvatore. I won't admit to doing something I didn't do. But I'm taking my medicine, and writing this essay, because you told me I had to do it, and you're doing what you think is right. It doesn't matter whether, in this case, you're wrong. You're the principal, which means you're like an umpire, and you have to make tough calls, and once in a while you're going to get one wrong. That's how the world works. Principals have to make tough calls, and students have to live with them. If they can't live with the calls, then students have to accept the punishment. That's the principle of the thing. Being a good citizen means knowing that the world is bigger than you are, and life isn't always fair, but people are doing their best to make the right calls.

I slid the paper under the door to Principal Salvatore's office, as usual, and then limped upstairs to homeroom.

Half an hour later, after old Mrs. Griff had finished her slow-motion list of morning reminders, Miss Medina was waiting for me in the hall outside the classroom. She pulled me aside as I walked out with Beverly, and she handed me back the essay I'd written. Principal Salvatore had written on the back:

The ump says you're safe. You can stay in Fast Track.

Miss Medina stood there while I read Principal Salvatore's note. When I looked up afterward, she leaned over and said in my ear, "Congratulations." Then she turned and walked off.

Beverly was waiting for me at the end of the hall, next to the stairwell. When I caught up to her, she asked, "What was that about?"

"Eighth grade," I said. "I can skip it."

"So all's well that ends well, right?"

"Yeah," I said.

"Then why are you still sad?"

"Please, Beverly . . ."

"Did I do something wrong?"

"No," I said. "I've just got a lot of stuff to think about."

I glanced in both directions. No one was paying attention to us, so I gave her a quick kiss on the lips. She smiled at me afterward. "If you ever want to talk about the stuff you're thinking about . . ."

"I know," I said.

Bobby Murcer on the Block

Bobby Murcer's real first name is Bobby: Bobby Ray Murcer. That's how he got to be my favorite baseball player. Which is a dumb reason, if you stop and think about it. But you latch on to things for dumb reasons when you're eight, and that's how old I was when I first heard of Bobby Murcer.

He was going to be the next Mickey Mantle. That was what my dad said, which made me remember the name, since my dad also said (pretty much every time a Yankee game came on TV) that Mickey Mantle was the greatest player he'd ever seen, and would've been the greatest player who ever lived, except he wrecked his knees, but I should still keep an eye on him, even though he was hobbling around, because greatness doesn't come along too often, and because one day I'd be telling my grandchildren that I'd seen the great Mickey Mantle.

Mickey Mantle did nothing for me.

The *next* Mickey Mantle, on the other hand, seemed like he was worth getting to know. So back then, when I was eight, I fished out Bobby Murcer's baseball card from the shoe box under my bed, and there he was, squinting back at me, holding a bat over his left shoulder, paired up with another Yankee rookie named Dooley Womack—which had to be the worst name I'd ever heard.

But what cinched it, what made him *my guy*, was when I turned the card over and found out Bobby Murcer's real first name was Bobby. Not Robert. Bobby. I mean, who names their kid Bobby? Bobby is what you're called, not what you're named. (Bobby Kennedy's real name, for instance, was Robert Francis Kennedy.) Except the more I stared at Murcer's face, the more I realized he *had* to be a Bobby. His face was round, like a lemon, and even though he looked real serious, squinting back at me, waiting for the pitch, I could tell, whether he struck out on three pitches or slugged a home run, he was going to trot off the field smiling.

That was the guy who pulled up in front of the Hampshire House at four o'clock. He was right on time, riding in a pin-striped blue limousine with a Yankees logo on the side door. We were lined up at the edge of the sidewalk. Quentin was in the middle of us, sitting in his wheelchair. We'd had just enough time to get Quentin off the bus, rush him home, rush back home ourselves, change out of our school clothes, grab our baseball gloves, rush back to Quentin's house, and then line up at the edge of the sidewalk outside the Hampshire House.

Jerry Manche was driving the limousine, and he hopped out first. Then he rushed around to the passenger side to open the door for Bobby Murcer, like it was supposed to be a big ceremony, but Murcer had already pushed open the door and climbed out by himself. He was wearing a suit and a tie, which looked weird. But his face looked just like his baseball card, except his hair was curled over his ears and a couple of inches longer in the back.

"How're y'all doing?" were the first words out of his mouth.

He said it to the group of us, but he was looking straight at Quentin, so we turned and looked at Quentin too. Except Quentin couldn't get a word out. He was staring up at Murcer with a stunned expression. I'm guessing the rest of us had an expression like that too. No one said a thing for a couple of seconds.

It was Lonnie who finally broke the silence. "We're doing all right, I guess."

Murcer squatted down in front of Quentin. He put out his right hand, and Quentin shook it. "I hear you're a fan of mine."

Quentin nodded. He still couldn't talk.

"Well, I'm a fan of yours, young man."

That made Quentin snort. "Why?"

"'Cause I hear you're a real fighter."

"You mean because I have cancer?"

"That's the rumor," Murcer said. "But you look like a tough son of a gun to me."

"I have to wear a wig," Quentin said.

"You want to know a secret? So does Joe Pepitone."

That made the rest of us laugh.

"He got traded," I blurted out.

"Well, now, that's true," Murcer said. "But Pepi hit twenty-seven homers for us last year, and he hit every single one of them in a wig. So what does that tell you about fellas who wear wigs?"

"They get traded?" Lonnie said, which cracked us up again.

Murcer got a big smile on his face. He stood up, walked over to Lonnie, and shook his hand too. "So you're the wisenheimer of the group. That would make you Lonnie, right? My pal Jerry warned me about you. He said you might give me a hard time. As for the rest of you . . . I'm guessing you're Eric the Red, right?"

Eric nodded, and Murcer stepped forward and shook his hand.

"Now, let's see. That would make *you* Shlomo . . . and *you* Howie."

He shook both of their hands too.

"How'd you know?" Howie said.

"Oh, I got a whole scouting report on you fellas."

"You left out Julian," Quentin said.

"I'm just getting around to him, Quent." Murcer stepped toward me and looked me up and down. "Speedy Gonzales, am I right? From what I hear, you're as fast as greased lightning."

He put out his hand, and I shook it.

"Why don't you race him?" Lonnie said.

That made Murcer smile. "What do you say, friend? I've got a pair of tennis shoes in the trunk."

"I can't," I said. "I hurt my leg last week."

"Hammy?"

"How'd you know?" I asked.

"It's always a hammy with you speed merchants," he said. "I'm thinking I lucked out, 'cause you might've made me look bad."

"Maybe you can come back next week," Lonnie said. "I'm sure he'll be healed up by then."

"C'mon, Lonnie!"

Murcer just laughed. "No thank you! I'm going to be real satisfied with a draw."

Right then, Jerry Manche popped open the trunk of the limousine and pulled out a baseball glove and a ball. "I don't think Bobby came all this way just to talk," he called. "I think he wants to loosen up."

Murcer stepped back and took the glove and ball from Jerry Manche. "How about it? You fellas want to toss it around for a while?"

"Sure!" Shlomo said.

"What about you, Quent? Think you can ditch that chair for a couple of throws?"

Quentin glanced up over his left shoulder. It took me a second to realize what was going on: he knew his mom and dad were watching from their window on the fifth floor. He didn't want to worry them.

"Can Quentin stand up?" Lonnie called up to them.

"Just no running around," Mrs. Selig called back.

Quentin's face lit up when he heard that. Lonnie stepped behind him and steadied the wheelchair, and Quentin stood up. He wobbled but then got his balance. Then he reached back for his glove, which was hanging off the handle behind the chair.

"You ready?" Murcer said.

Quentin nodded.

Murcer tossed the ball underhand, from ten feet away, and Quentin caught it.

"C'mon," Quentin said. "I'm not a baby."

He fired the baseball back at Murcer, a perfect chest-high strike.

Murcer started to laugh. "Hey, friend, I'm just getting warmed up."

He threw the ball back to Quentin, overhand this time, and Quentin caught it and fired it back even harder than before. This one was high and outside, and Murcer caught it in the heel of his glove with a loud pop. He took off the glove and shook his hand, as if Quentin had just broken his palm.

"Lord have mercy!" he cried. "I think we'd better work in some of these other fellas, or you're going to put me on the DL."

Shlomo asked, "What's the—"

"It's the disabled list," Lonnie said.

"Oh."

The catch lasted about half an hour. It was the six of us, plus Bobby Murcer, and even Jerry Manche pulled out his glove from the trunk and got in on the act. After ten minutes, Beverly came down the block. She shot me a look as if to say, *Why didn't you tell me what was going on?* I *should've* told her. I didn't think of it—maybe because I didn't want to think of it, because I felt bad about the situation. But I lent her my glove, and she joined in, and you know what? It wasn't so bad. Quentin had a good time, even if he ran out of gas toward the end and had to sit back down in the wheelchair.

Afterward, Murcer autographed our gloves with a black Magic Marker. He signed Quentin's glove first, right below the fake Willie Mays signature branded into the pocket, and never batted an eye. He signed my glove last, right below the fake Bobby Murcer signature, and then looked at me in a weird way. He said in a low voice, "So how come, if Quentin's such a big fan of mine, you're the only one with my name in your mitt?"

"My dad bought it for my birthday," I said. "I guess I kind of asked for it."

"Is there something on your mind, friend?"

"No." I stared straight down at the sidewalk.

He handed me back the glove, but as I reached for it, he took my right hand and squeezed it tight in his. "You hang tough. You hear?"

Jerry Manche pointed to his watch, which meant the two of them had to get going. Then he got in the car and started the engine. Murcer walked back over to Quentin and squatted down in front of the wheelchair again. "I know it's hard, young fella, what you're going through. But you got the best folks in the world in your corner. The best doctors and nurses, the best family and friends. You also got the New York Yankees." As he said that, he reached into his suit pocket and pulled out an autographed baseball. "The guys in the clubhouse wanted me to make sure you got this. Every guy on the team signed it, even the coaches and Mr. Houk. What do you think about that?"

Quentin's eyes were bugging out of his head. You could tell that he had a lot he wanted to say, but all that came out was "Thank you."

"Hey, aren't you forgetting something?" Lonnie said.

Murcer looked up at him and grinned. "All right, friend, let me have it. What am I forgetting?"

"You're supposed to promise to hit a home run for Quentin in tomorrow's game."

"Now hold on a minute—"

"Didn't you ever see the movie *The Pride of the Yankees*?"

"Yeah, but—"

"Don't you remember the part where Lou Gehrig promises to hit a home run for the sick kid?"

"Well, I promise I'll *try*—"

"But that's not how it works," Lonnie said. "You're supposed to promise to hit a home run for Quentin if Quentin promises to feel better. That's what Lou Gehrig did."

"In a *movie*."

"But it's based on real life," Lonnie said. "I looked it up."

Murcer laughed out loud. "All right, friend. You got me. I promise, I'll hit a homer for Quentin in the game tomorrow night. But here's the deal: whether I do or I don't hit the ball over the fence, Quentin's got to hit a homer for me. I'm looking for maximum effort. Not every homer shows up in the box score. When you give your maximum effort, come what may, you're hitting a home run. Maybe not in the ballpark, but in life. What do you say, Quent? I'll hit a homer for you if you hit a homer for me. We got ourselves a deal?"

"It's a deal," Quentin said before Lonnie could answer.

The Next Game

It's not Lonnie's fault, what happened.
I just wanted to get that down on paper. Even though
afterward Howie started saying how Lonnie shouldn't
have razzed Bobby Murcer to hit a home run for Quentin, and then, after *that,* Eric started saying how Lonnie
shouldn't have shot that paper missile at his bar mitzvah, there was no way to know how it would turn out.
How any of it would turn out, because one thing leads to
another.

It's like the world's full of dominoes, and they're
standing on their edges, and you're tiptoeing around them,
minding your own business, but sooner or later you're
going to trip into one, and then it's going to fall into the

next one, and then that one is going to fall into the next one, and then the entire setup comes crashing down in ways you can't predict—unless maybe you're staring down at the thing from above, which would make you God. But Lonnie's not God. He's just a guy, like the rest of us, tripping into dominoes. Maybe he should be more careful when he tiptoes. But then he wouldn't be Lonnie.

Plus, he feels pretty awful about what happened.

It was Quentin's idea that we watch the Yankees game together, at his house, to see if Bobby Murcer would come through and hit that home run for him—which meant the rest of us had to cut our last three periods and rush home, because the game started at one o'clock. But that was no problem. Ever since his wig came off during the fight, the entire school knew Quentin had cancer. Sure, we'd have to answer questions the next morning. But like Lonnie said: once you say the words "Quentin" and "cancer," what's your teacher going to do?

Quentin skipped school altogether. He likely would've stayed home regardless, on account of it was another bad-breathing day, but him not being there made it easier for the rest of us to sneak out between periods, meet up a couple of blocks from McMasters, and then hustle back to Thirty-Fourth Avenue and over to his house in time for the first pitch.

Mrs. Selig had laid out tray tables of potato chips and

honey roasted peanuts, and she made a big pitcher of Hawaiian Punch. We were jammed into his room—the entire gang, plus Beverly. (I wasn't going to forget about her again.) I was sitting on the floor between her and Lonnie. Quentin was sitting up in his bed, with his back against the headboard. Shlomo, Eric, and Howie were sitting on folding chairs against the far wall. Our jackets were thrown across the pinball machine. We were watching the game on the portable black-and-white television, which his mom had rolled to the center of the room.

Murcer was hitting clean up against the Red Sox. He batted for the first time in the bottom of the first inning. Roy White had just lined a home run over the right field wall, so Murcer stepped to the plate with no runners on base.

Suddenly, the room got real quiet. It felt weird to see him standing there, doing what he always did, waving his bat in a circle, shifting his weight back and forth from his front leg to his back leg, waiting for the pitch. It *shouldn't* have felt weird. But it did. It felt like he'd never come to Thirty-Fourth Avenue, like we'd never met him, or like we *had* met him but he'd forgotten about us and gone back to being Bobby Murcer.

But here's the even weirder thing: *I didn't want him to hit a home run.*

Since the first time I'd heard his name, Murcer had

been my guy, and I'd wanted him to hit a home run every time he came to bat. Until right then, sitting in Quentin's room. Because I knew if he hit a home run, the rest of the guys were going to turn to Quentin and start razzing him about holding up his end of the deal, about giving a maximum effort, about getting rid of the wheelchair, about beating cancer . . . and how could I listen to that, knowing what I knew?

Murcer walked on four pitches.

"I knew it!" Lonnie said. "I knew it!"

Shlomo asked, "What do you mean?"

"If you're the Red Sox, why would you throw Murcer a strike when you've got Curt Blefary on deck?"

Blefary struck out to end the first inning.

Murcer batted again to lead off the fourth inning. That made it tougher for Ray Culp, the Red Sox pitcher, to pitch around him, since you never want to walk the lead-off batter. The count ran to three balls and two strikes. But then Culp threw ball four, high and outside, and Murcer jogged to first.

"What did I tell you?" Lonnie said. "He's got no chance."

Blefary struck out again. Then John Ellis and Danny Cater both popped out to end the inning.

"Culp's not going to throw him a decent pitch all game," Lonnie said.

"You don't know that!" Howie said.

"Would you, if you had a choice between pitching to him or Blefary?"

Murcer's next at bat came in the sixth, with no one out. The Red Sox had scored three runs in the top of the inning to take a three-one lead. But Thurman Munson led off the bottom of the sixth with a single, and White followed up with a single, which put runners at first and third.

As Murcer stepped to the plate, Lonnie said, "Culp's still going to walk him. Even if it means loading the bases with nobody out. He'll take his chances with Blefary. You just watch."

But then, as Murcer was taking his warm-up swings, something strange happened. You could see it in the lower left corner of the screen. Blefary was getting called back to the dugout from the on-deck circle. He *wasn't* going to hit next. The manager was going to put up a pinch hitter for Blefary.

Culp noticed it too. He stepped off the mound and called time out. He took a good look to see who was going to pinch-hit—but no one came out to the on-deck circle. Culp waited and waited, but no one came out. Then, at last, the umpire pointed at Culp. You couldn't tell what he said to him, but you could tell the ump was annoyed and wanted to get things moving again.

Culp stepped back onto the mound, and Murcer stepped back into the batting box. For a couple of seconds, nothing happened. Then Culp glanced at Munson on third, and then at White on first, and then at the empty on-deck circle, and then, at last, he reared back and threw the ball. It came right down the middle of the plate, and Murcer swung, and as soon as he hit it, the announcer cried, "That's well hit! That's way back! That's *way* back!"

Lonnie and Beverly and Shlomo and Howie and Eric and Quentin started chanting, "Go! Go! Go!"

You know what? Right then, as the ball soared high into the air, at that moment, despite what I knew, despite everything, I changed my mind: I wanted it to be a home run.

"That's going . . . ," the announcer said.

"Go!"

"That's going . . ."

"Go!"

"That's *gone!*"

As the ball sailed over the right-field wall, the seven of us let out a yell. It was *one* yell. You couldn't tell where anyone's voice stopped and anyone else's started. I glanced over at Quentin, and he was yelling along with the rest of us, and his voice blended right in, and it felt like his voice was coming out of my mouth, and my voice was coming out of his mouth, and there was no difference.

I glanced back at the TV: Bobby Murcer was trotting around the bases. The Red Sox manager was walking out to the mound, signaling for a relief pitcher, and Ray Culp was walking back to the Red Sox dugout. Curt Blefary had come back out to the on-deck circle and was waiting to shake Murcer's hand.

Mrs. Selig came running into the room to see what the commotion was about. When she saw Quentin sitting up in bed, pumping his fist in the air, she got a huge smile on her face.

Then the announcer said, "That's a very special home run, folks. Not just because it puts the Yankees back in the lead. No, that home run had a lot more than a baseball game riding on it. You see, Bobby Murcer promised to hit a home run in today's game. He made that promise to a dying boy who lives in Flushing, Queens. Bobby spent the afternoon yesterday with him and his friends—"

I think that was as much as any of us heard. The announcer's voice became background noise at that point, and we turned to Quentin. He was kind of smiling, and his eyes were darting around the room. He didn't get why we were suddenly staring at him. But a couple of seconds later, you could see him working it through in his mind, replaying what the announcer had said, and then you could see the meaning start to sink in. He brought his hands up to the back of his neck and rocked back and forth. He took three loud breaths through his nose. It was maybe another second before tears started rolling out of his eyes and down his cheeks.

He looked up and cried, "Mom?"

Mrs. Selig ran into the room and knocked over both tray tables. Potato chips and peanuts went flying in every direction. Quentin was reaching for her as she got to the edge of the mattress, squeezing and unsqueezing his hands. She threw herself onto the bed and hugged him, and he buried his face in her shoulder. She was whispering, "No one knows for sure what's going to happen, Quent. Not even the doctors know for sure. Your father will be home in a few minutes. You can ask him." But she turned her head and said under her breath, "Oh God . . ."

By then, there were tears rolling down her cheeks too.

Lonnie stood up and said to the rest of us, "Let's go!"

Shlomo said, "Shouldn't we clean up—"

But Lonnie cut him off. "Let's go! Now!"

That's what we did. We grabbed our jackets and left. We left Quentin's bedroom with the Yankees game still playing on the TV, and with peanuts and chips scattered on the floor, and with Quentin hugging his mom, and with the two of them bawling their eyes out.

Sherlock Lonnie

Bobby Murcer felt real lousy about what had happened. He called Quentin's parents from the locker room after the game. I'm guessing one of the newspaper guys asked him about the "dying boy," and he put two and two together. Otherwise, how would he have known?

It was Mr. Selig who told me and Lonnie about the call when we went over to pick up Quentin in the morning. He told us how decent Murcer was on the phone, and how he said he'd do whatever he could to make things right. I was glad to hear that. I didn't want to think Murcer had blabbed about the nice thing he'd done for Quentin.

What happened was Jerry Manche had mentioned it

to a few guys who worked for the Yankees, and then one of them mentioned it to a couple of newspaper reporters, and then of course they started yakking about it. By the time the story got to the announcer, he didn't know it was supposed to be a secret.

So Lonnie knocked over the first domino, when he asked Murcer to hit the home run, and after that it was just one domino falling into the next domino. It was no one's fault.

We were still standing at the front door while Mr. Selig was telling us that. Lonnie waited for him to finish and asked if Quentin was going to school, and Mr. Selig shook his head. He told us that Quentin was back in the hospital, that he kept waking up during the night because he couldn't breathe. "I think maybe it's just his nerves," Mr. Selig said. "His mother's with him. . . ."

Then he started to sob and waved us away.

As Lonnie and I were walking back toward the bus stop, he turned to me and said, "You knew, didn't you?"

"How could you tell?"

"The way you were walking home afterwards," he said. "The rest of the guys were staring down, thinking about stuff. But you were staring straight ahead, like there was nothing to think about. Plus, *something's* been eating at you these last couple of weeks. I figure it must've been that. Magoo told you, right?"

"Lonnie—"

"That's okay," he said. "You don't have to say it. I figure it's got to be him. Who else from the block would know except Quentin's mom and dad? I figure they must've told him, because he's their rabbi, and because that's the kind of thing you tell a rabbi, and I figure he must've told you. I don't know why he'd do that—"

"Neither do I," I said.

Lonnie looked at me, and I looked back at him, but we kept walking.

"How long do you think he's got?"

"I don't know," I said.

"You *really* don't know, or you know and you're not supposed to tell anyone?"

"I really and truly don't know. I swear on my mother's life."

Those words kind of hung between us for a couple of seconds.

"Anyway," Lonnie said, "it's a good thing the truth came out."

"How do you figure that?"

"Because we can treat him like a king." Lonnie swallowed hard. "I mean, as soon as he gets out of the hospital . . ."

"Yeah."

"I doubt he's going to go back to school."

"Why wouldn't he go back to school?" I said.

"Because what's the point? I mean, why does it matter anymore if Quentin can change fractions to percents? What good is it going to do him?"

"What else is he going to do?" I said. "Going to school has got to be better than sitting around and waiting."

"Here's what I was thinking. What if, as soon as he gets home from the hospital, the rest of us just skip school until the summer?"

"C'mon, Lonnie!"

"Think about it, Jules. It's only a few months. We can just hang out at his house and get him whatever he wants. He wants a vanilla milk shake, *bam,* one of us can run downstairs to Vera's and get him a vanilla milk shake. He'll never be alone. It's the right thing to do."

"Lonnie, it's not going to happen. It's not realistic."

"Why isn't it realistic? My mom will write me a note. She knows what it's like to lose people."

"Even if she does, it's just a note from your mom. Who says Principal Salvatore will go for it?"

"Then we'll go to the newspapers," Lonnie said. "We'll tell them how we just want to spend time with our dying friend, and how our school principal won't let us. Let's see what Salvatore says with an office full of reporters."

"You just want to skip school."

"I never denied it, Jules. But I want to skip school *for*

a good reason. That makes a big difference. Don't you want to spend as much time as you can with Quentin? You said yourself you don't know how much time he's got left. He could die next year, or he could die next month."

"Lonnie, we can't talk about it like this. It's not right. It's just . . . not right."

"You're the one who says we should be realistic. I'm trying to be realistic."

"How about if we wait until Quentin gets out of the hospital and then figure out the rest of it?"

"That's fine with me," he said.

Twelve

Quentin died last night. Friday night. April 17, 1970. Eight days after the Yankees announcer messed up and said the thing he said. I want to remember that date, April 17, 1970. He never came home from the hospital. The last time I saw him, he was hugging his mom.

He was twelve years old.

I mean, he was *twelve*.

TWELVE!!!

Keep It to Yourself

Why do people get philosophical at times like this? Why do they have to go on and on about the meaning of it? I mean, you expect that kind of thing from your parents, and maybe even your sister. But the stuff comes at you wherever you turn. Your teachers. Your mailman. Even the guy who picks up and drops off your laundry. They've all just got to get in their two cents about how things will be all right no matter how much it hurts right now.

Yeah, Quentin died. Yeah, it's real sad. End of story. I mean, did we *really* need another trip to Miss Medina's office this morning? She's a real nice lady, but I doubt she could've picked Quentin out of a lineup. Do I need her to tell me time heals all wounds? I felt like saying, "That's it? That's the best you've got?" But I sat there in her office and didn't talk. None of us did. Not even Lonnie. He could have let her have it. But he didn't. My point is, why is it the guidance counselor's business? What's she going to tell me that I couldn't have figured out on my own?

You know what old Mrs. Griff did? She nodded as I came into homeroom. That's it. Just a quick nod, as if to say, *Sorry about your friend.* She made more sense than the rest of them put together.

April 22, 1970

Long Island

It was hot out this morning, like middle-of-summer hot. I think it was maybe seventy-five degrees, but it felt even hotter because we had to wear blazers to Quentin's funeral.

The cemetery was way out on Long Island. The ride was pretty bad. I was sitting in the backseat of the car, next to Amelia, and she kept reaching across and squeezing my hand. I let her do it because it seemed to mean a lot to her. But it just made me hotter. The sun was glaring through the windows, and my mom and dad were whispering back and forth in the front seat, and I was staring down at the buttons on my blazer, and the back of my neck was sweaty, and the middle of my back was sweaty, and it was the wrongest, sweatiest feeling I'd ever had.

We parked in a lot next to the chapel, which was a large beige building in front of the cemetery. There were a half dozen cars there already. The first person I noticed was Beverly. She was standing at the front door of the chapel. She took a step forward when she saw us drive up, but she held back and waited for my parents and Amelia to get out of the car and walk into the chapel. Then she ran up to me and hugged me, which would've been all right, except for how hot and sweaty I was.

She was weepy, of course. But she managed to get out, "It's so bad. . . ."

"Yeah," I said.

I didn't know what else to do, so I kissed her on the cheek. That seemed to work. She wiped her eyes and smiled at me and told me she'd see me later. Then she went into the chapel to sit with her family.

I waited outside for the rest of the guys to show up, which they did over the next ten minutes. We didn't talk much. Howie razzed Shlomo a couple of times about how shiny his shoes were, how he could see his reflection in them. He didn't mean anything by it. You couldn't blame him for doing it because it filled up the silence. The only good thing about standing there was that it was shady, and there was a breeze blowing, and I started to cool off.

Lonnie was the last guy to arrive. His mom and dad were walking in front of him, and I expected Mrs. Fine to be crying her eyes out, but she had this stiff look on her face. Her eyes were flat. Her mouth was straight. It was like she had no expression at all. What was even weirder was that she didn't stop to hug us, and she's the biggest hugger I know. But she and Mr. Fine had their arms locked together, and they were looking straight ahead, and they walked right past us as if we weren't there.

Lonnie came over and said, "You're going to say something, right, Jules?"

"What do you mean?"

"After the service, when we go out to the grave, Magoo is going to ask people to come forward and say stuff. That's how funerals work."

"How do you know?"

"My mom told me. She asked me if I was going to do it."

"Then why don't *you* do it?"

"Because I'm not the word guy. You're the word guy."

That was as far as we'd gotten when a blue limousine pulled into the parking lot. I thought at first it was a funeral car. But then I noticed the pinstripes and Yankees logo. The limousine rolled to a stop, and out stepped Bobby Murcer and Jerry Manche. They were wearing dark suits and sunglasses. They walked around to the trunk, popped it open, and pulled out a huge horseshoe of flowers. I mean, the thing was just enormous—at least six feet tall. It wasn't heavy, though. Jerry Manche was carrying it by himself as he and Murcer walked toward us.

Murcer took off his sunglasses and slid them into his pocket. Then he put out his hand and shook each of our hands. "How're you fellas holding up?"

"We're doing all right," Lonnie said. "Nice home run."

"Thanks."

"I didn't think that guy would ever throw you a strike."

Murcer smiled. "Neither did I."

Jerry Manche said, "Hey, Bobby, I'm going to bring the flowers inside. You take your time."

Murcer nodded and then walked over to me. I was looking off to the side because I didn't want to have another conversation, but he ducked down and made me look him in the eye. "How are you doing, young man?"

"I guess I'm all right."

"Life's tough to figure out, isn't it?"

"I guess so," I said. "I don't know."

"Just hold on to what's important."

I didn't want to keep looking him in the eye, so I nodded and said, "All right."

He shook my hand again and headed into the chapel.

As soon as Murcer was gone, Lonnie started in on me again. "C'mon, Jules, you're the obvious one to get up and talk."

"I think *you're* the obvious one to get up and talk. I don't know what to say."

"You're not supposed to think about it," he said. "Just speak from the heart."

Shlomo was nodding. "It doesn't matter what you say. You say whatever you feel like saying. When my *bubbe* died, people got up and told stories about her, or they talked about what a nice person she was, or they just said how much they were going to miss her. It's not a big deal. You say something, and then you sit back down."

"Then why don't *you* do it?" I said.

He shook his head. "Not going to happen."

Lonnie said, "Be logical, Jules. It's got to be you."

"What if I say the wrong thing?"

"You're not listening. There's no right or wrong."

I took a deep breath. "All right, fine, I'll do it."

"So what are you going to say?"

"Lonnie!"

"It's a *joke*. I'm just trying to break the mood."

Out of the corner of my eye, I saw Danley Dimmel and his mom walking up the path from the parking lot. It took me a second to realize it was the same guy we egged last year. Danley towered over his mom, who was maybe five feet tall. The sight of him in a dark blazer and a tie was strange. He looked like a grown-up, like a guy who worked on Wall Street. Except the closer he got, the less grown-up he looked. He looked like a guy who wasn't used to wearing a blazer. It was too tight on his shoulders and too short on his arms. Also, his tie was crooked, and he kept fidgeting with his hearing aid.

I gave a quick wave to Danley, but he didn't notice me. Which you could understand. He was sobbing, and his mom was sobbing even worse, so he was kind of distracted.

The next car to drive up and park was a clunky green Rambler. Out of it stepped Principal Salvatore and Miss Medina. The two of them saw us standing off to the side. They walked over and told us how sorry they were for our loss. Their voices were different outside of school. "We're so sorry for your loss" were the exact words Principal Salvatore said, and then Miss Medina said, "So sorry." That was it. But it was real dignified, the way they said it. Like they really and truly were sorry for our loss.

As we watched them head through the front door of the chapel, a tall guy in a dark suit poked his head out and called to us, "You boys need to come inside. We're about to start."

The service was pretty much what you'd expect: a blur of Hebrew words, lots of standing up and sitting back down, with sobbing and weeping in the background. From the second it started, I wanted it to be over. But Rabbi Salz-berg dragged it out, getting in his two cents about how none of us can know God's purpose, how we have to accept God's wisdom. Like I said, it was pretty much what you'd expect.

After the last "amen," the tall dark-suited guy who'd called us into the chapel cracked open the side door, and sunlight blazed into the room. Rabbi Salzberg stepped off the stage, and the rest of us followed him out to the cemetery. It was maybe a hundred-yard walk to the grave site, which was where Quentin's coffin was.

That thing was beautiful. I just stared at it. I mean, you take wood shop, and you make a two-foot book-shelf, and you step back and look at it, and you feel kind of proud. But then you see something like that coffin, and you realize how rinky-dink your bookshelf was. The way that thing was put together, the way the wood was polished—I mean, it was gleaming in the sun. So were the brass handles. I couldn't take my eyes off it, even when Rabbi Salzberg started to speak.

We were sitting in metal folding chairs on the grass next to the grave. I was sitting between Lonnie and Howie, staring at the coffin, and not much listening to the rabbi. I knew there were prayers going on, and more sobbing and weeping, but I wasn't paying attention. I did hear him winding down, though. I looked back at him right as he was asking if anyone had anything to say about Quentin. But for some reason, it didn't register. I just sat there.

Lonnie gave me a quick elbow, and I stood up.

Rabbi Salzberg smiled at me. "Yes, Mr. Twerski?"

"I just wanted to say . . ." I swallowed hard, twice.

"Yes?"

"I mean, I just don't . . ."

That was it. That was all I could get out. There was a long, painful silence as I tried to say something else. Words kept buzzing and fluttering around in my head, but I couldn't get hold of them and put them together into sentences and make them come out of my mouth.

It was maybe a half minute after I stood up that Lonnie pulled me back down. Then he stood up. His legs were shaking as he started to speak. "I just wanted to say that Quentin was the greatest guy. He was just the greatest guy I ever knew. I always tried to be nice to him, and I think . . . I remember the time he got his eyebrows burned off on the Fourth of July. Except it was the fifth of July. That was real funny. Not because of what happened. But because of *how* it happened. The way he took it. I remember it so clear. . . ." Then, suddenly, Lonnie started to cry. It was the first time, the *only* time, I'd ever seen him cry, in all the years I'd known him. But you could understand it, getting up in front of all those people, staring at Quentin's coffin. What I mean is you couldn't hold it against him. I sure couldn't, because I was doing it too.

Plus, by that time, pretty much everyone there was bawling their eyes out. But you know who was bawling the loudest? Danley Dimmel! He was the next guy who got up and spoke. He did a better job than I did. It turns out, before Quentin got sick, he'd been going over to Danley's stoop and playing cards with him. I guess he wanted to make up for how bad we egged Danley. That's how come it got to him, Quentin's dying. Quentin was that kind of guy. The only person who wasn't bawling her eyes out, or at least the only one *I* saw, was Mrs. Fine. That was another thing I couldn't figure out. With how emotional she got about other stuff, you'd figure she'd be going through Kleenexes about a mile a minute. But she was just sitting there, a couple of rows behind us, taking the entire thing in, and not even batting an eye.

Maybe ten people got up and said stuff. Except for Lonnie and Danley, I didn't know any of them. I'm guessing the rest were Quentin's aunts and uncles and maybe a couple of older cousins. They just kept saying again and again, in different words, what a sweet kid he was—which no one was arguing about in the first place. Really, looking back, Danley's saying how Quentin used to play cards with him was the most interesting thing anybody said.

Once the talking part of the funeral was over, Rabbi

Salzberg gave a signal, and four large guys in dark suits lifted Quentin's coffin onto a machine that lowered it into the grave. That started another wave of loud bawling. Mr. and Mrs. Selig leaned forward and kissed the coffin on its way down. Then Rabbi Salzberg asked the rest of us to pick up a handful of dirt from the mound next to the grave and toss it onto the coffin.

Lots of people backed away when they heard that. They couldn't do it. But I did it. I figured after messing up the talking part, I owed Quentin the tossing-dirt part. The dirt was wetter than I'd thought. Flecks of it stuck to my palm, but I got most of it onto the middle of the coffin. After I did it, Beverly did it. Then the rest of them came forward and did it. First Lonnie, then Howie, then Shlomo, then Eric.

Each one of us tossed a handful of dirt onto Quentin's coffin.

April 25, 1970

Choosing Up Sides in Ponzini

It's the never-ness that gets you.
The thing is, it doesn't hit you right in the face. It comes in waves

Kissing Beverly

Beverly stopped by late in the after-
noon, around five o'clock. She didn't tell me during school
she was going to stop by. She didn't even call first. She
rang the doorbell, came upstairs, and said she wanted to
go for a walk. We had just enough time before dinner
to walk over to the Bowne House. We sat down on the
grass behind the house, next to the oak tree. We didn't
talk much. But we kissed six times. It was pretty good. I
mean, it was pretty good

May 2, 1970

The Coffin

When you think about it, it was a beautiful coffin. Why would you bury something like that? I know you're not supposed to think about stuff like that, but the thing is

Definitions

Addleeoonee: the topsy-turvy way the world is, with bad things happening to good people, and good things happening to bad people, and guys like Quentin dying.

Fiffle: the stuff that distracts you from what you should be thinking about.

Horgonk: the white paste that sticks to the cover of a composition book after you peel off the price tag.

Quilby: how your heart feels when you're carrying your friend on your back.

Zeetoosk: the back-and-forth sound shovels make in the dirt.

Tribute

It wrecked me that I never came up with those definitions while Quentin was still here, that I never got a chance to show them to him. I stared at them in the composition book afterward, and I teared up. How could I have been distracted by all the *fiffle* when I could've been figuring out Quentin's definitions?

Beverly and I walked home from school together this afternoon, and I told her about the words. She just listened and didn't say much. Except then, as we turned the corner onto Thirty-Fourth Avenue, she came up with an idea . . . maybe the greatest idea I'd ever heard.

We arranged to meet up again after dinner, in front of the Hampshire House. That gave me enough time to copy

Quentin's words and their definitions onto my mom's good stationery. I mean, you should've felt that paper. It was as thick as a bar mitzvah invitation, and it had classy ruffled edges.

I wrote out the words and definitions as neat as I could. Not in cursive. I printed the entire thing. It took a few tries. I did it twice before dinner, but the lines came out slightly crooked. I guess maybe I needed food, because after dinner, the third time I tried, my hand was steadier, and the lines came out almost perfect. They were as straight as I could get them.

Beverly was waiting for me at the Hampshire House. It was eight o'clock and real dark. No one was outside on the block except the two of us. The wind was blowing hard, and it was whipping her hair a thousand ways at once. I showed her the paper, and she nodded at it. That meant a lot, given how good she was at art.

Then we started to climb the tree.

Quentin's sneakers were dangling by their shoelaces four stories up, right below his window on the fifth floor. Four stories might not sound like a lot, but it *feels* like a lot when the branches get thinner and thinner, and the wind is roaring in your ears, and you know there's just sidewalk underneath you. The old oak at the Bowne House is a higher climb, but at least there you're climbing over grass.

I started getting jittery about three stories up. Beverly

was out in front of me by then. From where she was sitting, she could reach up and grab the branch the sneakers were hanging from. She glanced back at me, and I shook my head. I couldn't go any higher. I pulled the folded paper from my pocket and held it out, and she shinnied down the branch, took it from me, and stuffed it into her pocket. Then she shinnied back and caught hold of the branch with the sneakers. She chinned herself up and shinnied out. It scared the daylights out of me, how thin that branch was, and how much it drooped. But I figured she'd gotten out that far before to hang the sneakers, so she could do it again. Sure enough, she got to the sneakers and took the folded-up paper from her pocket.

I felt my eyes welling up as she slid the paper into the right sneaker. But I fought it off. I didn't bawl.

Neither did she.

"I hope Quentin's got a good view of it," Beverly whispered.

"I hope so too."

After that, we started the long climb down.

June 6, 1970

Manhood, I Guess

My bar mitzvah was last week. I figure I should mention that. I'm tired of writing stuff down, but I didn't want to end this thing without a real ending. I'm not going to say much about it, though. It was a bar mitzvah. I got dressed up in the same blazer I wore to Quentin's funeral. I did what I had to do. I said my haftarah. I said the words. I didn't glance down even once at the crib sheet. I could've recited it with my eyes closed, standing on one foot. After I was done, while I was still at the podium, Rabbi Salzberg walked up behind me, grabbed me by the shoulders, and said to the congregation, "Today, Julian Twerski is a man."

The congregation applauded and filed out to the

reception in the banquet room at the end of the main hall. I wanted to climb down from the stage at that point, get done with the hugs from my mom and dad and Amelia, get razzed by Lonnie and the guys, maybe get a kiss or two from Beverly. But Rabbi Salzberg didn't let go of my shoulders. He led me back behind the stage, out the back door, and then through the side hallway to his office.

As he sat down behind his desk, he smiled at me in a satisfied way. He said, "You have a question you want to ask, Mr. Twerski. I suggest this is the right moment to ask it."

I thought hard for a couple of seconds, then realized what he meant. "Why did you tell me about Quentin? Why did I need to know beforehand? Why didn't you let me find out with the rest of them?"

"Because memorizing your haftarah and living your haftarah are two different things."

That was all he said. I'm still not exactly sure what he meant. But I'm working on it.

After that, I walked out of his office and closed the door behind me. Then I headed around the corner and down the main hall to the banquet room. The rest of the day went like I thought it would. Hugging. Razzing. When the music started, I had to dance with my mom, in front of the entire crowd, while the band played an old song called "Mr. Wonderful." That was the worst of it. Lonnie's never going to let me live that down. But after the dance was over, Beverly caught me by the arm and pulled me behind a purple curtain. She kissed me, and I kissed her back.

Then she said, "You did it."

"Yeah, I did it. I passed."

That made her smile. "You always pass."

"So do you. Why do you think that is?"

"I don't know, Julian. I guess it just *is*."

She kissed me again, real hard, and then let me go. I walked out from behind the curtain and back to the reception. I didn't think much about Quentin for the rest of the bar mitzvah.

But I thought about him when I got home, when I saw my Bobby Murcer baseball glove in the corner of my room, and I've thought about him for the last week, because there are reminders wherever I look. What I'm worried about is what happens when the reminders are gone, when I'm grown up, when Thirty-Fourth Avenue is maybe just a place I once lived, and the guys are maybe just guys I once knew.

I don't want to stop thinking about Quentin: I loved him. I love him.

It *is* the never-ness that gets you. It gets you right in the gut. I never even thought about *never* until Quentin got sick, and now, since he died, it's all I think about.

What a teensy-weensy thing *now* is, and what a gigantic thing *never* is. It's like we were sailing together on a boat, Lonnie and me and Eric and Shlomo and Howie and Quentin, and then, for no reason, Quentin fell overboard, and now he's drowning in the *never,* and we're still sailing ahead in the *now,* and I can't throw him a rope, and I'm standing at the railing, and I'm leaning as far out as I can, and he's still bobbing up and down, but he's getting harder and harder to see. It's like I'm losing him over and over again, minute by minute, hour by hour, day by day.

How can that be?

On the other hand, how can it *not* be? I'm sitting here, at my desk, staring at Beverly's painting of the Bowne House, and I'm thinking about all the dead people who were once alive inside that house. Dying is part of the big picture. It's like the frame. You can't have a picture without a frame. Well, I guess you could, if it was one of those tape-it-to-the-refrigerator jobs little kids draw. But real pictures, *big* pictures, have a frame.

You just have to remember you're not on the outside of the frame looking in. You're right smack in the middle of the picture, but it's not a picture of just you, because if it were a picture of just you, you'd never be able to fill it up. The things you do, the stuff you learn, the people you love—that's what fills up the picture. Even when the colors start to fade.

Acknowledgments

If not for the New York Writers Workshop, Julian Twerski would never have drawn his first breath. My gratitude to the organization is enduring.

This book wouldn't have been written without the suggestions, criticisms, proddings, and occasional hisses from the usual crew: Linda Helble (along with Spencer and Spicy Jane), Charles Salzberg (friend, mentor, and third-base coach of dubious judgment), Eric Rosenberg (memory jogger and lifelong friend), Allison Estes (whose literary insight is exceeded only by her psychic resilience), and Mississippi Luke.

It wouldn't have been sold without the patience and diligence of Scott Gould of the RLR Agency.

It wouldn't have come together in its present form without the wisdom and guidance, and the gentle editorial hand, of Chelsea Eberly of Random House.

About the Author

Mark Goldblatt is a lot like Julian Twerski, only not as interesting. He's a widely published columnist, a novelist, and a professor at the Fashion Institute of Technology. *Twerp* was his first book for younger readers. He lives in New York City. Visit him online at markgoldblattkids.com.